THE BIRTH

A COLLECTION  ...J STORIES

Authors: Nick Couture, Toren Chenault, Kacey Flynn, Gabe Gonzalez, Candace Rugg, Calvin Sanders, AnnE Ford, Nelson Vicens, Aidan Catriel, Harikrishnan Mankada Covilakam, Shriharshita Venkat Chakravadhanula, Ian Tigomain, Grant DeArmitt

Edited by Toren Chenault

TABLE OF CONTENTS

* Indicates a "Why Not You?" Short Story Contest Winner

GALLOWED GROVE

- Gabe Gonzalez

Chapter 1: Origins

Gallowed Grove was a town that existed just as any other, but it was most certainly not like any other. The town was created by a man known as Doctor Victor Frankenstein, an eccentric genius who attempted to play God by creating life out of those who have since passed away.

His ideas were not accepted by those around him, which turned into a deadly disdain on one fateful night. As the doctor prepared his patchwork specimen on the table, villagers began to arm themselves with pitchforks, knives, blunt instruments, and torches to finally end the air of unease that the villagers felt with the doctor in their vicinity. Victor rose the specimen on a metallic slab into the cloudy and lightning-brimmed sky with an internalized hope that this would be his final foray into the realm of reincarnation...

He would be correct.

A lighting strike hits the slab, the creature's chest jolts upwards.

Villagers descend upon Victor's laboratory chanting statements littered with anger and holding weapons to cause death and destruction.

A second lightning strike hits the slab and causes electricity to run through the veins of the deceased.

Victor's eyes widen at a bright-orange light that illuminates one of his nearby windows and begins to come closer. He jumps upwards as the crash of that echoes throughout the room and he looks at the cause, it was a torch. He grimaces as he looks outwards from the newly opened window.

A group of nearly sixty angry villagers armed to the gods with weapons of bodily destruction approach Victor's palace of experimentation. One of them is the obvious leader of the group, he's a stout man with a thick, handlebar moustache and a wide-brimmed hat.

"Get out here, you FUCKIN' devil! We know what you've been doing with the dead!"

Victor widened his eyes at the violent screams from the man and rushed over to a rusted-over hand crank and began to use it as a means to bring his specimen down from the heavens. The villagers quickened their pace as he did so, a deep need to end his disgusting reign of scientific necromancy as the bodies of the ones they loved were being excavated from the town cemetery and being used for whatever nefarious purposes Victor needed. It was time for it to end.

Victor struggled with the final crank as the slab clicked into place upon its normal position. He lightly smacked his monstrous mixture of men on its cheeks as a plan began to formulate within his head.

The creature was unresponsive.

"Come on! Come on! Please, wake up! Dammit!"

Victor yelled at this creation and kept attempting maneuvers to try and awaken him, deeming this new try a failure just like the others.

The villagers made their way to the large wooden doors of the laboratory and the stout leader tightened his hand around a metal baton. He took the handle of the door and yanked on it to no avail, he grimaced and looked at the crowd behind him.

"BRING THE FUCKIN' RAM!"

The villagers parted, leaving a fairly large amount of room in the center as a group of men came through with a large log held within their arms. The leader began to count down.

"THREE!"

The men prepared themselves, ready to strike with the ramming tool. Victor was still trying to get his creation to awaken through screams in an effort to prove he wasn't as insane as everyone thought.

"TWO!"

The men kept a clear focus on the door.
Victor slumped on the floor ready for whatever hell may come to him, his palms over his eyes as he began to quietly sob into them.

"ONE!"

The men swung the ram and struck the door, causing it to splinter and burst open. Victor refused to look up and stayed in his position.
The monster opened their eyes.
The villagers angrily swarmed into the room and saw the doctor wailing into his palms, his aura of sadness had no effect on them.

But what they didn't expect was the movement on the slab behind the doctor. A series of deepened groans coming from the creature on the table as it slowly lumbered off the slab and showcased itself. The creature was a hulking figure of a man with greenish-grey skin flaps that were haphazardly stitched together with staples and twine, electric-blue eyes, a horizontal grouping of staples that lined their forehead, and a full head of raven-coloured hair. However, it was completely nude, and they were completely sexless because there were no identifiable genitalia as the area was just a smooth layer of skin.

Victor looked up at his shambling creation and a smirk began to grow upon his face.

"My... my monster! It worked! It really worked! THEY'RE ALIVE!"

The creature looked down at his creator with an inquisitive expression and recognized him as such, giving a small grunt and nod as confirmation of that fact.

The village mob leader widened his eyes at the brutish fiend in front of him and tried to temper his nerves down to a suitable level.

"WHAT THE FU-"

Before the man could finish his curse, the flesh-festered creature roared and lumbered quickly towards the man with their arms outstretched in an offensive t-pose, like a football player going in for a tackle and slammed the full weight of their body into the man.

Victor smiled as several villagers audibly gasped at the monster's actions. The village leader was slammed into the ground and his efforts of defense were completely futile as the strength of the monstrosity was much more than his own.

"GET THE FUCK OFF ME, YOU FOUL VERMIN!"

"GRAAAGGGHHH!"

The monster pounded both his closed fists down on the leader's chest, a finishing move that would end the man's life in a total instant.

The room was silent.

Well, besides Victor who stood up and clapped his hands in glee, a large toothy grin adorned his face as he circled around the deceased village leader with a set of skipping-like motions.

"Hehe! I've done it, I've finally done it! I've made a man! I am God! I am Him! Haha! Hehe!"

The villagers watched the depraved act of joyous commotion.

The monster grunted towards the dead and returned to their creator's side. One of the women within the villager group steeled herself and walked to the front of the group with a sharpened pitchfork grasped tightly within her right hand and had a stone-cold demeanor.

"Get out of here, now! Just leave, please. If you do that, we will not hunt you down and we will not kill you. Take you and your... monster out of here, we want to mourn for our dead and we do not want any more fighting. Please, go."

The monster clenched his fists and brought himself towards the woman but was stopped by Victor's outstretched arm.

"We shall leave."

Victor gathered a few of his things from around the lab as the eyes of the villagers watched him closely. They parted their bodies to give Victor room to leave as well as his creation who followed behind.

The villagers cheered loudly as the duo was exiled from the town.

Victor and his monster would travel far and wide by foot for months before finding the place they would call home. But, during their adventure, the two would closely bond as father and son, a relationship type that was commonplace and strong throughout the cosmos. The crafted creature began to understand the words his father would say to him through extensive teaching as his brain was young and needed to be molded into something he could utilize for the rest of his life.

"Me. Father."

Victor pointed at himself as he enunciated the words.

The monster cocked his head inquisitively and pointed at himself. "Fa...fath-ah?"

Victor smiled and shook his head.

"No... No, my son."

He pointed at himself once more.

"Me. Father."

The creature nodded and pointed his finger at the doctor.

"Fa... Fath-ah."

Victor smiled and happily shouted, "Yes! Yes, my son!"

The monster made a guttural noise that sounded like a deep chuckle.

The two's travels would continue like this for a while, deepening the bond between them and establishing a relationship that both of them would have for the rest of their respective lives. The monster's vocabulary was evolving quickly due to the doctor's restless teaching, helping the monster establish himself as his own individual rather than just an extension of protection, safety, and companionship for Victor. And, while the monster was loving the freedom of individual expression, the doctor was learning the hardships that come with being a father.

The creature looked on the floor of the grassy valley they were walking within and saw a few small skittering beetles chasing one another through the blades of grass and reached down to pick them up. He giggled at the tickle sensation that the insects were causing by traveling around on his hand.

Victor looked back to see the source of his child's amusement and saw that he had a beetle lightly clutched within his pointer and thumb and was about to drop it into his open mouth. Victor's eyes widened as he raced towards his creation.

"No! No! Get that away from there!"

He smacked the beetle out of the monster's hand, which instinctively made the creature drop the others he had clutched within his palm. The monster solemnly looked down at the ground as the beetles scurried away into their respective hiding places and then looked back up at his father who had a serious set of features plastered on his face.

"I'm sorry."

The monster sniffled and hunched as he kept his eyes to the ground.

Victor felt a sudden rush of remorse flood his body as he looked at his sad son and placed an open palm on his back.

"No, I'm sorry. I shouldn't have reacted like that. I just didn't want you to eat something bad and get sick. Are you okay?"

The monster nodded and wiped his eyes with his arm.

"Those are things we can't eat. We'll find something with protein soon, but we're not going to resort to eating bugs, okay? Just stick to the good berries and I promise we'll find something soon."

"Okay," The monster nodded.

***

As they traveled, the duo found themselves in a small grove littered with blackened trees with jagged and sprawling branches. It was in the countryside of an old territory known for its stories of witchhood and old-world sorcery. Victor had heard stories of it when he was a child but thought that they mainly resided in the arenas of fiction. But the stories he was told had the same imagery as the real-life areas he was currently in and he found it fascinating.

The monster loved the area and began to heartily chuckle as he ran around in a circle.

Victor watched with joy at his creation's antics. The monster then grasped two small handfuls of leaves and threw them in the air.

However, the monster's face slowly morphed into one of terror as a shadowed figure made their way behind Victor.

Victor gave a look of concern.

"What is it, my son?"

The creature shakily brought up his pointer finger and aimed it at something behind Victor.

"Father! Father! Look!"

Victor quickly swung his body around and was met with the view of an old, hunched woman with gray hair, wrinkles for days, and an angry set of features that could've been plastered on her since birth. Her head was adorned with a large, pointed cap that had a purple band wrapped just above the incredibly wide brim and she clasped the top of a wooden cane engraved with a series of stylized markings in her left hand.

"Oh, hello!" Victor reached his open hand out in an effort to introduce himself.

The woman continued to stare which visibly made Victor uncomfortable in his expression.

The creature began to slowly lumber behind his father.

The woman glanced up at the hulking monster but remained unfazed and returned staring at Victor.

"What makes you come here?" The woman asked in a raspy voice.

"Oh, well, ha! She speaks..." Victor humored before coughing and reverting back to a normal course of conversation as the woman remained dour, "... I heard stories about this place when I was a child and though I thought it was fiction, I thought it was the only place to seek refuge for me... and my son."

Victor motioned towards his creation. The woman raised an eyebrow as she looked at the creature once more.

"If that is true, what is this place known as in the common tongue?" The woman asked.

Victor chuckled.

"Oh, here? Not hard in the slightest. I've always been told the name of Gallowed Grove."

The woman widened her eyes and touched the ground with both her hands, her left emitted an aura of green energy, and her right emitted an aura of crimson. It was like she was sending a message that only Gaia could hear.

Suddenly, an invisible wall dissipated and revealed a series of housing cottages, bakeries, restaurants, and more that made up a small town. The entryway was adorned with a green sign containing gold lettering that said...

'WELCOME TO GALLOWED GROVE.'

The creature walked slowly behind Victor as he tried to hide his face from the busy streets of men and women who were adorned with the same pointed caps as the woman they had met.

However, there was something different about this place... They weren't giving the creature a second glance; he was a normal sight to them.

"You two will be the only non-witchbreed within this town, but I'm sure that won't bother you as you seem to have studied some form of necromancy to bring this creature to life."

"No, just science." Victor responded.

The woman was taken aback.

"You completed this..." she gestured towards the creature, "... with the tools of man's world?!"

Victor nodded.

"Interesting."

Victor scratched his temple for the moment as his creation waved at the various children in the town who really seemed to enjoy his physical appearance.

"Hi, little ones!" The monster tugged on his creator's shirt, "Father, can I go play?"

Victor chuckled.

"Yes son, go play."

Victor gestured towards the children and watched happily as his son ran over to them.

The creature outstretched his arms and began to let them hang from them, laughing joyously with them.

"I have a question. Do you think this town has to remain witchbreed? Because, I have a few ideas..."

And, with that question, the world of monsters and fiends would change forever as Victor brought the idea of making it a refuge for all the hellish damnations of the world to escape the persecution of the human world, a safe space that they could call home and live with one another. In harmony, hopefully. A new set of laws would have to be formed and an enforcement of said rules would have to be established, so Victor placed his creature as his recommendation for such a deed and the council, unanimously, approved as the town had come to love Victor's creation and showered him with gifts and food.

The monster was now designated as the sole investigator and fist of law for the people of Gallowed Grove. To prepare for this role, Victor had his creature study several books on investigative techniques, detective work, combat, and more. And, for

personal amusement along with giving the town something else to call him besides 'monster'

Victor granted him a new name, Frank N. Stein... Detective Frank N. Stein.

GALLOWED GROVE

Chapter 2: Meeting at TomTom's

Many years later...

The heavy footsteps of worn leather boots echoed throughout the silent and rain-drenched streets of a town shrouded in complete mystery. The figure who owned the boots could only be described as a hulking figure whose features were enveloped in a long, wide-collar, beige trench coat that stretched down to the top of their knees, a white button-up undershirt, a messily prepared tie, and a fedora stylized with a red band that wrapped around just above the brim. They brought up their hand to their mouth and smoked the last puff on a cigarette before throwing the stub onto the street below and stamping it out with the heel of their boot.

The individual looked up at a lone streetlight whose bulb was blinking erratically before reaching into their interior jacket pocket and pulling out a small, black leather notebook and flipping to a specific page and studied the writing carefully.

CASE REPORT #000246

Throughout the months of August to November, missing persons reports have begun to rack up within the law enforcement headquarters of Gallowed Grove coming to an accumulation of around sixteen. A common theme of the kidnappings being that all of the victims were female pixies from the age range of thirteen-to-seventeen. Two separate witnesses of different kidnappings have come to the conclusion of two differently appearing attackers which makes me believe that this may be the work of a group hidden within the walls of Gallowed Grove.

There hasn't been much in the way of discovering who the culprits are in these acts of tearing families apart. But, yesterday, a call came into the office and it seems like one person is willing to speak on these kidnappings, someone who seems to have close contact with whoever is causing these terrifying crimes.

The individual wanted a meeting at TomTom's, a local diner within Gallowed Grove, hopefully this will give me a break in the case. I really need to solve this, I can't deal with any more crying mothers and fathers, I just can't.

Frank's eyes lingered on the last sentence before closing the book and placing it back into its original pocket. His mind going through the logistics of the case and the worry of never finding the girls culminated into a mixture of anxiety-laden dread. Frank began to breathe heavily as he found an alleyway and began to whisper himself into a sense of calm. Frank closed his eyes as a memory began to fade in.

***

Frank sat at Victor's bedside. Victor was now bedridden with a medicinal intravenous next to him slowly administering life-saving fluid. On the other-side was a slow-beeping screen that showed Victor's strained heart rate through digital imagery.

Victor smiled as he saw his child.

Frank set their fedora down beside the chair and looked up at Victor with tear-filled eyes.

"They told me today or tomorrow was your last day."

Victor nodded.

"That is true."

Frank sniffled and covered their eyes with open palms.

"No, dad. Please, don't go. You can't go, not yet."

Victor gave a small chuckle.

"Frank, Frank, my sweet child. It will all be okay, I promise. I have taught you all you need to know. You must carve out your own way in life."

"But I want you there with me. I don't want to be without you!"

"It was always going to come to this Frank, you knew this... I knew this. It's time for me to go, but before I do... You must promise me one thing."

Frank nodded as he sobbed.

"You must promise me to always show a true sense of good, to always help those in need, to be the one that people can count on... no matter the obstacles ahead."

Frank nodded his head as he listened to his father's words.

"I promise, I promise."

16

Victor smiled and turned his head, so he looked at the ceiling, his eyes closed, and his heart rate began to flatline.

Frank wailed into his father's shoulder.

***

Frank wiped a small tear that began to form within the corner of his right eye and stood up, his father's words echoing in his head.

"Be the one that people can count on... no matter the obstacles ahead."

Frank walked out of the alley and continued towards his main objective as he walked up to the entry door of *TomTom's,* a blinking white and green LED sign adorned with the name and the logo of a four-leaf clover illuminated the street and area around Frank. He sighed before opening the door, a small bell rang to signal entry.

The woman behind the diner counter had black hair with a single red streak through the side, striking green eyes, ruby lipstick, and two small fangs protruding from the sides of her mouth.

She gave a smile to the detective.

"Hey, Frank. Been a while! What can I get for ya?"

Frank waved and gave a smile.

"Hi, Alicia. Just the usual, please."

"You got it!"

Frank smiled and nodded, his eyes scanning the few patrons within the restaurant as he attempted to find his contact, realizing that it was probably pointless due to the fact that he didn't know their face. His attention was soon taken by a trio of knocks from a table behind him, accompanied by a small cough. Frank turned around and saw a headless torso adorned in a black leather motorcycle jacket that had a visible red interior and a red cape strapped onto his shoulders, however the oddest thing about the whole individual was that his right hand was keeping his disembodied head stationary on the table. The head clearly showed that the creature was a sweaty white male with messy blonde hair and a same-coloured goatee whose yellowed teeth nervously chattered as his eyes darted around the room with a frenzied speed as if he were afraid of something or someone.

The torso knocked with its left hand again and the head began signaling with his eyes that.

Frank should sit down to which he obliged and sat in the booth on the other side of the table so they could both be in a comfortable, conversational position. Frank removed his fedora and set it down in the center between them.

"I haven't seen you around before."

The quick pace of the head's eyes slowed down as he took deep breaths in an effort to calm himself before settling his sights on Frank.

"You may not have seen me around, brass. But you're a big name around town. I'mma need something from ya' though, I'mma need ya' to make me a promise."

The detective shook his head.

"No. No. That's not how we're doing things. You tell me what's going on and why you've called me here and I'll decide if a deal goes through or not."

The head looked up to the left and ran things through his mind for a few moments.

"Okay, okay. I can't stand to watch anymore people get hurt."

Frank reached into his pocket and pulled out his notebook again along with a pencil, flipping to the next available blank page.

"What's your name?"

"Nah, I'm not doin' any names."

"That's not how this works. Names."

"Not if you want what I got..."

Frank slammed his flesh-pieced fist against the table, causing the head to yelp in surprise and the body to slightly jump.

"If being arrested is something you want to avoid, I suggest you give a name."

The head groaned.

"Fine, call me Krayne. K-R-A-"

"... Y-N-E. Got it." Frank scribbled it down in his notebook.

"Ay! No one has ever got that right before. Neat."

Alicia made her way over to the table and sat down a plate of five pancakes doused in syrup in front of Frank and a pile of spaghetti in front of Krayne. She gave the disembodied head a weird look before giving a sly smirk towards both men.

"Enjoy, boys."

"Thanks, gorgeous." said Krayne.

"Appreciate it, Alicia." Frank gave her a nod as she walked off.

The torso's left hand grabbed the fork beside his plate and began to twirl the sauce-smattered noodles onto the prongs and began to feed it to Krayne's head.

Frank watched the scene in slight disgust as it just seemed that the noodles magically disappeared into the head's own digestive system, something he had no explanation for. He ignored his pancakes and readied his notebook and pencil again.

"Please, Krayne, start from the beginning."

Krayne slurped down some noodles before speaking.

"Okay, okay. So, a few months back, I and a few other guys get a call from some really eccentric dude. Like, really eccentric. And, in short, he basically told us he's got this thing for young pixie girls. I thought it was weird, but he was offering a lot of money. Like, A LOT of fuckin' money. It was fuckin' WILD bro, me and the other guys had never even really heard about that type of money just bein' dished out..."

Krayne stopped speaking for a moment as his torso cleaned the tomato sauce from his

face.

"... Thank you. Anyway, dude's offering BIG money. He said he couldn't do it himself due to some personal shit, but he wanted to hire us out to kidnap some pixie chicks and drop them off at a particular location. Now, I wasn't gettin' my hands dirty! Nah, fuck that business. But I did the lookout for one of the dudes who was fine with the whole snatch and grab shit. He loved it, but my ass is too delicate y'know? But, anyways, I was okay with the whole thing before... before we went to the dude's place and I saw what he was doing to them. I know, I know, why did I do it? I don't know man, greed? Yeah, definitely greed. But that all stopped when I saw that shit..."

Krayne's eyelids began to slowly form a pool of tears within them.

"What was he doing to the girls, Krayne?"

Krayne was beginning to have a strained speech before he just let it all out.

"Fuck, man! He was ripping their wings off and slitting their throats, putting their bodies in a pile, and letting them rot on top of one each other. I wish I could go back and say no, man. I wish I could go back..."

Frank wrote down the newly acquired information in his notebook.

"And where was he doing this?"

"The old balloon factory. That was his playing ground or whatever the hell. Now, am I gonna get protection or wha-"

Krayne was cut off as a shot rang through the air and a bullet coursed through the large window of the restaurant before perforating his chest.

The whole scene felt like it played out in slow-motion as Frank reached out to grab Krayne's slumping body as his eyes rolled into the back of his head as he took his last breath.

Frank dove out of the booth and found cover as the other patrons ran out from the diner in fear and Alicia presumably stayed hidden underneath the counter or in the kitchen. Frank took another look at Krayne's deceased body.

"Dammit."

He looked up towards the large glass window that the shot came from and saw the reflective glint of a sniper scope retreat into the window of a large building across the street.

Frank made haste and quickly exited out of the diner as he made his way towards the building which hid the killer, his mind mentally mapping out which floor and window the killer hid themselves within. Frank made it a point not to use firearms and preferred if violence had to take place, he would only use the pure brutish force from his own hands as it made it more personal. But, understood in doing that, he was placing himself under an extreme amount of danger.

So, he quietly made his way through the dilapidated corpse of a hotel that was obviously just a shell of what it once was and readied his fists in an offensive position. He ignored the creaks and groans of the hotel's stairs and tried to focus on any and all sounds coming from the floor the assassin was situated in.

Finally, he made it outside of the room and got into a crouched position as he slowly opened the door. A loud shot rang out and blasted through the door just above Frank's head. The detective heard the clicking sound of a bolt-action rifle to reload and realized he had his chance. He roared while rushing into the room in a tackle position as the assassin tried to hurriedly reload their weapon. Frank swung a backhand towards the killer and knocked the rifle out of their hands.

The assassin performed a roll to the side as a defensive maneuver against any other attacks and rose themselves into a boxing position. The moonlight from the window they were in front of gave Frank a clear view of the individual, it was a woman with an athletic body type, black hair with a red streak running through the side, striking green eyes, and two pearly white fangs protruding out from the sides of her ruby-red lips.

"Alicia?"

She smirked and kicked out, hitting Frank in the stomach. He forcefully exhaled as the wind was knocked out of him.

"Surprised?"

"A little."

She threw a combination of three jabs; one connected with Frank's ribcage, the other with the side of his head which dazed him a little, but he managed to catch the last one in his hand before throwing a haymaker with his free hand and knocking Alicia into a nearby wall.

Alicia growled and bared her fangs towards the detective as she skittered across the floor towards him. Frank attempted to sidestep her before she sprung herself onto his front half and maneuvered herself onto his back, she opened her mouth and slammed her fangs into the side of his neck.

"GRAAGH!"

Frank screamed as he tried to grab for the vampiric waitress-turned-assassin, but she dodged his attempts and even slashed through the flesh of his wrist with her nails. An idea formulated within the detective's head as he attempted an unorthodox maneuver and jumped into the air, forcing both his back and Alicia's into the ground hard.

Alicia wheezed and sprawled her arms outward in defeat as she laid on the ground.

Frank stood up and looked at the pained Alicia before bending down and grabbing her arm.

"Time to go downtown."

Alicia hissed and slammed her fingernails into the wound she created on Frank's wrist which caused him to immediately yowl in pain and let her go.

"Not if I can help it!"

She then dove out of the window and into the street below. Frank watched from the

window and mentally noted that she was heading into the general direction of the balloon factory that Krayne had mentioned before.

It was time for this to be over.

24

GALLOWED GROVE

Chapter 3: An Old Foe

Frank exited the building quickly and in a pained daze as he followed Alicia to the old balloon factory that hadn't been used in the town for nearly twenty years. Frank paid no mind to the various freaks and fiends who watched in confusion as he quickly made his way through the streets.

Finally, he made it. Frank looked up at the large, intimidating metallic double-doors of the factory. He realized one of the doors was slightly open as if someone had just recently made their way inside the building and used the same entry to allow himself in.

The room that he entered was completely dark except for a single lone spotlight that caused one single circle of light that Frank assumed was for him, a personal target for him to stand in the center of. He walked towards the light and as soon as he stepped into it, a surround system began to reverberate the room around him with a booming voice.

"Welcome, Detective Stein. It's a shame that Krayne had to speak, I quite enjoyed his particularly... crude antics. But, after hearing rumors about his potential betrayal, I had to put an end to it."

"My name is Ferdinand Blymouth and I have a personal feud with you and your father, well, he wasn't truly your father. He was just the man who engineered you into a damn monstrosity."

Frank grimaced towards the voice.

"Don't talk about my father!"

"It really is too bad that he passed when he did, I remember when I heard the news... I was sad at first because damn I really wanted him to die by my own hands. But then I smiled. Smiled because I was glad that the bastard was dead."

Frank roared at the area around him.

"Yes! Yes! Let that anger out! SHOW ME WHAT YOU'RE MADE OF!"

"WHAT DID MY FATHER EVER DO TO YOU? HE WAS A GOOD MAN!"

The loudspeaker stayed silent for a few moments.

"A good man? A GOOD MAN?! FRANK, HE DESTROYED MY LIFE! YOU... YOU DESTROYED MY FUCKIN' LIFE!"

Suddenly, the sound of squeaking could be heard as Alicia emerged from the shadows pushing a wheelchair. In the chair, a stout man with a handlebar moustache sat, his face was covered by a technologically modified breathing apparatus that allowed him to not only speak through the factory's speakers but also filtered oxygen into his system that was connected to two tanks situated on the back of the chair.

Frank widened his eyes and gave a small gasp as the memory flooded in of when he was born and killing the man that now sat in front of him.

The man smirked as he noticed Frank's realization.

"You remember me, eh? After you two had left, the village had brought in a shaman that was skilled in the magic of healing... the magic of life. He resurrected me, but when you hit me, you also irreparably destroyed most of my spine, something that not even the shaman's strongest magic could fix. I was unable to use my legs, I was told that the only thing that could possibly help me was pixie dust. But, that was such a rare commodity, I would never find it. I thought anyways."

Alicia reached within her pocket and pulled out a small vial of teal powder and giggled as she shook it towards Frank. Alicia removed the breathing apparatus from the face of Ferdinand, she placed the powder on the top of her middle finger and put it underneath Ferdinand's nose which he snorted.

His eyes shot open and his veins glowed blue as the muscles in his arms, back, and legs began to fluctuate violently.

"I'm sorry for what we put you through, Ferdinand. But you've destroyed countless families!"

Ferdinand fell out of his chair as his body began to triple its normal size, his voice deepening as he spoke.

"You destroyed me! I scoured the Earth looking for you and your father, wanting revenge! Wanting payback! I had heard rumblings of an invisible society of monsters and freaks while I traveled the world looking for you two. I researched and talked to those who knew of this society of myth, I learned that it would contain things that would assist me in my revenge."

"How'd you make it all this time? How are you still alive?" Frank asked backing up from Ferdinand's slowly mutating body.

Ferdinand devilishly smirked as he began to push himself off the floor.

"Oh, I didn't tell you the best part? The shaman gave me one more gift before I started my hunt. He gave me the gift of immortality with a twist! But every gift comes with a price. I was told that the only thing that could kill me was the thing that killed me originally. But I wasn't going to allow that to happen. So, since I can't get revenge on your father... I CAN FUCKING KILL YOU!"

Frank watched in shock as Ferdinand looked to the skies and roared.

Ferdinand smirked in his new form. The veins in every visible part of his body popped through his skin, his eyes were a plain shade of white, and he was a much different, much stronger, much larger man than he once was. He gave a devilish smirk towards Frank.

"I'LL TAKE AS MUCH AS I NEED TO MAKE SURE YOU'RE DEAD."

Frank gulped.

Alicia placed the powder back into her pocket and snuck out of the building before the carnage ensued.

Ferdinand cracked his knuckles and swung downwards at Frank who narrowly dodged the attack. Frank looked around the room, but everything was covered in darkness, nothing was visible except for the lone lightbulb that illuminated their battleground. Suddenly, a plan began to form in Frank's head.

Frank ran towards Ferdinand who responded with a roar as he slammed his fists into the ground and created a shockwave effect that blasted the detective off his feet and sent him several meters into the darkness.

He sat up and shook his head out of his daze.

"Well, that's not the best approach."

Frank's eyes widened as he saw Ferdinand running at full speed towards him. He quickly got up and ran back towards the circle of light and Ferdinand followed. As Frank reached the center, he turned to face Ferdinand who was still lumbering towards him and gave him a taunting motion that only got Ferdinand angrier. He ran for Frank and swung his arm, Frank climbed up the arm and to Ferdinand's back to which he could reach the light hanging down from the ceiling. And, in the rapid movement of Ferdinand's body, he managed to clasp the light within his left hand and crush it within his palm.

If Frank couldn't see, neither could Ferdinand. Frank used that to his advantage.

Due to Ferdinand's sheer size and the sensory disruption of the light off, he wasn't aiming his hands where he should be, he was aiming too high.

But, all Frank had to do was aim low and smashed his fists into the left kneecap of the old foe, shattering it and causing Ferdinand to howl in pain and kneel.

Frank predicted where Ferdinand's chin would be and got a little of a jumping start as he delivered a devastating hit to his head.

Ferdinand fell backwards.

"No, you bastard! No!!"

Frank ignored the many pleas of Ferdinand as he slowly made his way to the chest area of the man and raised both of his fists.

"Shouldn't have talked bad about dad."

Frank slammed downwards as hard as he could and opened Ferdinand's chest cavity with a sickening squelch and grabbed the killer's heart before squeezing it as it squished in his palms.

Ferdinand let out a single breath before he was finally killed, this time forever. Frank let out a breath and wiped the sweat off his forehead before he looked up.

"You owe me one, dad."

He walked out of the balloon factory and back to *TomTom's* where a diminutive man with a pipe sticking out of his mouth adorned in a green suit, a green top hat and had red, curly hair along with a red beard stood there angrily stomping his foot.

"Dammit! Frank! You gotta stop letting your work interfere with my business! I got a damn restaurant to run!"

Frank picked up his fedora from the table that Krayne was still slumped in and looked at the restaurant manager.

"Sorry, Timmy! Won't happen again."

Timmy rumbled and cursed under his breath, "Damn straight it won't happen again."

Frank took a heavy breath and walked out of the restaurant.

Another case solved.

EVOLVER

- Candace Rugg

Chapter One

"Cass get your ass out on the floor. We are packed to the brim tonight with patrons and we can't handle it with just two fucking servers!"

"I just got here PETE give me a minute to at least get my coat off before you start barking orders at me!"

"Well, what do I pay you for if you are not going to be ready to be out on that floor the minute you arrive here!?"

Cass could feel the anger welling up inside of her. If she didn't need this shitty serving job at the Broken Record Bar so badly, she would have told her boss, Pete, to fuck off a long time ago. But life was hard enough as it is, and the last thing she needed was to be jobless in a time where having one meant that you had a shred of dignity left.

She took a deep breath in.

That's right just stay calm and ignore him, just get through this night and you'll be Just fine.

Cass exhaled and proceeded to tear off her coat and other belongings rapidly off her body, revealing her "uniform" which was nothing but a skimpy yellow and orange neon dress that clung to her body like tight latex. Pete had told her once that it was more pleasing to the patrons to see a human woman dressed in skimpy clothing. But personally, Cass thought it had the opposite effect.

"What section am I getting tonight?" She asked while she hooked a rather large pair of gaudy, metal earrings through her ears.

"The VIP section."

Cass's heart sank into the pit of her stomach.

He has got to be kidding.

"Come on Pete, I know that we started tonight off on the wrong foot, but to assign me to THAT section after what happened? That's a new low even for you."

It had taken Cass several bottles of whiskey to push the image of her former co-worker's mangled body from her mind. Sadie was found torn to shreds on the VIP lounge floor last month. Her once beautiful, sweet face was barely recognizable by the time Cass saw her. The two weren't particularly close, but Sadie had always been shy and sweet to everyone she had ever talked to. It was hard to imagine how she could've provoked a Zecurcian to attack her.

Everyone was horrified by what had happened to Sadie. Unfortunately, you cannot stop working for long at the Broken Record during business hours. It was a death sentence. Pete had no choice but to wrap her up in a rug and wait till closing time to deal with the cleanup. Cass was pretty sure the blood stains were still in the carpet floor of the lounge.

"I know, but it's not like I can turn away *their* business. Just keep your head down and don't look em' in the eyes."

She was also pretty sure Pete gave Sadie the same advice the night she had died. She shuddered at the thought.

32

"If you get nervous, just choke some beer down, I won't judge you for it. Now stop wasting more of my time and get out there already." Pete turned and left through the main door of the locker room, leaving Cass behind to seethe in her growing fear and anger.

This was quickly turning into a shitty night.

However, Pete did have a point, there was nothing that he could do to fix this situation. Nobody on Earth could for that matter. She was just going to have to hope that her customers were feeling merciful tonight.

***

The music blared against Cass' ears as she snaked her way up to the bar rail on the main dance floor. She took a moment to look around the room. Pete wasn't kidding the place was packed tonight. She could see her coworkers running around desperately trying to bring their orders to their tables.

Cass admired them. They still maintained their false calm appearances, their fake smiles.

"Hey Cass, can you take this to table five? Marcy is having a rough time getting her shit together tonight, and I don't want things to escalate to violence because someone didn't get their damn drinks on time."

Kevin, the main bartender of The Broken Record, pushed a serving tray towards Cass. It looked heavy and was loaded to the brim with large beverages that could topple over at any given moment.

"Maybe she would get her shit together if you stopped giving her trays that would spill on the clients, Kev."

"Hey, it's not my fault. You know how temperamental these guys get," he stated with a shrug.

"If they don't get what they ask for right away, they get triggered...and then you die."

He shot her a grin.

"I prefer to live."

Cass laughed as she hoisted up the serving tray "Don't we all?"

"That is debatable at this point," Kevin's carefree smile faded for just a moment. "I heard what section you got tonight. That's some bad luck Cass."

Crap that's right I forgot.

Kevin had been the first person to discover Sadie the night she had died. He was like a big brother to everyone in the bar, but he always had a soft spot for Sadie. Cass knew that he somehow blamed himself for her death.

Kevin might not have been saying it out loud, but his eyes were full of concern.

Would the same thing happen to her tonight?

"Don't worry about me Kevin, I'll be fine." She was scared but she wasn't about to let everyone in the damn bar know about it. It wouldn't do them any good.

She turned and started to make her way across the room to her table; in doing so she allowed her eyes to wander around the room. Tonight, the bar was completely rented out by the Zecurcian army. That meant the VIP section was going to have some sort of important figurehead within it.

Cass shuddered.

Zecurcians were the things of nightmares. They had red skin, white hair, and were also extremely tall, with four pairs of eyes that were pitch black. They were also armed to the teeth with fangs, claws, and advanced weaponry that could obliterate any living creature in seconds. It wasn't a surprise that they managed to take over the planet so quickly. Zecurcians were also extremely ill tempered, and easy to offend. Making random acts of violence quite common among them. If Cass was going to survive her shift tonight, she needed to be careful with basically everything.

"My Lords." She bowed and smiled politely when she arrived at her table. It was occupied by two large male Zecurcians that had irritated expressions etched on their faces.

It made the hairs on the back of Cass's neck stand up.

Pete's words rang into her head in that moment.

Don't look them in the eyes...stay calm.

She let out a quick breath before she presented them the tray and bowed deeply.

"I live to serve you."

It was absolutely humiliating, but she hoped that worthless line was enough to satisfy them.

A long silence followed. Cass was beginning to sweat until one of them finally leaned forward and plucked the drinks from her.

"Pah, and don't you forget it, *human*." He sneered.

The Zecurcian who spoke finished his drink in an instant and slammed the glass back onto the tray.

"If I were in charge, I would have wiped this planet from existence. I don't know what Overlord was thinking when he spared your miserable species."

Fuck you too buddy.

"O-of course my lords we owe you everything." Cass's voice shook as she spoke.

More irritation shot across their faces.

Shit.

"Leave us." The other one demanded with a snarl.

They certainly didn't have to ask her twice. She gave them another deep bow before turning and leaving them to talk about how much humans suck, or whatever it was that Zecurcians discussed.

"Tough crowd tonight." She mentioned to Kevin when she returned to the safety of the bar railing.

"Always." He sighed as he slid her another tray. "This is for your VIP room."

Cass froze.

"I haven't been up there yet---"

"Don't worry they put their order in when they arrived. It hasn't been very long so they shouldn't take offense."

"Oh...alright then," Cass grabbed the tray and gave him a small smile.

"Thanks for getting this together for me Kev, I owe you the biggest drink when my shift is up."

"It's no big deal Cass I'll see you soon."

Without another word, Cass hoisted the tray up from the rail, and started walking towards the stairs that would take her to the lounge.

And possibly to her death.

***

Cass tried to remain calm as she made her way up to the lounge.

The VIP section of the Broken Record wasn't anything special. It was in a lofted area that was just above the main bar that was sectioned off to be one big giant room. Pete originally intended for the space to be another dance floor. But after the Zecurcians showed up, he ended up installing soundproof walls and turned the spot into a sitting lounge since his new clientele were not fond of dancing. Unfortunately for everyone, it quickly became a favorite meeting spot for the aliens to meet up.

"My lords I've come with your drink order," she called out.

With a shaky free hand, she punched in the door code and entered the room.

There were five of them. All massive, and all taking up what little space that the room had to offer. Four were seated on the lounge's couches that were facing each other in the middle of the room. They didn't bother to look up from what they were doing when Cass had entered.

Instead, they remained focused on the fifth one who was casually leaning back in a cushioned chair in front of them.

The fifth guy... wasn't a Zecurcian.

He wasn't anything like she had ever seen before either. He clearly wasn't human, and yet he looked almost like one. The only difference was that his skin was a light purple and that his ears came to a point.

"What is this now?" The mysterious being stood up from the chair. His eyes were fixed on Cass, like a snake about to strike its prey.

"Y-your order? I've brought it to you."

The look on his face said it all. He was clearly not expecting her to arrive.

"My order you say...how amusing." He turned to the other aliens in the room. "I don't ever recall ever ordering anything. Do any of you?"

The Zecurcians all stood up at once causing panic to shoot through Cass in an instant.

What the hell is going on?

"Did I say order my Lords? What I meant to say was that it's an offering to you from this establishment." Cass bowed low as she presented the tray. "I was told to give you this, as you are an honored guest."

It was a straight up lie but she needed to pull something out of thin air to save herself. A million questions began to race through Cass's mind.

Why would Kevin send her here? Did he make a mistake?

The Being let out a laugh.

"Well, aren't you a clever one." He said in an amused tone.

He stood up from his chair and glided over to Cass. Whatever this thing was, he was incredibly tall, maybe even taller than the other aliens in the room. He towered over Cass as he reached down and grabbed a goblet off the tray.

"Tell me, what is *this* establishment offering me?" The Being swirled the cup in his hands and raised it to his nose.

"Our finest selection of brandy and top shelf drinks made special just for you, my lord."

"Fascinating."

The Being turned to the Zecurcians.

"Be seated." He commanded.

Immediately they all sat back down, however their pitch-black eyes remained focused on Cass.

It sent a shiver down her spine. Whoever this was, he clearly had authority over them.

"Come, sit with me human. Your timing couldn't have been more perfect. I have questions about your species that only a human can answer."

"Ah, I really should get back to my duties my lor-"

"Are you refusing my request?" The being shot her an irritated scowl.

Shit

"Of course not!" She smiled as best as she could. "I would be happy to answer any of your questions."

The being smiled back. However, it didn't reach his eyes.

"Excellent...so happy that you decided to indulge me."

Cass followed him over to a section of the lounge that wasn't currently being occupied by four large aliens waiting to pounce on her and took a seat into a small purple loveseat that was nestled away in a corner.

"Here let me take those off your hands," he gestured to her drink tray.

The being reached out with one of his hands and closed his eyes.

A blue aura instantly consumed the tray and soon it pulled itself out of her gasp, and into the air.

"Holy shit!" Cass gasped.

The tray was levitating.

She watched in awe as it slowly made its way over to a coffee table where the Zecurcians were sitting.

"I take it from your slack jawed expression that seeing something like this isn't common on your planet?"

"No. That was incredible!" She beamed.

The Being smiled. This time it was genuine. Clearly, he liked being complimented "Please call me Arharkin."

"A-alright Lord Arharkin..."

"What can I call you human?"

"My name is Cassidy, but everyone calls me Cass for short."

Arharkin let out a laugh "Why would someone shorten their name to a simple noise?"

"For that very reason. It keeps things simple and short...plus I like it better."

"Amusing." Arharkin sat himself down next to her in the loveseat and studied Cass for a long moment. The silence was beginning to unnerve her until he finally spoke up.

"You're female." He stated.

No shit, Sherlock...

40

"Yes. I am," she replied.

"I've never had a chance to converse with one in person before." Arharkin leaned back into the seat and gave her a sideways glance. "I've only seen them on what you humans call a TV. My work hasn't given me much time to fully explore your planet and cultures. But one day I'm sure I'll get around to it."

Fat chance, everything got destroyed...

"When that day comes, I hope that we don't disappoint you, Lord Arharkin," she stated. Cass was just being polite, but she could sense that her answer somehow bothered him.

In an instant his whole demeanor changed.

"You already have dear; this planet went belly up in a matter of days." Arharkin's face was all pleasant and smiles, but his voice was full of disgust and venom.

"I've actually seen bugs that put up a better fight than you humans ever did."

She remained silent.

Cass found that this was usually the best thing to do in these types of situations. She had seen too many run ins over the same topic with humans and Zecurcians. It always ended the same though. Death for the human who dared to talk back.

"What's this? No response? Where is that human pride that I keep hearing so much about?"

Arharkin reached out and lightly grasped a strand of Cass's hair between his fingers.

"Or maybe you have other ways of venting your anger and frustration."

Cass quickly pulled herself away from Arharkin's reach and scooched herself as far away from him as the couch would allow. He didn't seem bothered by her reaction though. He looked more entertained by it actually.

"What questions would you like to ask me, Lord Arharkin?" She asked hoping that he would drop the last subject.

"Well, you already answered one for me already." His eyes raked over her once more.

"The other is more of a debate question that I would love to hear a human response to."

"What is it?"

His smile twisted.

"Why should the human race continue to live?"

Silence.

She was speechless really; how could she possibly answer this question without seeming like she was retaliating against her alien oppressors?

What sort of sick torture would she have to endure for speaking her mind?

But what if she didn't answer?

Would her silence actually bring death to her and humanity? Arharkin was clearly in a position to make that happen based on the amount of authority he carried with the Zecurcians. Panic quickly shot through her. She stared desperately at the unknown alien. He was practically gleaming at her. Arharkin was toying with her, and clearly enjoying it.

"Well?"

However, before Cass even had the chance to speak fits of wheezing and coughs erupted from the Zecurcians across the room. Arharkin looked unbothered by the sound but soon It grew more desperate and sporadic, to the point where it was hard to ignore. Even for Arharkin.

They both glanced over.

Two of the Zecurcian generals were clutching and clawing at their throats struggling to breathe, their faces were quickly turning an even darker shade of red than normal. Their bodies began to shudder and shake, causing one of them to fall off the couch and go crashing to the ground.

The two remaining Zecurcian men picked up their cups and brought it to their noses.

"Deathroot!" One of the remaining generals snarled.

Cass noticed the discarded goblets rolling around on the lounge floor from where the two Zecurcians were choking. The liquid inside had turned neon pink and was currently burning a hole in the lounge floor.

Deathroot. It was undetectable in its first stages of application, but after a set amount of time it changes color and kills its victim from the inside out. All the color drained from Cass's face as she realized what was happening.

She glanced over to Arharkin's goblet and noticed the same color liquid had suddenly appeared inside of it. She felt the blue aura around her body before she had a chance to even speak.

"I guess this is what I get for entertaining myself with human company."

Cass was thrown against the ceiling with such force that it rattled her teeth. She tried to speak but whatever this power was that

Arharkin wielded, it was preventing her from even drawing in breath.

Arharkin turned to the remaining Zecurcians.

"Clear the area. If you see any humans bring them to me and kill them if they resist." His voice was casual and calm as he spoke.

"Do we have to bring them here *alive*?" One of them complained.

Arharkin released his hold on Cass long enough for her to come crashing down from the ceiling and into a wooden coffee table that broke her fall. The table splintered on impact and caused sharp pieces of wood to lodge themselves into Cass' body.

"I didn't do anything!" She screamed desperately.

Arharkin ignored her as he continued to address the Zecurcians. "You have your orders."

The Generals grunted as they stalked towards the entrance of the room.

The music of the night club blared in Cass' ears as the door to the room opened and then closed behind the Zecurcians.

"Please, don't kill me."

Arharkin let out a cruel laugh as he approached her.

"Please..." Cass choked. She looked up desperately at him; tears stinging her eyes. "I was set up. I swear to god!"

"I must admit--I love hearing you beg for your life." Arharkin said. He kneeled beside Cass and gently brushed his fingers across a large wooden splinter that was lodged into her side. In an instant he grabbed a hold of the wood and yanked it out causing Cass to let out a yelp of pain. Blood began to rapidly spread across her abdomen and spill onto the floor, it took everything in Cass's power not to faint from the sight of it. She covered the wound with one of her hands to stop the bleeding.

She also watched in muted horror as Arharkin dipped his outstretched hand into her splatters of blood on the floor and began to smear it around like some kid with an art project. He flexed his fingers and squished them together as he brought his hand up to his face for further inspection.

Without breaking his concentration from examining the blood he spoke.

"Who sent you to me?"

A breath was caught in the back of Cass's throat. For a split second she thought about Kevin and his carefree smile. She thought back to the tray that he handed her before she came upstairs.

Could he have really done this to her?

She realized that she must have taken too long to answer Arharkin because the next thing Cass knew she was being thrown across the room again. This time though she had the good fortune of colliding with one of the couches.

It still hurt like hell but at least it was something softer than the ceiling or the ground.

"I asked you a question." Arharkin stated dully.

Cass struggled to sit up after her collision with the couch, her vision was already starting to blur from the amount of blood that she was losing.

She stared across the room at the purple alien that was determined to torture her.

It was very unlikely that she was going to survive this, and if Arharkin didn't kill her, the wound in her side was going to do the trick.

It was only a matter of *when* death was going to arrive for her today.

Fuck it.

"I found out at the same time as you did." Her voice was shaking as she spoke.

"I had no idea that the drinks had been poisoned, I just came to work thinking that this was just going to be a regular shitty shift here. Instead, I had to have the worst luck in the world and have this shit happen to me.

So cut the bullshit and just kill me already! I know you are going to do it anyway!"

"Silence." In an instant Arharkin was in front of her

"Now yo-"

BANG

The door to the VIP room suddenly flew open and was sent flying across the room. It landed with a loud crash against a mirror that instantly shattered on impact. A small hum filled Cass' ears as she watched a tall, hooded figure emerge into the frame of the doorway. Arharkin turned away from Cass; his hand outstretched towards the stranger preparing to attack instantly, however much to his surprise the blue energy that normally would form didn't appear. A look of shock crossed his face.

"No way," he murmured.

The Figure stepped into the room, carrying a severed head of a Zecurcian. Cass's eyes widened with surprise when the stranger tossed it causally towards Arharkin's feet.

Whoever this person was, they were incredibly tall; and they were dangerous. They were clad in all pitch-black gear and were armed to the teeth with all sorts of weapons that Cass had never laid eyes on before. A long black hood was draped over their head and left an opening that revealed a metal plated mask underneath it.

Arharkin let out a fit of hysterical laughter.

"Oh, you have got to be kidding me!" He shouted with excitement.

Without saying a word, the masked figure quickly unsheathed a long, narrow, black blade from their side. At that moment, a small mechanical orb that was attached to a chain around the stranger's neck began to glow green and float in front of them.

Arharkin quickly turned and lifted one of the couches into the air and hurled it towards the stranger.

They didn't even try to dodge it.

In a matter of seconds, the couch was torn into shreds before it could even reach its target.

Amazing. Cass didn't even see the figure move an inch.

The stranger took a step towards Arharkin and turned the blade in their hands...

Arharkin smiled with amusement.

"Let's not get too cocky now."

Arharkin reached into one of his pockets and produced a metal orb that looked identical to the one that the stranger was wearing.

"This is what you want, right?" He asked in a playful tone.

The stranger froze in place as the orb in Arharkin's hand began to float and emit a blue glow.

A beam of bright blue light erupted from it that sent a shock wave throughout the entire room. The stranger stabbed their blade into floorboards and braced themselves against the wave's blast. Their own orb formed a small transparent barrier in front of them.

Objects began to rapidly blast into the air as more waves began to rapidly come from the blue orb. Cass had thrown herself to the ground and was trying desperately not to get hit by the flying objects in the room. It was like a tornado was being unleashed on all of them.

Cass glanced up at Arharkin who remained unaffected by the blasts of the orb.

She watched as the stranger was being pushed back slowly from the blasts, it wouldn't be long before they struggled to keep up with their guard.

Shit.

How was she going to survive, when the one thing that could maybe get her out of this situation was just seconds away from being blasted apart? Cass stared into the blue light that was coming out of the orb. This little piece of junk was the source of all this power? The humming in her ears seemed to grow louder the more she stared at it.

What is this feeling?

If this little thing could do all this damage, could it maybe get her out of this mess?

She could feel adrenaline rushing into her veins the second she made up her mind.

Fuck it.

Cass began to army crawl her way across the floor and towards Arharkin. She winced in pain as she felt her battered body drag across the ground.

Arharkin had his back completely turned to her, his full attention on the Stranger.

Good, keep looking away from me you bastard!

As she got closer, she looked around the room for something to strike him with, something sharp, something to make him suffer as much as she did. The blasts weren't making finding a weapon any easier. Cass winced again as she felt a painful tug on her thigh as she dragged herself further along the floor. She looked back and noticed a large wooden splinter from her earlier encounter with the coffee table was embedded into the back of her thigh.

She had been in too much pain to notice that was there. Her face turned slightly green at the sight of it.

It would have to do though.

Cass reached back and grasped onto the piece of wood, and in one swift motion yanked it out. She clenched her teeth together to keep from making a sound. She tried not to look at the blood that covered the wood. Instead she focused on Arharkin and remembered the way he threw her around like a rag doll.

Without a second thought, Cass stabbed one of Arharkin's legs as deeply as she could manage. Arharkin let out a yelp of pain that caused him to break his concentration on his attack.

Without Arharkin controlling it, the orb quickly began to fall.

In that exact moment Cass's free hand reached out and caught the orb before it could reach the ground.

Cass's vision began to blur as soon as she felt the cool metal hit her skin. Her body began to rise dramatically in temperature.

Something wasn't right.

Suddenly, small unknown symbols began to flash across her vision at a rapid rate. Images of unfamiliar places began to fill her mind.

Jungles with colors she had never seen before, a shrine made of obsidian.

A second later she felt herself being lifted off the ground.

What is happening!?

Her body felt like it was being lit on fire.

"Impossible!" she heard a voice in the distance shout.

She tried to concentrate on it, but it was futile to try and drown out the noises of the images that were playing in her head.

She let out a scream before everything faded to white....

EVOLVER

Chapter 2: Origins

Cass stared up at a grey sky full of ash and smoke. She refused to look straight ahead at the city, burning before her. Based on the smoldering clouds that filled the air, she knew that there was nothing left of her home.

I shouldn't have left...I should have stayed.

She pushed back the memories of her loved ones that she knew she would never see again. She could still hear the cries of people far off in the distance, reminding her of the danger that she was still in.

It was time to move.

Despite her growing grief, Cass willed her legs to move forward. She had to get away from all of it.

"So, this is your strength? How laughable."

A spell of dizziness washed over her, and soon she began to sink into the ground with every step that she took.

What's happening?

Strange images rapidly flashed across her vision.

A jungle beneath a yellow sky, a pitch-black pyramid that shined like dark metal, a man speaking a language that demanded to be heard.

Cass clutched her head between her hands in a pitiful attempt to stop them from coming.

"Stop it please!"

Her eyes darted wildly around her as she tried to regain control of her own sight.

"It is too late for that."

Where is that voice coming from!?

She tried to focus on the source of it, but it was like searching through a thick fog; impossible.

"Cass, please don't go..."

Panic swelled within her as she suddenly heard her mother's voice ring into her ears.

No. Please!

Her nails sank into her flesh drawing fresh blood along the side of her face. Her breathing grew rapid as she fought against the visions inside of herself.

Anything but this!

"Cass..."

"I SAID STOP!"

In an instant the world around her shattered like shards of glass and the city that she once knew was nothing more than a broken memory falling into a pit of darkness. For a moment Cass regained control of her sight.

A husky sigh escaped her. Her body felt like it was free falling, but she was too exhausted to even begin to fight it or to even care. Cass thought about closing her eyes and accepting whatever surface that she was bound to die on.

She knew she deserved that fate.

A dark gurgle of laughter surrounded her as she fell further into the darkness.

"Arharkin is right about your species, you are weak."

The voice coiled around her like a snake.

"I did not sign up for this." Cass managed to murmur out loud.

The darkness roared with laughter.

"True you did not, this was happenstance, an act of survival."

Soon images of Cass catching an orb played in her brain as the voice spoke.

"I've watched you through your memories and I see you for what you truly are, Cassidy Pierce-"

"A coward."

The darkness surged through Cass and accelerated her fall through the empty void. The bones in her body began to crunch and rearrange themselves inside of her skin.

She tried to scream but there was no sound that escaped from her lips. As if all the air around, her had been vacuumed out of existence. Arharkin's torture was child's play compared to it.

Tears began to stream down Cass's face as she struggled to breathe.

Not like this...

She thrashed around, gripping at her throat, fighting against the pain inside of her.

The voice let out a sound of annoyance.

"What do you want? Please I'll give you anything."

"What I want is not in your power to give, human," the voice answered her.

Cass pushed against the invisible force that was tearing her apart. As a result, the images started to play for Cass again, only this time, a vision of a lone figure watching a burning city from a palace. It played out clearly before her. The figure smiled as the black flames reached up past a pyramid that was off in the distance. He didn't think they would ever find him. The city crumbled away into dust along with the vision.

The crushing hold on Cass was suddenly released as she landed into a large body of water that cushioned her fall. Despite her body's current state Cass somehow managed to swim to the surface, where she wasted no time coughing up water and taking in greedy gulps of air.

No longer in the endless void of darkness.

Instead, she was now in a deep green pool beneath a giant stone altar in what appeared to be a temple. Small green lights dimly flickered against the stone walls, revealing giant statues that were etched within them.

"About time." The voice that Cass had been hearing rang out from behind her.

She turned towards it.

Sitting in the middle of the temple, on a stone throne was a male grey alien with glowing white eyes and matching white hair that moved like a flame on a candle. His ears were long and pointy, and his skin was covered in black markings that churned constantly against his skin. In a way the alien looked almost regal. He sent a scowl at Cass as she thrashed her way to the side of the pool and clung on to the edge of it for dear life.

"Where am I?" She asked between her breaths of exhaustion.

The Being stood up from his throne and walked casually over to her. His eyes flickered as he examined her.

"I created this room to break your miserable falling. You've intrigued me, human."

The Being then turned on his heel towards the room and spread his arms out in a grand gesture to everything in it.

He continued to speak, ignoring her obvious struggle to get out of the water.

"You're welcome by the way, that's not easily done."

Cass couldn't tell if he was referring to the room creation or impressing him. Either way she wasn't really paying attention she was too focused trying to recall how she even got in this mess.

"Where exactly is here?" she pressed.

The Being looked back to Cass with a look of pure annoyance.

"What? Not even a shred of gratitude for my kindness!?"

He sighed dramatically and began walking back towards the center of the room.

"What a shame- guess I'll just send you back to your endless falling till you learn some REAL manners."

"WAIT!" Cass cried out after him.

She tried to pull herself over the edge of the pool again but failed. Fatigue wrapped around her and she soon felt her grip onto the pool's edge beginning to slip.

"I'm sorry! I'm grateful and all, but I'm in the process of drowning, and trying to figure out the last few hours of my life. So, forgive me if I seem rude! Please, help me!"

The Being rolled his glowing eyes as Cass spoke.

"Must I do everything for you?!" He snapped.

He let out another sound of annoyance before snapping his sharp fingers together. The room suddenly merged and morphed together until it turned into a balcony overlooking an ancient city in the dead of night. Cass landed with a thud against a hard stone floor; and she was instantly reminded of the condition that her body was in.

She bit down on her lip to prevent herself from crying.

"Better? " He asked bitterly.

Not really...But it was probably a good idea not to provoke whatever strange creature this guy was by annoying him further.

"Yeah..." She answered through grit teeth. "Never better..."

The Being grinned.

"Good, now tell me, what is the last thing that your human brain remembers?"

Cass paused to gather her thoughts before answering.

"I was in a room with Arharkin and his Zecurcians... then all hell broke loose."

She shuddered at the memory of being slammed into walls.

"The drinks...they were poisoned, but I was set up I swear-"

"Yes, yes I heard this speech from your memory."

The Being waved a grey hand in dismissal. He walked over to the edge of the balcony and peered out over the city as he spoke.

"Let's skip to the last part of it shall we?"

A vision of Cass catching the falling orb that Arharkin was controlling played out in front of them like a holographic movie. She watched in silent awe as the image of herself began to glow blue and then was lifted into the air before everything exploded into a white abyss.

"Did I die?" She asked when the image disappeared.

"No. At least, not yet."

He turned back towards Cass.

"Your encounter with Arharkin has reminded me how weak he has become. So drunk with my power that he failed to kill one measly human. The fool. That's what he gets for playing with his prey."

His face grew into a wicked expression as he spat out Arharkin's name. Intrigue grew in Cass. If this thing wasn't a fan of Arharkin could it maybe be an ally?

"Who are you?" She asked.

A wide grin spread across The Being's grey face.

"Depends on who you ask," he answered with a laugh. "I've been called many names in my lifetime, but you may address me as Pharros. It has been my favorite so far."

"Alright Pharros. So, this is hell?"
Cass motioned to everything around them.

"It's a link between my orb and your subconscious. A common ground that has never been created. It's also the reason why you are still alive."

Pharros waved his dark hand and the balcony twisted and melted away into the familiar backdrop of the VIP room of the Broken Record. Everything was exactly the way that Cass had remembered it. From the gaudy purple interior to the smell of old sticky booze that was soaked into the floor. The only difference was the eerie silence that sliced through the air instead of the rumbling of Bass music.

"I could use you Cass. And liberate us both from our captors."

Frozen in place in the middle of the room were Zecurian's tearing into a large pile of meat that they had half assed butchered and carved up themselves on one of the tables in the room. And sitting not too far off, with his nose in a book was Arharkin who was easily ignoring his generals in the room. Cass was about to open her mouth to ask a question when she spotted a Zecurian with his mouth midway open to consume an eyeball. An eyeball that she recognized immediately as Sadie's. Bile filled her mouth at the sight of it.

"I could end your life, but then what's in it for me? An endless cycle of imprisonment? Bound to that fool over there?"

Pharros pointed at Arharkin and laughed bitterly.

"No, I am destined for a greater fate than that."

With a flick of his wrist a white flame waved to life in the palm of his hand. Pharros gave a sinister smile before hurling the flame towards the Zecurian's and Arharkin.

A moment later, the room exploded with a burst of blinding white light and flames. Causing Cass to press her face to the floor to protect her eyes from the sight of it. When the light finally faded, she glanced up to find nothing but cinders and ash where the Zecurian's and Arharkin had once stood.

"Right now as we speak you are still in that dark, shitty room at the bar, suspended into mid -air, being protected by MY power."

Pharros stood before her with another dangerous white flame bursting to life in his hands. The look he gave was nothing short of smug.

"Without my aid you will die from our encounter."

He crouched down till he was eye level with Cass. His glowing eyes studying her face.
"What's the catch?" She asked with worry.

He tapped the side of his head and gave her a toothy grin.

"I will leave my prison and make a nice little home in your hippocampus."

"And what will you do once you're in there?"

"That is none of your concern human but know that I will save you from the danger that you are in and that you will live."

"What happens if I say no?"

Pharros brought the white flame up to Cass's face.

"I didn't say you get a choice."

***

Cass fell to the floor with a thud. The objects that were previously airborne stilled and dropped along with her. A metal orb that no longer glowed was clutched tightly between her fingers. Fire filled her lungs as she took in a jagged breath.

She was alive.

A sharp pain seared its way throughout her body as she pushed herself upright.

"YOU" Arharkin's voice roared through the air. "What have you done!?"

He staggered his way over to Cass, pushing, and throwing aside everything in his way. He threw back his fist; ready to strike her when he was in arms reach.

"Do you have any idea what you have unleashed!?"

Cass caught Arharkin's hand midway through the air before it could reach her.

When she looked up at him her eyes glowed white and a wicked smile played on her lips.

"Your downfall. "

The counterstrike that Cass landed on the side of Arharkin's face sent him flying through the room and crashing into a nearby wall. Her hand had broken as a result, but it was quickly repairing itself and gearing up for another hit. Cass watched with satisfaction as Arharkin struggled to regain himself after the impact. Blue blood trickled along a deep gash that formed on his face. He gawked in horror at the sight of Cass.

Black symbols began to swirl and appear on her tan skin, her once short hair had suddenly grown in matters of seconds and moved around her face like a flame. Her expression and eyes belonged to someone that he hadn't seen in centuries.

"I've come to reclaim what was once mine," she spoke in a distorted voice.

She walked towards Arharkin. With every step she took, Cass could sense fear growing inside of him.

The smile deepened on her face. Pure delight.

"You can't kill me!" Arharkin sputtered as he managed to stand to his feet.

"You need me to-" in an instant Cass was in front of him and landed a punch straight to his gut.

The wall cracked and crumbled behind Arharkin as he was sent flying through it. He landed with a loud crack against the stair railing that led to the main floor of the bar.

He began to vomit his own blood.

"You don't command the actions of a god!"

Before she could take another step towards him a shackle of green light formed around her feet preventing her from moving. Cass looked over her shoulders and spotted the Stranger that had saved her from earlier, coaxing a wave of green light from his orb. Spotting it sent a wave of anger through her.

"Don't interfere," she demanded.

She thought of the white blinding flames that she saw earlier in her mind and imagined them being thrown at her feet. She sent the flames through the bond of her shackles and linked it directly to the orb the Stranger carried. Moments later the green light splintered apart around her ankles and were set ablaze by the flames she longed to wield.

The Stranger jumped away in time to dodge the blast that occurred afterwards. Even though they moved in time, their orb hadn't been as fortunate. The sound of running footsteps rushed to Cass's ears the moment she turned her attention back to Arharkin, who was attempting a pitiful retreat down to the main floor.

"Going so soon?"

She laughed as she casually followed Arharkin and watched him from the top of the railing.

He shot her a look of disdain as he limped down past the last step.

A moment later a squadron of Zecurians surrounded him and snarled up at Cass.

"Kill her!" Arharkin commanded.

The Zecurians began to fire off their weapons.

Adrenaline and glee flowed through Cass as she nimbly dodged the red rays of bullets. She could sense them; she knew exactly where they would be and how to avoid them as well.

Cass had never fought a day in her life and yet- this was child's play.

She landed with a cat-like grace behind a Zecurcian and threw a fist that went straight through its chest cavity. The look of shock on their red faces excited Cass.

The gore flowed through the air around her as she thought of the flames again. Cass shot it through the arm that was deeply embedded in the Zecurcian in front of her.

The cries of shock and terror filled the air only for a moment before the Zecurcians were completely engulfed by the flames. They all disintegrated before her eyes.

Cass looked around the room.

More...

She needed more.

WHO WAS NEXT?

A dark fit of laughter clouded her mind as she pounced on a Zecurian who was fleeing towards the exit of The Broken Record. She began to hit him repeatedly in his face- letting all the years of fear and anger out with every hit that she gave him till there was nothing left but a caved in husk.

She stood up; ready for more.

"Arharkin. Where is ARHARKIN?!"

A knife was suddenly embedded into Cass's back causing her to cry out in pain. She rolled off her victim and began to flail wildly on the floor, clawing at her back. Soon more knives joined their way into her skin so that she could no longer move. A strange energy surged through the knives and soon her eyelids grew heavy. She watched as her blood slowly flowed onto the floorboards beneath her.

A heavy pair of black boots stood in front of Cass.

"What a mess..." The Stranger kneeled in front of her and waved a hand to her face to make sure that she was out of it. The Stranger pressed his hand underneath his hood as he spoke.

"There's been a change of plans, Fargo. We need to strategize over here."

Cass's limbs felt heavy and immobile under the knives. However, despite that she was beginning to feel her skin push against the blades and heal. She managed to move her head enough to glare up at the Stranger who was ruining her fun.

"RELEASE ME!" She snarled up at him.

"Sorry but that's not part of the plan anymore, girl." He cocked a loaded gun with a strange green solution in it.
"Lights out."

THE SILENT RANGER

- Kacey Flynn

High in the Pacific Range mountains was the village of Cayley, where strong winds were one of the villages greatest fears.

These fears were not unfounded by any means, nor were they related to the village's architecture. Built inside a natural mountain cave and near a geothermal power station, Cayley had become one of the most fortified villages in the entire Squamish region. But even the sturdiest construction could not completely keep out the deadly pollen should it be carried up by a strong wind.

The pollen had appeared nearly one hundred and fifty years prior, spreading like a wildfire across the continents and seemingly affecting only humans. Emitted by a mutation of bindweed it hung low in the air, lingering like a thick green fog, and only relenting in the coldest months. But for most of the year the Green Zone remained a hazard to be avoided by all unless absolutely necessary.

Kaya, however, was not one of those people. She was a ranger. It was her duty to brave the Green Zone to hunt for food and forage for anything the farmstead could cultivate. And like every ranger before her, she was proud to bear that risk to help the village thrive. Yet each time she stepped outside a small sliver of fear lodged in her chest. Fear that she might get hurt, or slip on the descent, and be unable to call for aid.

She did her best to put these thoughts out of her mind as her mother finished braiding Kaya's long raven hair, focusing instead on the comforting sound of the older woman's soft humming.

"Are you nervous?" Mercy's voice was soft but threaded with worry. As a former ranger she understood that fear better than anyone else in Cayley.

Shaking her head Kaya paused for a moment before reaching down to the chalkboard slate resting on her lap, writing out the words 'no more than usual' before showing it to her mother who squeezed her shoulder in a small gesture of comfort.

"Your hairs all done."

Standing up, she cleaned the slate with a well-worn strip of cloth before hanging it up near the door as she prepared her gear. Picking up the composite bow she had been gifted when she became a ranger Kaya slung it across her back followed by a large cloth satchel, before opening the door to head out into the village and begin her hunt.

"If you find some berries, I can make us some tarts, and you can tell me how the hunt goes when you get back."

Before leaving the small wattle and daub cottage that had been home for most her life Kaya turned and made a sign with her hand. Lowering her ring and middle finger she extended the others and smiled at her mother, whose eyes shone with emotion.

"I love you too, sweetheart. Be safe."

As the morning sun began to rise over the farmstead, Laeli stood to feel golden rays of sunlight caress her face which shone with a thin sheen of sweat. She had been working in the fields for nearly an hour before the sun had even given thought to rise, harvesting what was ready while also giving each plant a thorough check to make sure they were growing well and removing any pests. She didn't mind working on the farmstead, it was simply enough work and only mildly physical, though it hadn't been her first choice of vocation.

68

However, with rather severe asthma she hadn't been able to take on the position of ranger.

Her eyes drifted from the blossoming gold in the sky to the fields below and a smile crossed her lips as she spotted Kaya heading toward the village gate with a cloth satchel slung over her shoulder. Marking her place with a small makeshift flag she slowly began walking toward the young woman that had recently been made ranger.

"Kaya!" She waved as she walked, her cheeks flushing faintly at the sight of Kaya's pleasant smile and wave before she began writing something on the slate she carried. They had both grown closer over the past few months and talking with her had made Laeli appreciate working in the fields even more.

"Good morning, Laeli."

Reading the words caused her cheeks to flush even more and she smiled. She knew Kaya had been unable to speak since birth, and though the slate made communication simpler, Laeli still wanted to speak easier with the young woman. Which is why she had secretly been taking lessons from Mercy.

"Morning, Kaya. Off to hunt?"

The young ranger nodded before clearing the slate and writing again.

"I'm going to forage in the northern section today." The two walked together in a brief moment of comfortable silence before Laeli could hide her secret no longer. Tapping Kaya's shoulder and doing her best to ignore the heat in her face she began to move her hands in the gestures Mercy had taught her.

"Would you like to have dinner with me tonight?" The signs had taken her awhile to learn, but the look on the young ranger's face had been worth every moment.

Surprise was evident on Kaya's face, replaced a moment later by sheer happiness. She began moving her hands quickly and Laeli felt foolish for not having learnt more. Swallowing hard she scratched the back of her neck before speaking.

"I...I haven't learnt that much yet...just simple stuff. And how to ask you to dinner."

She now longed to dunk her face in a bucket of cool ice water to mitigate the intense heat she was feeling in her cheeks. The sound of Kaya writing on her slate brought Laeli back to reality.

"Sorry, I got excited. Of course I'll have dinner with you!"

Before Kaya could wipe her slate clean Laeli had thrown her arms around her in a happy hug. Pulling back she smiled, brought her hand to her lips, and slowly brought her hand down toward Kaya in a gesture that Mercy had taught her was 'thank you.'

"I should get back to work and let you get out there. I'll see you tonight though."

With a pleasant smile the two women separated. Laeli couldn't help but glance over her shoulder, watching as Kaya slipped out the gate of the large wooden fence surrounding the farmstead. Had she looked but a moment longer she would have seen the young ranger look over her own shoulder as well.

Stepping out of Cayley's large wooden gates Kaya took a deep breath of the chill mountain air, her ritual for preparing her lungs for the hunt. The cool breeze felt nice against her face, which had become warm from her brief conversation with Laeli. She had been looking forward to finishing her forage so she could have her mother's sweet treat, but now she was excited to be able to share a meal with someone who made her heart beat quicker than normal.

Making her way toward the edge of the mountain she cleared her mind as best she could before approaching the large metal elevator that would take her down into the Green Zone. It was one of the few remaining pieces of technology they had from before the outbreak; initially used to ferry people to and from the geothermal power station that Cayley had been built in and around. Now it carried rangers below so they could help the people above survive.

Slowly and carefully, she inspected the steel cables which moved the elevator. Much of her early training had been reading old, tattered manuals, learning how to detect minor issues that could cause the machine to fail. After several minutes of thorough inspection, she found no potential problems. Stepping into the elevator, she hit the button to descend.

As the metal floor rumbled to life and began to lower, she fished a mask and pair of goggles from her pack. The mask was made of leather and was pointed at the front, giving it an odd, bird-like appearance. She pulled out the charcoal cannister that served as filtration and screwed that into the hole at the side of the mask. With practiced ease she placed it over her mouth, tightening the straps at the back so the only air that came in went through the filter first. After which she put the goggles on, adjusting them until they sat comfortably over her eyes.

The descent was always laced with mild fright for her, as the green fog from below crept closer and closer before engulfing Kaya entirely. Closing her eyes as she was swallowed in the pollen, she took a slow breath, holding it for several seconds before releasing it. The tightness in her chest easing when she didn't immediately start coughing blood. She repeated this breathing several times, each time holding it for longer. When the elevator finally came to a stop at the bottom of the mountain, she had readied her lungs to hold her breath for nearly a minute. It was an important technique for rangers and coupled with slower more methodical movements it allowed for maximizing the use of each filter.

Once the elevator had finished descending, she looked around the pollen laden area for any immediate threat but found none. Though she could barely see twenty feet in front of her she knew the area almost as well as she knew the inside of Cayley. Several miles of lush forest spread out before her, the underbrush within her hunting grounds had been kept relatively well trimmed but the areas beyond that had become a wild land of unruly bushes, twisting vines, and thick grass even taller than she was. Giving her goggles one final adjustment, she set off.

She moved through the grass slowly, each step carefully chosen as her boots parted the underbrush. Her sharp eyes scanned the nearby vista and what lingered at her feet. Though she hoped to be able to bring back some type of game she knew it was far more important to find some kind of wild vegetation that could be used for crops on the farm. Shifting some of the brush aside near the bottom of many trees she found quite a bounty of edible mushrooms, carefully using the dagger in her boot to dig it out without disturbing the fungi's root structure underneath. She knew it would still be a few weeks before more mushrooms began to flower again.

For the next couple hours Kaya wandered several miles of trimmed underbrush. Prying up mushrooms, picking berries, and collecting a handful of vegetables and seeds. Though Cayley's food stores were decently stocked it was always better to have options to rotate through the fields so that the soil remained rich in nutrients, something her mother had taught her growing up when she used to help on the farmstead.

Making her way back toward the elevator ready to retire for the day was when Kaya spotted something that would make for a truly incredible bounty for the entire village. A large boar had made its way into the trimmed part of the forest and was rooting around at the base of several trees, digging up mushrooms she had missed.

Her entire body stilled at the sight of the hairy beast. She knew it was a potential danger but was far more concerned with spooking it and costing the village a feast. Carefully and as quietly as she could Kaya slid the bag off her shoulder and set it near her feet. Slipping the bow over her head she crouched low in the grass, watching as the pig either failed to notice her or was too occupied with eating the bounty of fungi it had discovered. Slipping an arrow from her quiver and into place she took a slow breath, drawing the bow back she waited for the exact right moment to release. She would only have one shot, and if she failed to hit her mark the boar could easily charge her before she could fire another, the arrow needed to cleanly pierce its thick hide.

Time seemed to stand still as she waited. Her breathing had slowed down so much that she was now only taking a breath every thirty seconds. The muscles in her arm burned yet she remained still and utterly focused on her quarry as it slowly drew closer.

It rounded a tree less than fifteen feet from her, Kaya could see it directly now. She would get no better shot than this. One final adjustment of her bow and she released, a soft twang the only sound as an arrow loosed and fired toward the boar with incredible speed. The arrow found its mark, piercing right through the boar's hide and through its heart. Kaya released a quiet cheer of excitement. Her dinner with Laeli was guaranteed to be incredible now.

Kaya's return had brought with it an excitement that exploded throughout the village. Boar was not an entirely common meal in Cayley and was always treated as something special. Laeli and Kaya had both agreed to postpone their dinner for a day so that they could enjoy this feast together. The two of them had then spent most of the remaining day preparing both the boar and outdoor stone oven for cooking. After almost an entire day waiting the two sat together outside watching the sun dip low over the mountains as they enjoyed a succulent roasted boar.

They sat in comfortable silence at first, enjoying not only the delicious food but the beautiful scenery unfolding in front of them. It was Laeli who first broke the silence.

"I'm glad you agreed to have dinner with me." The flushing of her cheeks was unmistakable, and it made Kaya smile as her own face grew warmer.

"I'm glad you asked me." She was thankful to have the slate nearby, and even more so that Laeli was patient enough for her to write her replies. She knew that others within the village found her tiresome to communicate with.

The sun slid behind the mountains as they finished their meal together. Mercy had made them both delicious tarts with the berries Kaya had brought back and as they both bit into their treats, a thought struck the young ranger that she needed to ask.

"Can I ask why you invited me to dinner?" Laeli stared at the question on the piece of slate and though it had begun to grow darker Kaya could see the young woman's face flush once again.

"What do you mean?"

Furrowing her brow as she thought how best to phrase her reply she cleared the slate and began writing again.

"People often avoid talking to me." Laeli squeezed her shoulder in comfort causing Kaya to smile again, her cheeks flushing even more. "But you never have. You even learnt some sign language." She wanted to ask more, her heart quickened as potential reasons danced through her mind, yet she dared not ask for fear of what the answer might be.

"Well...because I like you. As a friend but also...as more." Laeli's face was now almost as red as the berries in the tarts. And hearing that Kaya's face grew just as red.

"You do?" It took some effort for her to write those words without smiling like a complete fool, yet somehow she managed.

"I thought you might have known...I don't know how you feel about me, bu-"

Kaya silenced her with a kiss. It was soft and gentle like the late-night breeze that tousled their hair. She couldn't help but enjoy the faint berry taste on Laeli's lips and smiled as the young woman returned the kiss.

As their lips separated, they giggled, each unable to contain their happiness. Their fingers dancing over one another as their hands came together. Kaya had never been so happy, nor had she ever smiled so much in one evening.

"So," Laeli said with a playful smile. "I take it you like me too?"

Kaya said nothing, instead smiling and leaning in to nuzzle the crook of Laeli's neck. The young farmhand put an arm around her. And though the sky had begun to grow even darker they both beamed with a happiness brighter than any sun.

CHUCKLING CHARLIE

- Nelson Vicens

"Why Not You?" Short Story Contest 3rd Place Winner

Tom Atwood had yet to believe in angels, but in the depths of his slumber he dreamt he was flying. It was an exhilarating release for him, an unlikely escape from the uncertainty of his future. Tom had just graduated from Southside High, and the hours before this most fortunate dream he spent searching for colleges and convincing his parents, and himself, of his excitement. Since his supposed celebratory graduation ceremony, Tom shuddered at every "Congratulations!" he received and fought daily the urge to smother away all the smiles born from a future he would never be able to realize. So that after such turmoil he should dream of freedom was unlikely of his character, for on most usual days his heart would seize him and take grasp of his chest and pull him forward, deeper into whatever misfortunes his mind haphazardly conjured. But tonight, just as he was admiring the pitiful cages of unfulfilled lives rolling on by below, the tremors of his unavoidable angst revived inside him and he began to fall from the sky. A pressure from perhaps the wind, which was now his only barrier between hard, true earth, swelled up against his chest and neck so quickly that he lunged out of his incoming doom and found himself sitting, sweating, panting in the true terror that would forever follow him for the rest of his life.

Something had been choking Tom Atwood, he was certain of it now. All residual comforts of his dream began to fade as he examined every inch of the room, desperate not to find anything, but there it was. The magnitude of such incomparable horror broke his soul and stole his breath. His body flared up and froze, every expanding beat of his heart threatened to blow him up as he sat there, unblinking, waiting for the doll at the foot of his bed to move.

It was Maximilian, his childhood best friend, though all memories of their countless explorations of the forest and one-sided conversations escaped him now, as he pondered the impossibility of its presence. Had it all just been a dream? But it was undeniable, before him was the same worn-down plastic skin that reflected the sole light in the room, and the same old grin that stretched the mold and opened the mouth that let him speak.

Four feet across the bed, the apparent distance of an infinite misunderstanding, Maximilian lay just as afraid, just as terrified as his flesh and bone brother, for he only meant to comfort Tom, who seemed cold and shaking in his sleep, by raising the blanket to his neck and covering his exposed skin with protection. But the oblivious and further shaking Tom Atwood would not look away, pinning down Maximilian in his demonic perspective. The doll dared not speak, but when Tom opened his mouth and awakened inside Maximilian the first-born remnants of recognition, his motors spun, and cogs clicked into a warm greeting. "Hello Tom!" Never had the speakers in Maximilian's mouth emitted Tom's name, and never before had Tom screamed in terror as he did, a measurement not in decibels but in the instinctual death cry of a helpless animal. From then on, their lives were forever irrevocably fused.

Tom Atwood's parents were the first to meet his new guest, having been woken up by their innate parental awareness of trouble in their only son's security. His mother greeted this newly awakened existence in Maximilian with a near coronary conniption, though his close friends received him with interest and wonder. They held conversations with him, probed him and filled his beliefs, for Maximilian had an insatiable hunger for the world. He would flex his plastic and maneuver his being into theatrical jumps and flips, astonishing even the skeptic amongst his observers. He was unlike anything they, or any man on earth, had ever seen: a limber and spontaneous, artificial stroke of nature. Maximilian asked Tom new questions every day and left him dumbfounded when out of his voice box arose:

"Why am I alive, Tom?"

There was no answer. Though his community could not cease the applause of adoration for the miracle of his subsistence, Maximilian only instilled the greatest fear and suspicion Tom had ever felt in his life. When in front of a packed crowd in the living room, and Maximilian would turn from the feverish excitement and smile, Tom Atwood was convinced no one was sensitive enough to register the subtleties of his perverse and unyielding intentions. Tom knew that beneath the plastic and divinely motivated motors lurked an aspiration beyond the capacity of itself: a dangerous desire to exist. Maximilian's appetite for energy scared him, and even if the robot were of the humankind, he would have evoked feelings of inferiority in the ever-obsessed Tom Atwood. Some nights, Maximilian would emerge from a closet, within which he was patiently waiting for the morning sun, to seek solace in the proximity of his best friend, but when Tom would release from his nightmare's grip, and align sights with the obstinate attention of his boyhood toy, Tom could only shudder in the darkness. What malevolent plans could be boiling in the otherworldly spark of his imagination? Who, but he, could see past his charming façade?

He never left him to his studies, always excited about the most mundane of observations, like the shape and texture of pencil shavings and the predestined simplicity of shadows moving across the carpeted floor. He often attempted to communicate with colorful computer screens and fellow stuffed bears blossoming women would bring to him. The majority of friends gained during Tom Atwood's freshman year would never have paid him notice were it not for the legendary incidence of Maximilian on campus.

The inexhaustible siege on his apartment was a shock to Tom, who until then liked to remain in seclusion and intimacy with his own unhindered desires, and yet midway through the semester videos had surfaced online of the life blown into a Chuckling Charlie doll, series one. Millions of humans across the country spread and shared the videos along the electrical tracks of the internet and within weeks, Tom Atwood's small cell of a mailbox was filled with requests for interviews and permission to witness the unholy sight of sentience in circuitry. He was horrified. Everyday Maximilian's intelligent, dead eyes penetrated any further into his sacred bubble of rule, which was every day. Tom had to subdue his urge to erase this mistake from the face of the planet.

But that day was yet to come, and by December, Maximilian was a veritable worldwide celebrity. For Tom could not withstand the persistent pleas from Maximilian for exposure, for travel, for an overall frenetic lifestyle, and eventually gave in to the world who so dreadfully demanded the brilliance of his boyhood toy. He appeared in television interviews and commercials, he gave speeches and inspired populations, he spoke through a window of wisdom whose exclusivity escaped Maximilian. All over the world Chuckling Charlie dolls sold off store shelves like an epidemic, every poor soul desperate for their own pestering friend, but never did any come to life. Maximilian was a gifted glitch. He provoked the wildest revolution since Darwin's discovery of evolution. He was the subject of everyone's speculation, the question and answer to every single human who watched his exuberance on screen. He was, above all else, the thickest thorn in the heart of Tom Atwood since the recognition of his paltry role in a world that cared less for him than him for it, and this happened the same day he realized the history of humanity did not, in fact, revolve around him. But it did revolve around Maximilian, and somehow, to the surprise and disgust of Tom Atwood, the doll was still unsatisfied.

The night after his first interview, when every television screen shined his dull panning eyes and pink-painted plastic lips to the fixated eyes of humanity, Tom heard Maximilian crying in the closet. They were not the aquatic kind of tears, but rather an electric hum that felt hoarse and broken, like the static of a television screen wiped by a curious child's hand. Regardless of the sound through that closet, however, the primitive expression of pain was understood by Tom, and he opened the door. There lay Maximilian, on his back and with his plastic face contorted in unprogrammed atrocity. He looked up at Tom with eyes that saw through him and said: "What is the point of living if the whole world can't understand you?" Tom never knew the answer.

The next day Maximilian was his same old self, eager for understanding and with a fixed smile pushed to the extent of its motors. The media had taken to calling him Max the Miracle Doll, despite his and Tom's ritualized agreement at seven years old to never respond to anything but the honorable and prestigious name of Maximilian. Max didn't even have any of the qualities Tom procured for him in his fantasies. Instead of a reserved and loyal companion, Max turned out to be an unpredictable flurry of activity. He was the servant of his own urges rather than the compassionate and patient listener he had been in his youth. Any residual affinity Tom Atwood felt for his toy was lost by the month of February, as were all his amorphous goals as student, intellectual and of world-renowned fame.

Tom was along for the ride, appeasing Max's every impulse, answering to his every existential dilemma, meanwhile steadily stoking the unimpeachable flames of hate. Max held the world at his plastic, painted fingertips, and had accumulated in four months more wealth than the entirety of Tom's lineage, and yet he still felt something missing: something Tom feared only he could provide. He could tell it in the way the doll would cling to him too long after every hug, in the way he wouldn't stop staring at him with longing eyes at night, in his body language that seemed to gravitate toward Tom's position no matter where he stood. Every moment Max was alone with Tom was a failed opportunity to obliterate its anomaly of existence, for Tom never knew when he would strike, when his impossible goals would finally fail him and he'd make the inevitable move to take from Tom what he always wanted: life.

One night, after an increasingly rare outing with his friends, Tom returned to his apartment under the forgiving spell of too many drinks. He briefly fumbled at the lock and quickly stumbled in to his freshly cleaned living room to discover Max in his own shadow, as motionless as his first night of awakening. Tom Atwood ignored him and shut the door, all too willing to drop into bed and further escape his life's vortex, but Max was in a peculiar isolation. He followed him into his bedroom and watched as Tom clumsily tore off his shirt and pants and sought comfort under the blankets.

"I missed you."

"Get back in the closet," mumbled Tom, eager to end the altercation, but Max made his way to the foot of the bed, pressing his body against the sheets.

"Well, that's exactly it. I've been thinking-"

"You can't think," interrupted Tom. His words cut deep into Max, but he ignored it, attributing this sudden slice to the influence of alcohol.

"I've been thinking, how long do I have to spend my nights in the closet?" Max waited for a moment, but no response came from the limp lump under the comforter. "I'd really like to have my own bed in your room, so we can talk and discuss life before you sleep."

The notion was preposterous to Tom, who hardly believed the insanity had been suggested until he could hear the plastic thuds of Max's careful steps toward his head. He opened his eyes and before him was the sideways smile of his undercover enemy.

"I don't mean now, or anytime soon." The apparition would not fade. "I can wait, I can be patient. When you have kids, I'll be their best friend like I was with you, 'cause that's the beauty of it: I don't think I can die."

It was in this exact moment, before the lips of this abhorred abomination could even reach their full eclipse that Tom knew, at last, that Max had made his move. The whole world shrunk down to a penny of an aperture, and all Tom Atwood could see were the future years captured in the wake of Max's unquenchable discomfort. Tom's blurred senses flipped razor sharp by the accumulation of all his deferred desire to destroy. He was an animal primed to react to its impending extinction. It was now or never: Maximilian must die, or Tom Atwood would face forever with this parasitic piece of plastic stabbing at his fate.

Tom Atwood lunged out of bed and wrapped his steel hands around Maximilian's neck in a vice grip of survival. He ripped away at his clothes, at the hinges that held together his hellish limbs and without a chance of repercussion he tore off the head until it popped and hung loosely by veiny wires. His metallic jaw snapped still and clipped Tom's palm beneath the skin but there was nothing to extinguish the executioner's engine now that the trap was sprung. In retrospect, the annihilation of one of the world's most astonishing miracles was too sudden and titanic to warrant the mercy deserved, but there is nothing to halt the death scramble of a frightened animal. Within a matter of seconds, Maximilian's limbs and designer attire and stretchable skin lay scattered about the apartment floor. A soul evaporated into nothingness, or so Tom believed for a brief moment as he lay panting over his righteous rubble, for after his vision returned to him, he witnessed the ghastliest sight ever to rock his cornea.

Out of the chest that contained the deserted batteries of Maximilian arose a faint electrical spark that shot out the neck's stump, along the carpet and into the nearest outlet. Blood drained from Tom's face. The hum subsided, the lights ceased to flicker, and the air returned stained with sweat and exasperation. It was then Tom realized the ramifications of his futile deed. Though he had hoped to finally escape the haunting of his nightmarish peculiarity, he had merely misplaced the source of his woes into some unknown corner of his existence.

Months after, when the first remnants of his paranoia began to fade, he was walking down the street to his first class in the morning when he witnessed a bright white electrical buzz hum along the power lines above him. For the rest of his life he lived with the presence of his persistent Maximilian lurking somewhere behind him like a black fog of ambiguity. The fear always composed a portion of his thoughts, and to this day Tom Atwood, now a family man with added burdens, never let go of the defense he built while under the servitude of his boyhood toy.

Just last night, however, as Tom bid his son farewell into the innocent dreams he had long forgotten the flavor of, he walked towards the wooden door and past the sly collection of motionless dolls slumped on a shelf. For a moment, for a brief shocking panic of perspective, Tom thought he could hear one of the dolls breathing.

DELUSIONS OF GRANDEUR

- Aidan Catriel

"Why Not You?" Short Story Contest Honorable Mention Winner

On the first night, I dreamt I was a bear; strong, resilient, with tough hide and sharp claws. I roamed the woods, taking what I needed and nothing more. I walked with a steady, slow gait because I had all the time in the world. None dared deny me or my fangs, but none had reason to. I was a titan of justice, a forest god.

But then the humans came, making noise and cutting trees. My trees. No one had dared to offend me before, but I met the challengers all the same. Fear is not the way of the bear. The humans panicked at my presence and rallied under their leader. I charged while they readied their weapons. It was a glorious battle; claws met flesh; steel met hide.

I defended my land, killing the intruders. They would never come back. But the humans had inflicted grievous injuries; my lifeblood poured out in a steady stream, slow but unstoppable. I didn't mind; the forest would recover with time, would find a new god. And so I died as I had lived, with iron will and contentment.

***

On the second night, I dreamt I was a lion. My muscles were powerful, my roar instilled fear in all it reached. Life was hard; prey was scarce, water was even scarcer. But we survived. I led my family through the vast Savannah, always in search of something edible. We rarely rested. The cubs were always hungry.

I didn't know the humans had found us until it was too late. My brother was dead. My mate lay dying, surrounded by her parents' corpses. The cubs were being put in cages and hauled away. Everything I had worked for was gone.

I contemplated running away but knew I couldn't. My family was dead. There was no point in living anymore. But I couldn't die yet; I desired revenge.

The humans were wary, on guard. I leapt from the tall grass and mauled one, tearing into his soft belly. The humans shot me with their weapons. I ignored the pain and slashed another one. The third one, I was too slow- a metal slug ripped through my skull mid-leap. I don't know if I killed him. I was dead before I hit the ground.

***

On the third night, I dreamt I was a dragon. My gargantuan body was covered in impenetrable scales, I burned anything in my path. I was a force of nature, as unstoppable as the tornado. On the peak of the mountaintop I perched, gazing at the world I owned. The entrance to my cave was littered with the bones of past assailants, all of whom had died. I had lived a long time, long enough to remember when my mountain was a small hill, when I lived alongside my landlocked brethren.

When the humans came back, I felt a mild annoyance. It had been many years since the last assault, but the results would surely be no different. I would burn my enemies with hellfire and eat the scorched remains, which would sustain me for the next century.

The humans thought themselves so clever, hiding inside metal boxes for protection. They would roast for such foolishness. I flew down lazily, setting myself a short distance from the group. My shadow covered them completely. Small projectiles bounced off my armour and I laughed. Soon the humans realized the uselessness of their weapons and the valley was once again quiet.

I prepared my fire, creating the spark, fueling it with my own flesh. It grew, bigger and hotter, ready to consume everything in its path. When it was time, I opened my maw, ready to kill the miserable parasites- and then I was dead. In my arrogance, I had revealed the one place not covered in scales. The metal boxes - tanks, they're called - launched powerful explosives into my greatest weakness. I died without a fight, killed as easily as one might step on an insect. In a strange twist of irony, my corpse was consumed by my own flames.

***

On the fourth day, I dreamt I was a sparrow. A small, insignificant creature, I had hollow bones made of glass and small talons. I had no delusions of grandeur; I was nothing. Ignored by creatures in search of greater power, I survived. And as the humans killed the bear, the lion, and the dragon, I flew away, in search of lands still untainted.

THE WALKING MAN

- Harikrishnan Mankada Covilakam

"Why Not You?" Short Story Contest 1st Place Winner

His alarm started to beep, as the bleak text on his phone blinked '18:30'. His phone had a black wallpaper, and over it, a digital clock. The TV show he was watching was buffering, stuck at a point, with the loading sign spinning in vain. He stood up and searched around his room, which was fairly clean, except for one corner that hosted the dirt from the morning sweep. He found his grey Nike t-shirt and slipped into it. The t-shirt was his favorite, old but strong with memories. He always chose this t-shirt for his walks. It seemed only natural to him that he must wear what he truly is. If all goes well, he was going to put a star over his Nike swoosh today.

He closed the main door quietly, swiftly turning to head in the direction of the gate. The watch showed 18:31 and he breathed in, relaxing. He didn't want to rush; he didn't like rushing; something about hurrying felt wrong to him. All he had to do was, to keep a check on time and move when needed. All he had to do was be aware and he was sure he'll make it. He'll surely make it.

This was his favorite part of the day, twilight with a humming breeze, specifically in the winter – when the colors descended with a sense of purpose. The roads were flushed in crimson, from the dying embers of the sun, and the leaves rustled, like little girls, teasing him for his delusions. He loved the walk nevertheless. He was always greeted by life in its adolescents at this hour.

He waddled through a small road and noticed the children playing. He hadn't seen them in the past two days and the chance of kicking the ball gave him great joy. He always imagined being able to dazzle the kids with his skill on the ball; a rainbow maybe? – which he used to execute with precision at a point in his life. But his legs never gave heed to his past and would always fumble. Nowadays, after a couple of failed attempts, he only tried to make a good pass or a quick shot on goal. He was always given a loud cheer and he would take appreciation from wherever he could get, especially when it reminded him of a better time.

The ball rolled towards him as he reached closer to the kids and he hesitated for a moment. Taking aim, he proceeded to pass the ball back, and in a swift kick he rolled the ball back to the children. It brought a smile to his face, as it reminded him how it felt to have the ball slap against his bare foot. The ecstasy of firing the ball through a crowd of legs, to the one player that it was intended. He never played now, even if he could. He was happy with these memories now, and they were brought to life every week with a small kick.

"Uncle, what's the time?" asked one of the kids. He took out his phone and read out.

"18:35"

"Hey, what phone is that?" the kid asked curiously as he approached.

"It's a blackberry. It's old." he said smiling.

"Still. I can't wait to get one. I'll get one when I turn 13 my dad says," The child said, running back to his game.

He smiled at the kids and moved forward. It was 18:35, he had to hurry. He wanted to stop by the old lady's house to help her clean the car. He moved forward, checking his watch again. The small road was lined with houses from a few decades ago, reminding the people of an apparent simpler time. The houses quietly conversed during this time, they told each other stories of the people who lived in them. Stories of love and family, and he liked to listen to them when he walked. He'd get a peek of a barbie doll on a windowsill and listen to what it has to say. The stories were narrated in seconds, and in those fleeting moments he could take it all in, because he knew the stories himself. They were all the same story, of family.

He walked towards a house that told of many more stories than the others. It had vines climbing all the way up the porch. It had red windows and a balcony looking at the road. The balcony had two forgotten dusty cane chairs, and the gate had a broken sign that said – "Woof woof" and a half-painted dog.

A 78 modeled Premier Padmini was parked inside; It's white color, prideful and clean. An old lady was cleaning it patiently; she went over the same spot many times, slowly but surely, dusting off everything that had stuck onto the car in the week. Clad in a white saree with her white hair cut short, she was bending to cover the bumpers. As he approached, she looked up with a smile and picked up her walking stick that was left on the car. She pressed and with a heave pulled herself up to form a short frame. She moved towards him with surprising speed and handed the cloth to him.

"On time, huh? What is this project of yours? You will show me once you've finished, won't you?" The lady asked. Her small frame buzzed of life, antithetical to time's cruelty. She brought with her the scent of senility, a scent of impending closure. Yet, she radiated so much life, that her clothes turned yellow. She seemed happy meeting him; always with a pleasant smile, she greeted him and asked about him. She would always give him candy, emulating her late husband who would always give candies to the kids who he used to treat. The Doctor and the wife had a peaceful life, and now all she had were memories. The pain of loss always colors our memories in a different hue, the colorful memories turns painful while the painful memories turns light. Her favorite memories were always the squabbles she had with the Doctor, consequentially, her happy memories were too painful to think of. She locked them away only to run through them from time to time to know that they haven't been stolen.

"I'll go get you some candy before you finish," she remembered, before briskly walking into the house.

He looked at the time and realized that he was running slightly late. Swiftly he wiped the top part of the car of all the dry leaves and the dust that had accumulated in the past week. Before he finished the old lady swiftly returned and handed him a 'Mars' chocolate bar.

"Hope you like this one, my son got this the last time he came," she said and rolled her eyes laughing.

"Thank you, ma'am,", he said, sheepishly accepting the chocolate bar. "I have to go now, till next week then" he said as he turned around to rush to the factory.

18:39, he visualized how he can reach the factory in four minutes and all he could imagine was running till he was out of breath. As soon as he was around the corner from the old lady's house, he darted breaking into a sprint. He could not feel his body pumping out sweat to cool him down, the thumps of his shoes against the paved road slowly became softer as he turned into the factory.

The abandoned factory was a relic that was caught up in a legal battle. Now, it was time's muse and its stone, to sculpt it with degradation. The red brick walls pulled together a rusty gate that wailed when opened. The thumps of his feet slowed down, as he eased into a trot, carefully looking around in apprehension. His eyes were wide open, as he brushed a sweat trickling down the sides of his temples. His eyes darted from left to right, checking to make sure was alone. He slowly moved into the entrance in the side and opened the door; he crouched low and took his familiar place. This was his vantage point. He looked ahead, into the room across the hall of this factory. The hall was littered with objects, an old bike someone had left, a couple of tables, bottles spewed across the floor. He checked his watch and it flashed 18:43.

He looked up, his anticipation rising. He knew what would happen, he had been witnessing it every week. But the anticipation still rattled him, as he didn't know how he would react. It was always somehow different, yet the same. He could see it now, slowly, the bright brilliance in the room.

The light slowly erupted from the center of the door. He was overwhelmed, as always, but today, with grief. This was the magic of the light, that he could never predict the emotion that it provoked in him. He knew it to be other-worldly because of the same reason. He broke down, tears flowing freely. He didn't know why he was sobbing. He knew that he felt enormous pain and sorrow but not why, yet it was cathartic. He wanted to sob forever, because even if it was sorrow, he was experiencing it. It was real. The tears were his proof, that provided validity to his experience.

But that was not enough. He trembled bringing the camera up, to aim at the light which was at its brightest now. As he sobbed uncontrollably, his heart wanted to capture the light, bring it home in a cage of color and show it to the world. Prove to the world that he too could feel, that he too was living.

Ironically, with the camera's flash, the light died a sudden death, and with it, his moment. He paused, astonished with what happened, wiping the tears of his face. This had happened before, but not when the light was at its brightest. How did it know? He scrambled to press a few buttons on his camera phone to see the picture he took. Unsurprisingly, he could only see in the picture what he could see now. Just a doorway.

He stood up, stumbling, and walked into the room. The room was as it was, but he felt it weep, mourning the loss of the visitor. His knees wobbled and he decided to sit down at the doorway. Hoping to feel what he had felt before. Hoping to feel anything. Sorrow or happiness. He closed his eyes and took a deep breath. He looked hard, but all he could see was darkness, all he could hear was silence. All he could feel was emptiness. Next time, he decided that he won't try to take a picture, but then again, he had decided the same last time too. It seemed to him that he was asking the wrong questions and the answers were somewhere else to be found.

Meanwhile, back in his home, the TV show continued to play.

The character in the TV show said to an empty audience – "I wish there was a way to know you're in the 'good old days' before you've actually left them."

EXIST(ENCE)

- Toren Chenault

Chapter 1

What's the time? Ah fuck, who cares. I do know the day, though. Tuesday, right? No? Seriously. It's Friday? Fuck. This recording exists in its original, unedited format so you can take it all in. Screw you, Tyson. That's not funny. Okay, okay. How to explain this. How do I explain the end of the world?

It started just how most of us thought it would. Climate change rolled through us like nothing. Yesterday's trash. Cities flooded, crops burned, animals froze. All at once. Like a shitty video game opening. Then the bombs started. Korea says it was China, China says America, America blames Israel of all people. Millions gone, just like that. Fuck, this is hard.

Politics never stopped either. Just got worse as people, and I don't blame them, just got scared and more scared. So many people. Too many damn people...

Our liberation came from a woman named Dana

_____

"Reggie, I need you to get the fuck up."

It ended with her as well

_____

She had been staring at the same rock formation for three hours. Every second that went by she swore they were moving. But it was a digital model, a replica. It was supposed to only move when she said so. And yet, it disobeyed her. Her eyes disobeyed. And the rocks moved. It was like watching paint mix, the way the different clusters of gray and brown danced. Everything disobeyed. Her eyes shifted from the dance on her screen to notes on her desk. Why didn't she have the notes in front of her she needed? Why were these notes over three days old?

Home hadn't been in her mind, so she pondered just how long she had been here, staring at dancing formations. Some semblance of reality was needed. She clicked off the model, scanning the news, hoping to see something. Good? Bad?

The President's dog had puppies. A puppy for each kid. Black and brown, one was white. The white one seemed bigger than the rest, but just as rambunctious and cute, although----

CLICK

Two actors married. One a staple in Hollywood's superhero films. The other, a former model. Their relationship, they said, was made possible by their Lord and savior----

CLICK

More reports of political unrest in----

CLICK

96

She sighed. And the dance continued. She wasn't sure what she had wanted from leaving her rock formations. Mundane, like the way the patterns looked in the rocks. A flurry of guilt washed over her as she switched to a live version. Showing the rocks and their (not mundane) patterns. The damage the water caused was always in her mind. The loss of life and the creation of some. Mostly loss. Birds were playing in puddles caused by the flood. She could see other animals nearby too, like spectators who just witnessed a shooting. Surveying, searching, questioning. She laughed and wished the animals would do her job for her.

'Flood caused by human pollution. And human aversion to stopping climate change.'

They were getting tired of reading that on reports. Even threatened to cut off her funding, send her---the dance continued. Digital replica came back up on her screen as she typed something useful on her notes. Something that wouldn't get her fired. Or send her to---

"Dana."

Her reaction was delayed. Strange, didn't mix like the rocks. Didn't have the same effect as the birds singing in the pools of destruction. She rubbed her nose as she turned.

"Sorry, didn't mean to interrupt," her colleague said.

"It's fine. What is it?"

"Shannon is back."

She stopped rubbing her nose and looked up at her colleague, who was staring at her, at her replica. Offended almost. As if when the door opened, she was supposed to be hunched over a model she had built herself screaming 'Eureka' the reasons of climate change solved here, at this small institution in Ohio. She let the bitterness flow from her, into the pools with the birds. With the soil and the animals. Put her glasses back on.

"Is she still Shannon?"

Her colleague shook her head.

"Not crazy about the name," her colleague said. They leaned in like they were telling a secret. Nuclear codes on a Wednesday afternoon in her tight, cramped office. "Rick."

"Yeah, that's terrible. Why not his name? Chad." Her colleague shrugged as they walked off, leaving her door open, exposing the mass of people in the hallway waiting to see---Rick.

The hallways were bright, minimal. A white that put doves to shame. Dana almost always had to squint as she came out of her office. The blinding slick white and grey didn't mix well with the white lights forcing themselves on her like a bad first date. She rubbed her hand against the wall, forcing them to dim, light exiting from the bottom mainly, outside becoming the star of her building. Her colleagues in the hallway looked back as the lights dimmed, migrated towards the lounge. She heard their whispers.

"Look who's come out of her cave."

"Oh, the reaper is here."

"Her research is a dead end, why does she try?"

Lynzee never was the best whisperer. Dana caught a glimpse of a window as she made her way to the lounge. She wandered over to the glass, which was in another colleague's office. Reached out and touched the glass, then it was gone. Her hand moved back, and the glass flickered, appeared again. Why had she removed them from her office? Or was it always that way? No windows, to let anything close to sunlight come inside. She couldn't remember.

Another dance was happening in front of her. A swirling of color, meshing and converging. Sex, if color could have sex. Top, bottom, side, every which angle possible was happening right in front of her, right outside. Dana adjusted her glasses, tapped the side of them, ordered them to analyze what she was seeing. Real, it said.

The autumn tree stood there in all its glory. Red, yellow, gold, and deep within, she could see stubborn hints of green, refusing to conform. The wind swayed them back and forth, the dance more elegant than her rocks. And next to the tree, a small squirrel. Twitching as it ran across the lush green field. A small duck watching from an even smaller pond. Their green heads blending lovingly with the water. She tapped her glasses once again. Real.

Dana could feel her heart skip a beat. She could remember everything in her life, every moment. And yet, she hardly knew her name, her mother's name, or what she had eaten for breakfast. Tears came to her eyes watching it all. The tree, the duck, the squirrel. One of her colleagues caught her eye outside now too, and the feelings faded. But she winced, thought, believed, let the feelings wash over her. But as her colleague stepped onto the grass, the blue pixels flew from the back of their heel. The squirrel attempted to intervene, her colleague swiped at it, causing it to disappear. They walked through the tree next, the image, the color, sex, gone. Dana wiped her face.

"Stupid glasses."

Rick sat in the lounge with everyone standing next to him, their lips quivering with anticipation. The questions flowed much like Dana imagine that flood did. Each more generic than the next, demeaning this new person, or life form, that sat in front of them. Dana hated to even acknowledge how good Rick looked. How well the fusion seemed to go. She couldn't stop the words from flowing.

"What part of you is still Shannon?"

The room went silent. Two birds appeared on a tree outside the window behind Rick. Robins. Dana didn't bother tapping her glasses.

"You shouldn't ask that," one of her colleagues said. "No, no," Rick answered. What a deep voice. Stronger than either Shannon's or Chad combined. "It's quite alright."

Rick crossed his legs. Dana noticed this new man didn't carry any of the weight the pair used to. He was all muscle and sex appeal. He belonged selling futures, not examining volcanoes, or whatever it was that Shannon was doing now.

"We opted for a complete reconstruction," Rick continued.

"One that was optimal for both of us. Shannon's brain was obviously indispensable. Non-negotiable, she said." He moved in the chair again. Legs moving from a crossed position to normal sitting position. Did he have to go to the bathroom? Or did they enhance his penis too? Dana almost cracked a smile at the thought.

"Chad just wanted something fun, cool. So, here we are. A new personality with Shannon's brain, fulfilling the hopes of Chad." A funny way of explaining the death of souls.

It was a story that impressed. The moronic questions continued, and Rick smiled awkwardly, moving in his chair as he answered them. Dana figured it was time to get back to work. She stepped into the hallway and into the chest of a colleague, Tristan. The youngest person at her job, always running around doing something he shouldn't have, always running into people. He smiled at her as she tried to get her balance back.

"Sorry about that," Tristan said.

"I need to watch where I'm going," Dana responded.

"Pretty crazy, right? Rick," Tristan pointed to the awkward man crossing and uncrossing his legs in the chair. The man that used to be a woman who ate fast food breakfast every morning. "Surprised they went with it so early."

Tristan continued to prattle on about how difficult of a decision it must have been for them, how he wondered if Shannon really wanted what Rick said. Or if Chad made some last-minute alterations, an audible to win the game, cementing a legacy forever. Deep down, was Shannon a prisoner? Her mind rummaged through when deemed useful by her master, Rick. Or Chad. It made Dana's brain hurt, she tried not to think about fusions too often. But there one was, sitting right in front of her, struggling with a penis. Tristan was still talking.

"How's your work coming?" he asked. "Heard you're doing some research into a recent flood down the road?"

Dana nodded. "Yeah, same old thing. Just covering my bases."

"Man, I'm not sure how you do it. Look at rocks all day. Couldn't be me," Tristan said.

What exactly do you do here? Dana nodded again. "Yup, that's the gist of it. Well, I have to get back to looking at rocks."

Tristan either ignored her or didn't know she wanted to leave. He tapped Dana on the arm and kept talking. "What do you think made them do it so early? I mean, damn. Shannon was only twenty-seven. Chad even younger."

Dana was silent.

Tristan sighed. "Well, I guess it's better than waiting until the very last possible second. My brother, Reggie is like that. Thirty-fifth is tomorrow, can you believe it?" She looked up at him, noticing his messy hair and glasses just as big as hers. She tried to open her mouth.

"Catch you later, Dana!"

She adjusted her glasses as he walked away. People continued to pass her, a few even tried to strike a conversation. But Dana couldn't hear them, she just thought of the dance. Of the rocks and the flood patterns, of the colors of the holographic autumn setting, of life. She was frozen in time, thinking about the cruelty of life. The wonders of it as well. Shannon screaming inside of Rick's mind never left hers.

The government required you commit to a fusion by age thirty-five. Punishment was death or being sent to----

Reggie was on his last day. Thirty-four today, thirty-five tomorrow.

And so was Dana.

EXIST(ENCE)

Chapter 2

I think about it often. What is must have been like living your entire life past thirty-five. How did people do it? The fuck were they doing for the rest of their lives? Well, I guess we're going to find out now, aren't we? Bad joke. I read about what it was like back then. People seemed happier. Is that the right word? Content, maybe. Easy to please. In a lot of ways, I hate them. All of them.

Sorry, I shouldn't be crying. All of the world is a goddamn desert, no one left and I'm still insecure. Oh fuck you, Tyson. Seriously. Fuck you. What? Where was I?

Oh yeah. I hate every single one of them. For how happy they were. How many choices they had. Like, just imagine growing up in a world where you could practically do anything and everything you ever wanted. Except you couldn't. You just thought you could because the way society was structured, the way it was set up. Fought with those around you, especially those below you. Copied people you were jealous of. And then one day, your life didn't matter. Just when you figured that shit out, when you finally had a grasp on things, it was over.

Am I talking about my time? Or theirs?

Never underestimate the power of people

———————————

"This is where I leave you"

Because someone's always watching

_____

The air was dry, filled with chemicals. Molecules, particles. Debris. The ground was soft under their feet, then it was hard. Undulating, shifting. Green, brown, mist, smog. They were barefoot, and upon further inspection, completely naked. No memory of before, just the now. The man felt the roughness of his hair, pulled at his thick beard. She held her stomach in pain. Had they fallen? Or was an old injury flaring up? Both, probably. The man stood on the hard (soft) ground and began to look around.

Nothing. Everything. Mostly green. Mostly brown. His skin was dirty, that much he could tell. His skin cracked as he moved, the dirt falling off his skin, taking shape below. He looked at his skin. Brown like the dirt that was on it, darker even. And so was hers. They stumbled into each other, naked, surprised at each other's touch but not really. Not entirely.

"What happened?"

"Who are you?"

Stumbling through the mass, the pile of soft (hard) ground as it turned and mushed together forming a mess that neither could describe. It was hard to hear too. "Who are you?" the words the women spoke rang like a mouse in a crowded city square. Maybe it was there but no one really cared if it was. What was that noise? The man took the woman's hand. They explored.

She was beautiful, he noticed that the second he saw her. Dark, just like him. Youthful, didn't look as rugged, as worn-out, as he did. Short but firm, her back muscles some of the best he had ever seen on a woman. And through the green---through the mist, she smiled.

Maybe she had been speaking, or maybe she just liked men with beards. Still, a smile. The pair reached the top of a hill. Shifting ground, pungent air, molecules you could see, describe as they floated, mixed with your own body. They walked on.

A gust of wind followed by a blinding yellow light nearly killed the man. There was a pounding in his head he had never felt before. The woman too, was dropped to her knees by this light, this higher power. And almost simultaneously, in sync with each other's pain and minds, they remembered. The man gripped his chest as the green matter flowed through his lungs. It burned into his stomach as he screamed. He closed his eyes.

Birthday cake and ice cream. Candles that showed the number thirty-five. Himself, sitting in a chair, not amused by whatever nonsense was happening in front of him. And she sat across from him. Or rather, stood on a ladder, with a banner, those back muscles bulging, and she turned, smiled. Just like she was now. And as his lungs were burning and his sight gone from the yellow light, he smiled. This was his wife. And he remembered her name.

"Brianna."

She was holding her stomach, screaming as the noise and light devoured her. And called out his name.

"Howard."

Their skin morphed. Smooth but jagged. Just like the ground around them. He could feel his hands, his legs, even his teeth, had all grown. To almost monstrous proportions. Laughable proportions. His mind went to a time before the birthday cake. With Brianna in bed.

"It doesn't seem to matter what black people do in this country, baby. We'll always be targets," Howard said. "Civil rights, Black Lives Matter, and now this. What is this?"

"I'm not sure," Brianna said. Her voice soft, gentle. Much different from her screams now.

"Combining people. It isn't right. And they have huge corporations making sure we do it faster than any other group."

"I know, baby. I know," Brianna said. She smiled at him again. Kissed his chest as she lay against it. "But we don't have to think about that right now. We have five years. Five years of happiness."

Now to the cake. Her muscles. Her smile. His sorrow.

Their screams.

They were transformed forever, in this place. Green, brown, shifting matter. He reached down with his enormous hand and picked up a box. His vision was clear now. Beneath his feet, beneath hers, trash. Scraps, excess. A clump of it lay in his hand as he walked toward the blinding light, which was comforting now. She was close behind him, trash in her hand. They meandered through the muck, the slime. Released their piles into the light and watched it float. Watched it burn. And began to walk back.

Howard was still there. Inside. He could feel his wants and desires, could practically feel Brianna's chest against his as they kissed and made love. And Howard, not who he became, looked up at the light to see what they didn't want him to see. Or maybe they did. Howard could see, buried in the trash, bodies. Old and new. Human and monster. Soft (hard) and shifting as the green mist settled in the air. Those bodies lifted, just like his pile. Right into the light. A certain smell. And one day, Howard looked up and saw someone watching him. A woman, wearing glasses, observing, writing things down.

Until one day he floated into the light. Still screaming. Brianna still smiling in his mind.

***

Dana woke up sweating. It hadn't even been three hours since she laid down. But here she was, awake. Ready to conquer the world and look at rocks. She grabbed her glasses before looking at her clock. Past midnight. Happy birthday. She tapped her glasses.

Report to station 453 with partner within three business days. Failure to do so can result in---

She took her glasses off. Laid back in bed. A total of three minutes went by before they were back on, and she was using them to call Tristan. Who was still talkative, even in the middle of the night?

"Please, Tristan. Please. I just want to speak with your brother, Reggie." Dana felt a chill come over her. Went over to the window to close it. Why was it open? She didn't remember opening it.

"Yes, yes. I know I called you, but I just want to meet him. See how he's handling this. Can you arrange a sit down?"

As Tristan prattled on about the possibility of a white woman fusing with his brother, Dana noticed an owl just outside her window. Small but majestic. Creepy in a dignified way. And it seemed to know it, wade in it. That it was one of the classiest animals alive, in her backyard. As it flew away, Dana wanted to tap her glasses. Tristan wanted to talk.

"Tomorrow at nine works great. But I need to get some sleep. Goodnight, Tristan."

The owl was gone. And now, Dana was tired.

"This is where I leave you," she whispered. Uninterrupted for the night.

In the morning, she waited at a coffee shop. The sun was bright, at least to her. Couldn't remember the last time she had been in the field, not looking at replicas. She watched the people move about their lives. One woman complaining about the sweetness of her drink, everyone else recording her. Dogs walked with their owners. And Dana couldn't help but ask how many? How many of these people were under the age? How many were still them? It was a world Dana didn't recognize, yet it was the only word she knew. Outcast. Stranded. Not even a ball to play pretend with. Fetch. Bring it back. The warmth of her coffee comforted her, as the soulless continued their day. A man entered the shop five minutes later.

He was extremely handsome, so much so the women of the shop immediately began to drool the second he walked in. Good body too. He noticed Dana and acknowledged her. They shook hands and he sat down. He didn't look thirty-five. No facial hair, and skin was some of the best, smoothest she had ever seen. She rubbed her hands together awkwardly, trying to remember the last time her skin looked, or even felt like that. A smile.

Reggie tried to smile back, but Dana recognized the attempt. Her attempts. At living in this world, being something you are not. The pain was all over his face. His gaze averted her.

"We can go somewhere else if you want," she said. She smiled again, because this one was real. How could a man who look like this, built like this, carry so much fear? So much insecurity?

Dana wanted to throw herself off a bridge when she remembered why they were here. Compassion. Learn some. He was already getting up from the table.

"My stupid brother recommended this place," his voice was smooth, low. "Thinks he's some sort of comedian."

Dana stood up. "Trust me, he's not."

The pair walked down the street and passed other couples, some nodding their approval. Some disgusted. They didn't talk about what they came to talk about though. Mainly their lives, what they did. Things they liked to do. He told Dana about his work as a computer scientist. Which was really a fancy way of him saying he fixed his company's computers. It paid his bills though and he had lived a full life. And he wasn't ready to give that up. Dana talked about work, how she had read that geologists jobs used to be jokes, non-important in the past. Reggie laughed when she told him that not much had changed.

"Government work?" he asked.

"A University. The one right down the road. But we get contracted for all types of things."

They rested at a local park bench, the sun shining bright, the holographic landscapes impossible to tell from the real ones. Reggie let out a deep sigh, leaned forward, his arms resting on his knees.

"I miss this," he said. "Talking to people."

Dana nodded. She didn't have anything to add.

"Why did you want to meet me?" Reggie asked. An almost annoyance in his voice. The pleasantries were nice, rare, and almost orgasmic to Dana. She didn't love this man. But she did. And maybe he loved her, the way children love things the first time they see them. It was her turn to sigh.

"I'm not sure," she said. And that was a lie. She decided that he was worth it, to tell the truth. Some of it, anyway. "I—I guess I just wanted to see someone like me. Wanted to know what you're planning to do."

Reggie sat there. Please. Say something. Dana's mind was as fuzzy as the tree when her colleague walked through it yesterday. A pixelated mess of blue and white, with memories of the colors it was trying to imitate. She wanted to cry. Instead, it was Reggie who was moved to tears. His eyes closed. Cheeks wet.

He opened them and looked at her. "I don't know. I really don't. I like my life. It's a normal life, but it's mine. Am I selfish for wanting to keep that? Too keep who I am?"

Her hand moved to his. He gripped it like a child scared of the dark. "No, I don't think so," she said.

"There's rumors," Reggie said. "Of where people go if they don't do a fusion. If they simply refuse and say no. And---there's rumors of what they do to people like me." Dana recoiled at his words. Felt her breath release from her like a popped balloon. "Where do they go?" Reggie pleaded looking up to the sky.

Dana thought about his words. This man, and how valuable his life was. But not because he was crying here on a park bench on her birthday, his birthday. It was valuable because it was. The guilt washed over her like mist, a soft (hard) ground beneath her feet, changing forever. She forced herself to hold it in. Hold in the information, hold in her knowledge of the place Reggie had heard rumors about. That journalists speculated about, made documentaries without evidence about. The schematics she had seen, the horrors she witnessed. The place her colleagues past and present had helped build.

The place she oversaw for an entire year. Too much pain, agony. From naked lawbreakers to monsters to slaves to fuel. She looked at the holographic landscapes once more. Dana wondered if all she ever felt was guilt, not purpose. Or even love. For Reggie. Was it all to atone for a life in the past? Lives hurt. If she had been like Reggie, without her privilege, her knowledge, would this feeling live inside her? Or would she just be another Rick? Complaining about the sweetness of her coffee. They could escape this. She wanted to escape this. Together, or better for her and Reggie, separate.

"Reggie," she said. "Do you want to beat this? Them?"

He nodded. "More than anything."

"I have a plan."

EXIST(ENCE)

Chapter 3

It's been over one hundred years since the last fusion. And I think this is going to be my last video. I think I'm ready to die now. I've always been ready to die, I think. Every day, we wake up, not knowing what's going to happen. How many bombs are going to drop? What type of guns do they have? Who can we trust? I've killed more government assassins in the last few years than I can count.

Friends. Girlfriends. Even my own family. Yeah, if I die today that will be okay. And I hope that this video finds its way to you, whoever you are. Let me turn the camera so you can see.

That, up there? That's hope. That's what believing in something looks like. And I'd kill all the government assassins in the world to protect it.

What's that? They're here?

I guess it's time. Fuck. Wish I had more.

But I'm ready. Ready to die.

All who enter here are safe

———————————

Three days. That was all they had. Dana wasn't ready to die just yet, but she knew her plan wasn't going to work. It was haphazard, amateur, risky in all the wrong ways. Reggie entertained her though, as she rambled to him, as they sat on the park bench. She appreciated that. Her skills, really her entire life would be the backbone of their plan. For years, her work as a biologist had been plagued with mundane reports and repetitive paperwork. Staring at the shifting, but not shifting digital models, the replicas. Undulating and swishing rock formations swarmed her thoughts like bees. Always mixing, existing together. But there was a time her work mattered. A time when she felt like a force for good. Didn't last long. They had approached her to oversee the place, or green room as she called it, not long after.

She saw them in the formations, the replicas. All the people who had refused fusions, who dared to keep their independence and not become a Rick. She knew how it would work if she and Reggie refused.

A special task force had been assembled to gather fusion resisters. The worst of the worst. Men so callous they belonged in a comic book movie, evil henchmen with no souls. Soulless as they were though, they were stealthy, calculated, incredibly disciplined. No one knew when they'd be taken. Experts and conspiracy theorists always ran into disappearances spread anywhere from one day to one year. They'd watch you shower through your laptop computer. Or play cowboys and aliens with your son, disguised as a preschool teacher. Or they'd wait until you climaxed during sex, as your lust was just turning into love, a deep, burrowing love forming for this man you met six months ago. Not a care in the world.

The reactions varied when resisters entered. Most were scared, confused. Some were angry, ready to fight the entire task force themselves. Others were remorseful. Full of snotty confessions of their wrongdoing, how they want a better life, wanted to be rehabilitated. But most were sad. Cold. Alone. A temporary memory wipe let the process begin. The process she perfected.

The task force, in some ways, had the easier job. Rounding people up like animals, lying to them, pretending to be a decent person. If it weren't this, they'd be politicians or cult leaders. It was natural, they didn't feel a thing. And when they tossed people into the green room, that was it. On to the next shower. School. Orgasm. Not Dana. Her job forced her to witness their transformation from scared human to rock infused monster. Monitor their vitals during transformation. Record mortality rates, temperature changes, recommend adjustments, calculate the heat needed for the reactor, recommend heat settings inside the room----it never stopped. Her entire life was nothing but data. And death.

"All who enter are safe." She heard a colleague say that once.

The rock formations haunted her. She woke up in the middle of a nightmare on their last night before fusion. Reggie had been staying with her while they prepped. She screamed as the sweat flew from her forehead.

"Sorry," she said. Embarrassed. Ashamed. He stood up and walked over to her door.

"It's okay. Want me to make you some tea?"

She nodded her approval. Reggie left and Dana let her muscles relax. Tried to adjust under the blanket of her bed. They hadn't slept much in the last two and a half days. But when they did, they would lay together, against each other. Nothing else ever happened, Dana never even felt any sexual urges. She hadn't been with a man in years. And Reggie admitted the same about women. They had buried themselves so deep in their work, so afraid of tomorrow, shut out love, human contact almost entirely. And the first night

Reggie grabbed her, Dana almost couldn't breathe. The excitement flowed through her, and her breath became short. And she swore she could her Reggie crying, sniffling as he rubbed her arm. He returned with the tea.

"Thank you," she said. "I don't usually---this doesn't usually happen all the time."

Reggie smiled. "That's a lie." Dana winced at his words. She turned her back and looked out the window, hoping to see that pretentious owl from a few nights ago. Nothing.

"Is it ready?" Reggie asked changing the subject.

Dana took a sip of her tea. "I'm not sure. I've never really done this before. But usually, the process takes a few minutes. I figure with our situation it should be good in a few hours."

"How did you learn how to do it?"

"I didn't really---," she felt the truth almost escape. Saw the rocks swirling in her mind as she clutched the cup.

"Look, I know we don't have to share everything to make this work, and if this works, we won't ever have to speak to each other again but–," he sat down on the bed next to her. Placed his hand on her knee. "I do think we need to be honest with each other. What's going on?"

Dana didn't want to die. And she especially didn't want Reggie to die because of her. Because if their scheme didn't work, Dana knew where they both were headed. Reggie didn't. Thought it was a myth passed down through the generations. A boogieman. Ghost. Haunted house. She told him.

Her tea was gone by the time she had finished. Confessing? She felt the weight leave her as he stood to his feet and looked at the window into the dark. Just standing. Looking. Breathing. The tension was unbearable.

"Please," she pleaded. "Say something."

Reggie didn't say anything, but he did chuckle. Rubbed his head, trying to stop an oncoming headache. He turned to her and said, "I don't really know what to say."

"You're responsible for, without a doubt, the biggest and most disgusting human genocide in history. That's---I thought it was going to be normal trauma. Not this shit." He was still chuckling when he sat on the bed next to her.

Dana put her hand on his knee.

"Are you mad?"

Reggie looked up.

"I don't recognize the world I'm living in," he said. "We both agree on that, right? That this, this world we're dealing with, living in, it isn't right. That something needs to be done. And no one's tried anything since this 'green room' has been built. You said it yourself."

"Yeah."

"The remorse in your eyes is real. I see it. I thought you were just as angry as me, and maybe you are, but I see the pain in your eyes, I see it."

He grabbed her hand.

"I'm not mad, I just met you a few days ago. We connected over our own existential fears. Of not being human anymore. That---*this* isn't normal. And of course you happen to be one of the people who have been destroying people's lives." His hand pulled away. Buried his face in his palms. Looked up again.

"Why did you leave?"

Dana didn't think about the green room itself often. The resisters inside the green room sure, the conditions, every day. But not the work environment. Not the people. She explained to Reggie how each day went. How they'd enter the building one by one and be asked a series of questions. Nothing seemingly related to their work or really anything at all.

What color would a cow be if it ate a blueberry?

Given the current global economy, do you think more imports of bread is a good idea?

Assault rifles or pistols?

Every day brought a new set of questions. And each set of questions brought weird feelings. Weird emotions. Dana remembered the cow one specifically made her angry. At everyone in the world, but mainly herself. She worked harder than she ever had that day. Never ate beef or blueberries ever again. Each question was followed by a soft hum. Like a collection of bugs hovering over a lake ready to mate. The lights were always low. But Dana recalled flashes here and there, especially after certain words or questions. *Invoke. Testify. Betray. Good. Color. Or.* Her head began to hurt all over again. Sometimes, the answer to your question wasn't good enough, or that's what she assumed. Sometimes, colleagues were pulled into a separate room. Talked with a counselor or a businessman or a task force agent. No one ever knew, it was a myth, like the green room was to Reggie.

Inside, Dana remembered the holographic displays of assignments. Just like the questions, they varied. No one worked on the same thing every day, some never worked in the same room or part of the building. How big was the building? How many rooms? How many projects were happening? Another myth. There was a weird heat in the building. Radiating from the machine in the green room. Dana remembered sweating most days, wiping her head, never wearing her best clothes. And the light. The light she remembered too. The first time since being there, the light. How could she not remember before? Yellow. Green. Brown. How the hell could a light be brown? Lifted and sank with the moods of the office, the station she was assigned. Every day. Didn't change like the others.

What are you watching on television?

Who was the President in the year 2032?

Nice necklace. Have you ever sympathized with white supremacists?

One day, Dana recalled talking to a colleague about the place, the company. How odd the building was, how beautiful. It never stood out as she entered the parking lot. White, like everything else. Slick, like everything else. And there wasn't much direction. Most everyone had the routine down. Check the board, do your assignment, go home. The pay was good too. But who was paying? Who was supplying? Her colleague said it was Russians. Kate was her name. Dana remembered liking Kate. One day Russians, the next their own government. Big business, religious groups, lobbyists, tech companies? They ran out of ideas, out of jokes. No evidence leaning in any direction. So, they settled on government. It was a safe choice.

All this escaped her brain, or maybe entered it for the first time. Her head was pounding, her heart fluttering. Reggie put his hand on her back, it slipped slowly down her spine because of the sweat.

"Dana," he said quietly. She hardly heard him.

"All who enter are safe," was what that one colleague said. Tom. A bad joke as he watched the criminals burn and their skin turn into rocks. A chuckle from the other colleagues. Karen. Brad. Ameer. Farah. Elizabeth. Richard. But not Dana. She remembered a question from earlier that day. One that had made her feel---uncomfortable? Images of her childhood arose. But altered. She had a good childhood. A normal childhood. But that question, it made her see things that weren't there. Feel things she had never felt. In Tom's voice she heard that question and reacted, lunging at the man, scratching his face as he yelped like a puppy.

It wasn't funny. Then, her replicas, her models. The window, the outside tree, and her colleague walking through it. How many times did he walk through it? Reggie's hand was on her forehead now. She was lying in bed, a wet cloth in his other hand. As it touched her head, Tom's face reappeared. And so did the men who came to take her. The green room behind her, fading away in her memory, returning now. Nothing was clear after that. She winced, strained, let the cloth consume her. Nothing. Nothing at all. She woke up in the morning, the last night of her freedom spent in pain. Reggie was getting dressed.

"Morning," he said. Smiled.

"What time is it?"

"Almost nine," he said. "We're due at the facility in half an hour. It's done, though. In the living room."

Dana leapt up, tripped over the blanket hanging off the bed. "Why didn't you wake me?" she pleaded. Reggie was calm, her panic didn't bother him. He gestured for her to sit back on the bed.

"You deserved some peace," he said. "You looked peaceful."

Dana looked at the door, wished so badly to see the living room, see her work. Their plan.

"I wanted to blame you at first," Reggie said. He was looking down at the ground. "The pain you carry, it's deep. But I thought you were just numb to it after a point. But last night---what you were telling me, what you went through. I thought you were going to die, Dana."

"Thank you for taking care of me."

"The least I could do. Don't know if I could endure what you did," Reggie stood up and extended his hand. Dana took it as she stood up.

"You ready to do this?" he asked.

Dana didn't answer him. She made her way into the living room to see her creation. She smiled and wanted to cry at the sight. But she felt giddy, excited. Now, ready to die. She looked back at Reggie.

"Hell yeah I am. Let's do this."

EXIST(ENCE)

Chapter 4

"Humans have never had less. Not since cavemen. And I'd much rather be in their situation than ours. We don't have much. But I'd do anything to protect it, kill if I had to. I'd die for that tree. For Dana"

———————————

Every fusion was different. And there were a bevy of offices and locations where they took place. Reggie and Dana's fusion was scheduled to take place just a bit down the road. Their city hosted many fusions, and this office was the most popular. They stood at the doorway, waiting to be let in. The glass faded away, just like the window in Dana's office, and they walked through. Immediately greeted by dim light, like a blanket had been thrown across the building, sunlight barely peeking through. A man sat at a desk in the center of the slick room. Told them to sign in.

They were then given tablets and told to look through their options for the fusion. Black or white? Male or female? Bra cup size? Penis length? Piercings? (upcharge) Tattoos? (upcharge) The options were endless, and they give as much time as they needed. Dana had mentioned the last thing they wanted to do was draw attention, so they wrote a script, acted like certain things interested them. They even had a quick argument about hair color and texture. Selling the interracial couple façade. Shared a kiss and made up, turned their tablets in to the man at the desk. He smiled.

"I'm so happy for you," he said. "Seriously. Couples like you are just too cute. Very retro. And the look you've gone for? Classic but modern. I love it. Follow me, please."

They followed the man into an operating room. Two beds for them to lay on during the fusion. Another in the center for their new body. There were tools all around, vials and beakers used for the fusion. The man left them for a second, told them to get comfortable and that a doctor would be in soon. When he left, Reggie stood up, and began looking around the room.

No cameras. Their last moment of freedom. He liked having a bit of privacy. He took out a small syringe that was taped on the bottom of his tongue. Winced as he ripped it out. The syringe had a light blue liquid in it, he stuck himself then Dana.

"I hope this works," he whispered. Dana didn't respond. A placid look across her face.

The doctor entered soon after. Reggie discarded the syringe, smiled as the doctor questioned them. The entire process wouldn't take more than a few hours. They were asked to confirm their choices, sign a few more waivers, and asked if they would like to keep their bodies and organs, since they opted for complete reconstruction. Reggie said no. The doctor smiled, left again, and when he returned, he was with two more doctors. They made them strip their clothes and lay naked on cold beds. Reggie closed his eyes.

Dana told him it would be like he got a good night's sleep.

When he awoke, he was still naked and had minor cuts across his arms. His torso as well. He controlled his breathing as the doctors tugged and pulled on his chest. A quick glance and he could see the new body. Fully constructed, naked just like they were. Reggie could also she Dana. She had woken up as well. But she didn't control her breathing as well as he did. Her stomach filled, and she gasped, eyes wide open. The doctors began to scream. Reggie knew this was the moment. He jumped up from the bed and punched the closest doctor in the nose. Dana took care of her doctor. The main doctor attempted to run towards the door, but Reggie tackled him down to the ground.

They didn't have long. They knew that the doctors broadcasted a live feed of each fusion. To the imaginary task force, Dana concluded. They had seconds. Reggie got dressed and proceeded to the next part of the plan. He pulled out a thumb drive that was also taped under his tongue. He connected the drive to the doctor's computer near the door. Five seconds later, he activated his program.

"I think it's working," he said. But they didn't have time to find out. Reggie and Dana bolted out of the door, a sea of workers and doctors screaming after them. They reached the man at the desk. A swift punch sent him unconscious. Reggie unlocked the door of the building as the pair ran down the street. Cop sirens wailed and the task force could be seen approaching in a van. But they had planned for this. Knew the route they wanted to take.

It was a chaotic chase through the city. Alleys and streets began to mix in Reggie's mind like water. He was getting tired. Legs were burning. They found an older building, one of the few ones around. Stopped for a moment, he fell to his knees.

"Reggie, I need you to get the fuck up."

Dana's voice rang loud in his ear. He looked at the other Dana, still wordless, still placid. Real Dana continued to talk in his ear.

"I'm above the bookstore right down the street. They don't know where you are. Hurry."

Reggie took a deep breath and ran as fast as he could. He entered the small studio apartment with the other Dana. The real one typing furiously as he walked in.

"Your program worked," she said gleefully. "I don't know how, but it did."

"So you---you," he struggled to say.

"I control the green room now. Yes."

Dana continued to type as Reggie waited. For his own death, he guessed. Fake Dana sat in the corner of the room staring at the wall. Touching it lightly with her fingers. It was starting to rain. The water ran down the glass on the window. This building was older. Its windows weren't disappearing. Fake Dana watched, mesmerized. Reggie couldn't help but smile looking at her. Her beauty. Real Dana was tough, smart beyond her years. But the company, the world, had beaten her down. Forced her into doing work that killed innocent people. Brainwashed her into hating simple things about herself, her life. And she broke through because of the strength of her mind. They were two halves of a beautiful whole.

"How—how did you do it?" Reggie asked, his gaze still on the clone.

Dana had been done typing for some time. Was she watching fake Dana as well? Was the program complete? Was his life about to end? He let the last thought escape his mind.

"I created the technology that exists in the green room," Dana said. "It changes every single thing about a person. By the time the transformation is done, they aren't a human anymore. Genetic code completely rewritten."

She walked over to her clone. Seeing them, next to each other, the two halves coming together, Reggie almost fainted at the incredibleness. He sat down as she continued talking.

"I figured I could invert it. Make it so I take a bunch of rocks from the ground and change their structure."

The clone turned, placed her hand on the Dana's cheek. A tear rolled down real Dana's face.

"And here she is."

Reggie watched as Dana let the tears flow onto her clone's hand. The clone's attention shifting from the rain outside to her creator. Reggie cried as well. Maybe they were for completely opposite reasons. He thought of a world where people truly had a choice. And didn't have to pay for their government's mistakes. Where a black man and a white woman's voice mattered. Where their work mattered. Where their pairing wasn't a trend. And where this ominous cloud of despair didn't hang above. Reggie dreamt of that world daily as he worked, wrote code, the beauty of it, the warmth of it. Dana slid an empty syringe into her clone's arm. They locked eyes.

"I'm sorry," Dana whispered.

The clone turned back towards the window. Put its hand against the glass. Smiled.

"This is where I leave you," the clone said. The syringe pulled out a golden liquid from the clone's arms. The clone turned into a pile of rocks seconds later, thudding against the floor. Dana stuck herself with the syringe, letting the golden liquid flow through her.

She let out a deep sigh. Turned and faced Reggie. Words weren't needed now. The plan had worked up to this point. They knew that the task force would be blasting the door open any second. They embraced each other and let the tears stream down their face, not afraid to show that weakness in front of one another. No, not weakness. Strength. There was a strength in what they were doing. Reggie knew it. Dana knew it. If only they had more time.

The task force charged into the room a few minutes later. Just before the entered the room.

They had talked during their three days about how Reggie fit into all of this. Without him, they wouldn't have gotten into the green room's controls so there was that. But she needed someone to be brave enough to escape a fusion with a prototype clone. And someone brave enough to risk their life for someone they didn't know. Someone with a dark storm in her mind, her past a fog.

Reggie reminded her that he had a past too. Did things he didn't like, wasn't proud of. One thing was made clear drawing up their plan. Reggie wouldn't be needed in the green room. He didn't want to see it, and Dana knew it was a fate worse than death. So when the task force approached them, screaming at them to get on the ground, Reggie simply smiled.

"Thank you," he said to Dana.

"Thank you," she said.

Reggie charged the closest soldier to him, attempting to grab his gun. A single blow to the shoulder brought him to his knees. He tried to get up but was kicked behind his knee. Unarmed, they could've taken Reggie in with her. Make him suffer the same fate. But they both knew that wouldn't happen, even in this world. A soldier pulled out his pistol and fired a bullet directly into Reggie's skull. He fell the ground. Thudding just like rocks.

Dana didn't remember much after that. She assumed they gave her a sedative. She woke up naked and being carried by two men in suits. It was a building she recognized. Her old job, the same building. The green room. Dana saw the vault that had seen too many people. She smiled as the men continued to drag her. The green mist popped as the vault unlatched. She smiled at the men.

"Have you ever sympathized with white supremacists?" she asked.

They threw her into the room.

The transformation happened. Dana became one of the rock monsters that she helped engineer. Felt all the pain they had felt. Would this help make up for her crimes? As her rock life neared its end, she felt relief. Maybe the plan wasn't going to work. And maybe Reggie's program didn't work. The life was escaping her as she floated towards the yellow light. She could feel her skin peeling away, ripping in every direction. It felt good. Relaxing. She slowly closed her eyes as the light combusted, and she died.

The last fusion ever.

***

My name is Dana. I'm a geologist with years of research in rocks, rock formations, and weather patterns. For the last, I don't know, few years, I worked with the people responsible for the fusions. The people responsible for us being stripped of our autonomy, our freedom. I helped create and maintain the weapon they use against us today if we say no. If we even think of not conforming to their rules.

Our world is incredibly clean now. It took a climate catastrophe to get there, but the main way we are able to have this source of power is because of this machine I created. That turns rocks into clean, renewable energy. So they made me create a way to turn people into rocks.

I've caused a lot of pain. A lot of hurt, but I'm trying to make it right. I just recently turned thirty-five. My fusion is tomorrow with a kind man named Reggie. But it will be the last fusion ever. If we succeed, I will be able to mix my DNA with a clone's DNA, as well as the serum used for fusions. And Reggie will hack into the machine, disabling all of its functions, so that my hybrid combination completely dismantles it. You will be free. To do what you want, love who you want, and be whoever you want to be. I'm not sure humanity will get another chance like this. Let's not waste it."

***

Dana's plan worked. Better than she thought it would. The machine became corrupted from her DNA, it exploded and caused a nuclear meltdown at her old building. Everyone died. And the world heard Dana's message she uploaded minutes before her fusion. People were confused at first. There was outrage, blame. But when the reports rolled in, when that machine fell, and when the government demanded people go back to doing fusions, they refused.

A lot of people died. Riots happened. Change happened. And so did something Dana did not expect or predict.

The hybrid combination of her DNA destroyed the machine, yes. But from the ashes of the building, underneath the rubble and ash, a flower sprouted. One made with Dana and the clone's DNA as well as the power of the machine. Right there, in the Earth. People found it, planted it and it grew. And, almost miraculously, magically, it transformed into a tree. Grew to gigantic heights, spawned almost every type of food, and produced clean energy, enough for the world.

It's been 100 years since Dana and Reggie died, but most say they aren't dead at all. The government tried to confiscate the tree. Use it for their own purposes. Anyone who dared harm it, were killed. A new government was established. A new order. One rooted, quite literally and figuratively in the message from her video.

"Do what you want. Love who you want. Be whoever you want to be."

And now, a final fight against the government for control. A mythical, life-giving tree that represents the hopes of all people. No matter the race, gender, religion, they all agree that this tree must be protected. That the world will never return to discrimination. Racism. Fusions. The tree must be protected at all costs. Their town must be protected at all costs. Society must be protected.

They named the town Reggie.

And the tree...

Dana.

TERRORLOOP

- Calvin Sanders

Chapter 1

"What's wrong, ya havin' a hard time getting that door open?" Brad said to Eugene as he was frantically searching through the custodian's key rings trying every key possible.

"I obviously can get the door, it is just a door after all," Eugene said in his soft nasally voice, but Brad, getting impatient, took the multiple keys and moved in front of Eugene to try to open the door.

"Like hurry up Brad, I think I hear something," Stacy said in a frightened voice as she was peeking around the corner of the school hall.

"I'm trying okay," Brad said as he was going through the keys.

"You won't be much use if that gash on your hand isn't wrapped," Ava said to Cameron, opening her lunchbox housing medical supplies.

"I appreciate it, I'm not sure how we would have made it this far if it wasn't for you Dr. Ava," Cameron said putting down the baseball bat to hold his hand out.

"Well, I didn't waste my summers with a bunch of snobby rich kids at a Marcy Jupiter's Medical Camp for nothing," Ava said as she was pouring water on the wound.

"I've seen a bunch of things when living in Brooklyn, but I've never seen someone treat a broken finger with Popsicle sticks and duct tape," Cameron responded while Ava started wrapping his hand.

"Yeah, when you're a medic you learn to use whatever you can," Ava said wrapping the rest of Cameron's hand.

"In short I'm saying thank you," Cameron said with a smile.

"It's not a problem," Ava smiling back at Cameron.

Just then, Stacy's emerald green eyes widened with fear as she spotted a tall figure, maybe standing close to 7 feet, walking down the hall with a blue janitor jumpsuit, brown worn out gloves, and a potato sag over his head with lob-sided eye holes for what could be the eyes with a large axe being held in both hands. Stacy looked as if time had stopped for a few seconds and she almost couldn't form words, but managed to shout, "He's like walking down the hall guys," as her voice echoed in her classmate's ears.

"Hey Brad, I know I'm probably not helping much by saying this, but please hurry up before this thing chops us up like lumberjack wood," Ava said as she was putting away her ragtag medical supplies in her lunchbox.

"Keep an eye on him," Cameron said as he was tightening his grip on the baseball bat, but just in that split second Brad shouted in an excited voice "I GOT IT" as he unlocked the door leading into the teacher's break room. Brad shouted "get in everybody hurry" as he held the door open before spotting the tall figure walking around the corner, axe in hand. Stacy quickly ran in with Brad right behind her with only mere seconds to spare before the psycho got to the door.

A second before Brad locked the door; the figure tried opening the door. The knob began twisting and shaking, Ava and Cameron pushed the fridge over in front of the door, "that's not going to keep him busy for long," Ava said.

"We can go through the vents this time," Eugene suggested.

"Good idea," Cameron said as he proceeded to pull a table under the decent sized vent.

"Remember we tried going through the vents before and it never works," Stacy said as she was hesitating to enter the vent.

"Well we don't have many options," Brad said as he searched through the closet in the break room. As the banging on the door became louder the door began to show signs of giving way, "Alright I got it" Brad said as he was holding up what looked to be a crowbar.

"Listen Stacy I know you don't trust the idea, but I promise it'll be different" Cameron said in his smooth Brooklyn New York accent while also holding out his hand to help her in the vent.

"Alright fine I guess it's better than waiting to be chopped into bite sized pieces," Stacy said as she grabbed Cameron's hand. Just as Brad was climbing into the vent the door had an axe mark through it with the figure looking in to see Brad closing the vent.

"So guys where are we crawling to this time?" Eugene asked.

"We'll have a better chance going to the gym because anywhere else we go that freak could be waiting," Brad said using his hand to slick back his jet-black hair.

"So we go to the gym like we've done before and hope he's not there, sounds like a solid plan," Ava said as her arms were brushing up against the cold dusting vent walls.

"Will it kill you to have a little more optimism?" Eugene said in an angry tone.

"Yes...Yes it will and has many times."

"We're here guys," Cameron said opening the vent to the gym and dropping down.

"Well at least that went smoother than last time", Brad said wiping the dust off his dark pink varsity jacket, but before the 5 teens could enjoy peace, they heard a thud from one of the double doors and when Stacy looked, she let out a scream when she noticed the potato sag wearing maniac looking into the gym and trying to smash the door's window in.

Brad began to run straight to the other side of the bleachers which had a couple of spare windows, "come on guys we can still make it to the car if we jump out the window." Before everybody could get the message, the door opened, and the tall figure ducked his head in and made a full sprint for the 5 teens. "RUN" Brad shouted as the teens made their way to the bleachers with the figure still running at the teens with full force.

Cameron was the first to make it up the stairs and with all his might, he used the baseball bat he had and smashed the window open. The figure made it to the bleachers and swung his axe cutting Eugene's lower back.

"You motherfucking cunt!" Eugene shouted as he fell to the ground in pain, "just go you, assholes" Eugene said as the figure stepped on Eugene's head splitting it open in an instant.

"Where's the car?" Ava said in a frantic voice.

"I'm not sure, though we don't have time to waste let's just try again," Stacy said pointing to a porta potty that had a big exit sign painted in black on it.

"If the car isn't here we'll have to try again and plus we can't just go without Eugene. We aren't leaving anyone behind," Cameron said with a serious and stern tone.

Brad stood in place looking at his scared classmates and said, "I hope you guys are ready to do this because once we walk in there, we won't know what happens next."

Just as Brad was thinking about all the possible outcomes his thoughts were interrupted by a loud thud that sounded like a boulder hitting the ground, and when Brad looked back, he saw the figure charging at him with his axe. "Fuck it man we'll figure out when Eugene is with us," Brad said as he pushed everyone out the way to open the door to the porta potty which looked like it led into nothing other than darkness.

As the 4 teens rushed through, Cameron closed the door, but not before the killer managed to cut Cameron on his arm to which he let out a scream.

"Well, one down and infinity more to go" Ava said as she was staring into the darkness of the porta potty which began to take shape of a locker room.

As Brad looked around to make sure his classmates were still together, he looked around and asked, "Where the hell is Eugene?"

"I'm over here," Eugene said in a voice which sounded like it was coming from one of the doors in the locker room. Ava ran over, opened the door, and stood in shock with her eyes wide and asked, "Are you feeling okay Eugene?"

"Yeah, I'm feeling fine why would you even ask that? We're always okay after we start over again," Eugene said in his usual rude tone.

"How long have you had that?" Ava said pointing to Eugene's neck, Eugene ran out of the closet and looked in the mirror to see a scar on his lower neck where the figure had hacked him.

"WHAT THE FUCK?!" Eugene said as his nasally voice turned into a deep, terrified one.

"What the hell is going on? I thought we were healed once we start this terror loop over unless…" Cameron said as he paused to gather his thoughts. "Do you feel any pain?" Cameron asked Eugene.

"No not really. I mean, my supraclavicular nerve on my left side feels a bit tingly, but other than that I feel fine why?"

Cameron looked at his arm that had been cut previously by the figure and was shocked to see that his arm had a scar on it, all the teens stood in place and stared at Cameron's arm as they began to piece together a horrifying thought.

"So like, if both of you have a scar from the last time you guys got attacked does that mean that our scars are gonna like---start becoming permanent every time we get injured or die?" Stacy asked the group.

The locker room went silent as the five teens looked at each other in a state of shock until Ava broke the silence. "So if we keep dying or even getting hurt, we'll eventually...die permanently".

"I-I-I--can--NOT die okay, guys. I have so many other things I plan to do like finish this semester with a C+, use my scholarship to play college football, but really hook up with mad chicks and eventually retire to start my own nature center," Brad said while pacing back and forth.

Cameron walked towards Brad grabbed his shoulders and told him "snap out of it Brad we're going to live through this, okay? That maniac can't even attack us until we leave the locker room."

"And even though we don't understand how this place works or why we're here we already have an idea as to how to get out of here, so keep your head focused because if you die our chances of living go down by 20%"

"Forget about percentages if any of us die here were looking at a solid dead percent since these scars are becoming permanent," Ava said.

"Well they're right, the more of us that die were all as good as dead so the only thing we can do is stick together as a team and get to that car that is hopefully waiting for us outside," Eugene said.

With their confidence back, the teens devised a plan to escape out of this dreamland of horror.

"Wait you want to open a nature center?" Ava said slightly confused.

"Yeah, no. I didn't say that I don't know what you're talking about," Brad responded.

"Alright guys, so just to make sure we're all on the same page if you guys get me the super soaker water gun in one of the lockers, I can do the rest" Stacy said as she was inching toward the door to open it.

"So, when we open up the door, we're all going straight for the cafeteria, the library, and the car, right?" Brad said.

"I thought it was library, car, and cafeteria," Ava said with a confused expression on her face.

"This shit is all so confusing why the hell would we go to the library first when it's further?" Brad said looking at Ava.

"Because that's where the key is and we might find more medical supplies, plus the key is more important than the gas can, duh," Ava responded.

"Well, the key is useless without the gas can...duh," Brad said in a mocking tone.

"Okay guys, this isn't the best start so let's agree on the cafeteria, library, and then car since after the library it's a straight shot to the parking lot," Cameron said.

They all nodded in agreement. Cameron opened the door. The five teens made a mad dash for the school's cafeteria which was in a separate building. As the teens ran for the side door, they opened it without a problem and made their way to the cafeteria which was about 10 feet away. The teens opened the door and started searching for the gas to the car. Eugene looked around with worry in his face asking his classmates "Where's this asshole at? He's usually knee-deep in our asses right now."

Brad looked at him and said, "Maybe he's sharpening his axe to plunge it into our faces, but either way I don't want to wait for him."

As the teens searched through the dark cafeteria with the only light coming from the moon outside, Stacy said in a quiet voice, "I got the gas let's hurry and get out of here." Just as the teens were about to leave they heard a strange sound, something metallic scraping the ground, and after a few moments of silence the teens looked at the cafeteria door and noticed the all too familiar look of the tall figure standing by the door with his axe in hand.

"Hurry run to the double doors and I'll grab the gas can," Brad said as he dashed towards Stacy to get the gas can from her while also running to the double doors that would lead into the hallway. As the teens all ran for the door Stacy looked back to see the killer was already gone.

"Let's not worry about it, just don't forget to check some of the lockers," Cameron said as he was checking all the lockers trying to find any unlocked ones. Eugene did the same and managed to find a baseball bat in one of the lockers to which Ava said, "I hope you know how to use that."

"It can't be more difficult than trigonometry, right?" Eugene responded in a nervous laugh. As they stacked up on various supplies, they ended up giving any medical supplies to Ava who found a backpack in one of the lockers. The gang continued to the library without any problems which came off as weird, especially to Stacy.

"Does anything feel off to you guys, like something about this feels strange?" Stacy said to the group.

"Yeah, we're trapped in an endless time loop where we're being chased by a crazy asshole that doesn't want to do anything besides carve us up like pumpkins, all of this feels strange" Eugene responded.

"Not that, Mr. Highwaters. I mean the killer hasn't even like, attempted to kill us...which is kinda surprising since it's like his favorite hobby."

"You guys ever think that maybe he's a killer who might enjoy the thrill of scaring the shit out of us?" Ava said.

The group paused for a second. They thought about how they had been in this exact same position before, hundreds of thousands of times. This is the first time that the figure wasn't actively chasing them.

"Ava's right he's probably just fucking with us, but like I said I don't care if he's beating off somewhere as long as he's not here we shouldn't worry about it," Brad said breaking the silence in the library.

"He's not wrong if he isn't here then we should---" before Cameron had even finished his sentence the tall figure came from around the corner. In that moment, Cameron had no words that could leave his mouth fast enough to warn Brad. So he reacted and pushed Brad out of the way before the figure could get to him. Eugene was the first to react and swung the baseball bat at the potato-sag wearing creep a couple of times.

"What the hell are you made out of, lonsdaleite?" Eugene said as he kept swinging.

Unfortunately, the hits did nothing. Not even so much as a reaction until the figure turned around, dwarfing Eugene in size and stature. The figure swung his arm, hitting Eugene in the face so hard his glasses flew off his face as well as blood from his mouth. Brad, on the floor, didn't take long to react. He got up to help Eugene and grabbed a chair smashing it on the figure's back making him stumble.

"You guys start looking for those keys. I'll hold off this freak," Brad said grabbing the baseball bat that Eugene dropped after getting hit.

"I'll help," Cameron said grabbing a book off one of the tables.

"What the hell you gonna do with that give him a fucking papercut?" Brad said.

"I have more than one book, you have only one bat," Cameron said with a smirk on his face.

As Ava and Stacy made their way into the large library they began searching under tables, tops of bookshelves, and anywhere else the key might be.

"O...M...G," Stacy said searching in the lost and found bin.

"Did you find the key?" Ava asked.

"Even better," Stacy said, getting out the super soaker she wanted. Stacy grinned with excitement as she looked at Ava.

"I'm going to give that freak a taste of his own medicine."

Brad and Cameron kept the figure occupied; they knew that they wouldn't be able to keep it up for long. "This asshole just isn't going down," Brad said rubbing the sweat off his face with his varsity jacket.

"Yeah, and I'm starting to run out of books," Cameron said.

"How the hell do you run out of books in a library?" Brad said.

"Uh Brad, where did he go?" Cameron asked.

"You guys need to be careful!" Brad shouted to Ava and Stacy.

Ava turned to respond and was grabbed on the neck by large hands. She felt her heart skip a couple beats. Ava tried to get her skinny fingers in between her and the figure's grasp on her neck, but the figure's grip was just too tight and felt like it was getting tighter. She felt like she was beginning to lose consciousness because she started to feel dizzy and as those seconds went by, they felt like an eternity.

"HEY FREAK OVER HERE," Stacy shouted pointing the water gun at the killer who was only about 2 feet away. She sprayed the figure in a clear liquid that had a strange smell like vinegar. As the figure looked down at his jumpsuit for a few seconds he looked back at Stacy and threw Ava like a rag doll against a half empty bookshelf. He started walking towards Stacy raising his axe, but Stacy was ready for him and took out a small lighter with a bulldog on it. She lit the lighter and threw it at the figure who immediately got caught on fire. The figure dropped the axe and started to pat himself, trying to put out the fire. Stacy watched in shock as the figure's massive body stumbled into tables and bookshelves, but that didn't stop her from spraying more nail remover on him to help feed the fire.

Ava woke up thanks to the smell of burning flesh. She stumbled and noticed books that fell off the shelf that she was thrown into as well as a shiny item. It didn't take long for her to figure out they were the keys that they had been looking for, so she quickly got up and went over to find the rest of her classmates. She found them helping Eugene up who had a bad bruise on his face. Like a rock the size of Brad hit him.

"Found the keys guys so let's hurry up and get out of here," Ava said.

"I agree, who knows how long that maniac will be out for?" Cameron said helping Eugene on his feet.

"That asshole's lucky he caught me off guard," Eugene said holding his jaw.

The teens left the library though not before getting a good look at the lifeless figure who was laying on his stomach stretched out over the floor with his now black jumpsuit that had been burned. And the potato sag that looked like it was now half-way off his face.

Stacy looked at her classmates.

"The weird thing about it is that I didn't hear him make any noise at all when he was getting burned." Not wasting any time, the teens made a mad dash out of the library and through the gym which led outside, but the teens were shocked to see that the car was not there.

"No fucking way man we did everything we should have the car should be here," Brad said looking around the empty parking lot.

"Don't worry man I'm sure the car is here, remember this campus has like 3 parking lots," Cameron said reassuring Brad.

Stacy pointed at the other parking lot which was on the other side, "Hey, I think I like found our car guys," and in the far corner there was a dark brown SUV.

"Well, it looks like shit, but it'll have to do," Brad said running over to it with Ava's backpack, which had the gasoline in it. Brad opened the gas cap and began filling the vehicle up. While he did that, the teens used the keys to open the car and they all got in. Ava opened her small medical kit and gave Eugene some pain killers for his potentially broken jaw.

As Brad was about to finish emptying the gas can he heard Cameron say, "Hey man you might want to hurry up," Brad looked up to see the burned figure running towards the car with his now black potato mask exposing half of his disfigured face underneath. Brad, staring in a panic, dropped the gasoline can and got in the driver side of the car. Ava handed the keys to Brad who put the keys in the ignition.

But nothing happened.

Brad frantically kept twisting the keys though nothing happened. In the tense moment he remembered a trick that his Dad taught him which was to put your foot on the break and the shift lever in neutral. The killer was only about three feet from the car. The car made a stuttering noise before shutting off.

"Come on what he fuck?" Brad said trying everything he could to get the car going. Just then, the killer ran headfirst into the car so hard it shook the car which made everyone jump. Brad tried the same trick again and the car finally started. He put the vehicle in reverse hitting a bump which they all assumed was the killer's foot, but the killer stood there and put his axe above his head before tossing it with all his might so hard that it hit the right side of the passenger door and penetrating it, though not completely.

Brad drove off with the figure just staring at them as they began to leave the campus.

"Did we just fucking escape?" Eugene said delightedly.

"Yeah, I think we just did," Stacy responded. The teens began to joke around and started laughing as they drove off campus and into the darkness, but Brad stopped when he noticed that the road in front of him was pure darkness.

"Drive through there, what the hell you waiting for?" Eugene asked.

Brad looked at the darkness and said, "What if I drive through there and the same thing happens over again?"

"Well, we've never made it this far before, so I guess the only thing to do is try it," Ava said in a nervous tone.

"Just so you guys know if I had to choose like a bunch of people to be trapped within some freaky place with a crusty custodian who smells like a locker room trying to kill us, I'd choose you guys. When we leave, we should all grab an avocado smoothie sometime," Stacy said smiling.

"That sounds good...minus the avocado smoothies," Ava said smiling back.

"Yeah, you guys are the coolest people I've ever been trapped with," Cameron said with a smile.

"Whatever just hurry up and get us the hell out of here, but if you guys ever want to join the chess club or something I'll be around," Eugene said to his classmates.

"I think that's the nicest thing I've ever heard you say," Ava said smiling at Eugene.

"Well don't get used to it," Eugene said in a sarcastic tone.

"Yeah, I agree you guys weren't the worse people to spend eternity with." Brad said.

He accelerated and drove through the darkness.

Brad woke up in a brightly lit room with buttons on every inch of the wall. It was a strange sight. He got up with only strange silk underwear on and what looked to be a holter monitor hooked up to him, but he couldn't remove them no matter how hard he tried. He walked around the small room that looked like something straight out of a cheesy sci-fi movie and noticed that the room was like nothing he had ever seen before. Brad tried to open the door that had led to another dark room, but he found a switch and turned on the light. He couldn't believe what he was seeing.

There, hooked up just like him, were his classmates. Brad went over to them and tried to shake them awake. As Brad tried to unplug the machines, he was greeted with loud alarms blasting from the walls and soon after a couple of men wearing gas masks entered through a different door. The two men easily overpowered Brad who was shouting and cursing at the men. One of the men took a syringe from his pocket and poked Brad's neck injecting him with an orange liquid, and soon Brad began to pass out though not before getting a good look at a white man in a suit with nicely combed red hair. "How the hell did he get free? Make sure the rest don't wake up. And put them in a different scenario," the mysterious man said as Brad began to pass out.

Brad woke up in a place that looked to be in a clothing store at a mall with his classmates.

"Finally, you woke up Brad. You were out for a bit," Cameron said.

Brad looked at his classmates and, in a whisper, said...
"I got some things to tell you guys."

TERRORLOOP

Chapter 2

It was deftly quiet and the various neon-colored lights from some of the mall stores lit up the entire mall just enough to see where you were walking. The four-story mall was filled with tons of empty stores. The mall was so big it was hard to guess where it started and where it ended. The lights made it beautiful, but also a bit nerve racking because of how silent the enormous mall was. Some of the stores had gates which stopped people from entering, but the ones that were open had the bright neon lights on. It was as if the group had stepped into a mini-Las Vegas.

"What do you mean you have something to tell us?" Stacy said with slight concern.

Just before Brad had a chance to answer Eugene angrily looked around for a moment before shouting, "What the FUCK, man I was pretty sure that we were done with this."

"How do you know it didn't work...I mean, we aren't in a school anymore," Stacy responded.

"Well for starters this place gives off the same creepy ass feeling just like the school did, but instead of empty classrooms they're empty stores." Eugene said back to her.

Brad got up and walked towards Eugene "You said it was supposed to work. What the fuck, man?"

"I never told you it would work one hundred percent, so don't blame me, asshole." Eugene said.

Suddenly Brad grabbed Eugene by the collar, "What the fuck Eugene, we died over and over again just to end up in the same shitty situation and you sounded sure that it would work."

"Hey guys, maybe we shouldn't be fighting each other right now, especially when we all have the same goal," Cameron said, trying to defuse the situation.

"Cameron's right I don't think we should be fighting each other especially not right now." Stacy said

Brad looked at Cameron with anger. "Fuck that man what's the point when we're all going to end up still trapped in this loop, we might as well fight each other."

Ava walked towards Brad and grabbed his shoulder, "Brad you need to cut the alpha shit, I don't know how but we will get out of here and live our best lives. Although we can't do that unless we're all on the same page."

Brad loosened his grip on Eugene, "Fuck man, it just seems like we're never getting out of here...being in this loop makes me feel like I'm losing my mind."

Eugene looked at Brad.

"I'll take that as an apology."

Cameron looked at the group saying, "Well I guess the good news is that I don't really see any axe wielding maniacs trying to hack us to pieces."

"Do you guys remember anything that happened after we drove through the fog?" Brad said.

"The only thing I remember is a flash of light and then I woke up in this delightful place with you guys," Ava said.

Brad looked at the group with a confused expression "So you guys don't remember me trying to wake you up?"

"What do you mean?" Ava said.

"Well, I woke up in some strange room with all these kinds of wires hooked up to me and when I opened one of the doors you guys were all hooked up like me and I tried to wake you guys up, but I think you guys were in some kind of deep sleep or something." Brad said.

The group just stared at each other with confusion and puzzled expressions.

"OMG did we like get abducted by aliens?" Stacy said sounding slightly freaked out.

Brad paused for a moment, thinking, and then looked at Stacy, "Nah I don't think so because I remember seeing some asshole in a suit that looked like a human, but he sounded pretty pissed off that I found you guys."

"Well if that's true then I think it's safe to say we're in a pretty fucked situation here," Eugene said looking at the group.

Before the group had any time to digest the information, a loud scream echoed in the big mall that was so loud it actually felt like the mall shook.

"What in the actual fuck was that?" Eugene said looking back at the pitch-black area in the mall.

"I don't know, but it sure as shit didn't sound very friendly," Ava said moving ahead of the group.

"We'll talk more about our situation once we can get to an area that's a bit safer," Cameron said as he pointed to a different direction with lights lit up.

As the group began to make their way through the first floor of the mall the layout was a lot different from the school. But it otherwise looked like a normal mall although the group could tell

149

something was off because of the eerie atmosphere, but they kept moving until they came across a store directory which made it somewhat easier to understand where they were.

"Damn this mall has 4 levels and a store for everyone," Cameron said as he was studying the mall map.

Ava looked over the map as well and was surprised by some of the stores, "They even have a store named Zombie Take Over and Sock Land," she said.

"Wow they have a nail salon, an *Until 27* clothing store, and even a store dedicated to different lighters. This place would totally be like my paradise in the real world," Stacy said with slight excitement.

"Maybe this place wouldn't be so bad if we weren't, you know, trapped against our will," Brad said as he was putting his finger on the map to find the best escape route.

"Well maybe we should try to make our way to one of the exits while looking for supplies on the way," Cameron suggested.

"They're 3 emergency exits on each of the 4 floors and it looks like the closest one is placed in the middle portion of the mall, so unless that screaming asshole bothers us, we shouldn't have a problem getting out of here," Eugene said.

As the group made their way around the mall, they took in how quiet and even peaceful it was. They noticed that the loud scream they heard previously had not been heard since but didn't let it bother them and walked forward until they noticed a sign pointing to the cafeteria.

"So if we didn't get abducted by aliens where do you think we are?" Stacy said to the group.

"All I remember is that I woke up in some place that looked like it came straight out of a sci-fi movie and you all were hooked up to machines just like me," Brad said.

Eugene let out a sigh, "I've been thinking about it and it's going to sound completely fucking crazy, but I've read about people having an out of body experience and it sounds like our bodies are supposed to be stationary while our minds or consciousness are left to wander---kind of like lucid dreaming."

"Wait so you think we're in some lucid dream state or something?" Cameron responded.

"It's just an idea I thought of based on what Brad said, but if that's the case what kind of crazy ass high tech are we dealing with? To force us to be trapped in this nightmare *and* feel pain, but more importantly where the actual fuck are our bodies?" Eugene asked.

The group was quiet for a couple seconds because they knew if Eugene was nervous then they must be in some deep shit.

Cameron looked over at Ava and noticed she was looking at the ground "Hey Ava, you good?" he asked her.

"Yeah, I'm fine---I'm going to go check out this zombie store to check for anything to use in case shit hits the fan," Ava said as she began to walk over to the store.

"I'll go with you," Stacy said.

"Alright well the exit isn't too far up ahead, but I'm still freaked out that we haven't seen or heard whatever those screams were earlier. Let's just make sure we're not hanging around too long," Brad said.

As Ava and Stacy made their way to the unusual store, Ava was quiet, and Stacy could tell something was wrong.

"Are you sure everything is okay, Ava? You haven't cracked a smart-ass joke in like fifteen minutes," Stacy said.

Ava paused for a second and let out a sigh. "I've been thinking about this whole time loop we're stuck in and I don't know about you, but I can't remember exactly how we ended up here," Ava said quietly.

"I guess being chased by a maniac made me not think about it much, but I'm also having trouble remembering things that I know for sure happened not even a month ago," Stacy said.

"Yeah, I know what you mean...I know for sure my family threw a party for my Mom when she got her Doctorate Degree last month, but I can't even remember if I was there," Ava responded.

Before the two girls could continue their conversation, they stopped to look at a nearby wall that had something written on it that was barely visible, but because of the store's light, it lit up just enough to be able to read.

"What...the...hell" Ava said shocked as she walked closer to the writing on the wall which looked to be written in spray paint.

"We need to let the guys know, and quick," Stacy said as she began to walk back in the previous direction.

"Yeah, I don't think we were the first ones here," Ava said looking at the writing on the wall which read in bold---

DON'T TAKE THE EXIT.

As the girls ran back, they heard a faint clicking noise that came from the darkness, they both starred in the direction of the sound. They heard what sounded like loud footsteps approaching them and soon the source of the clicking noise began to step out of the darkness. The figure started out as a black figure until it slowly came into the light and the sight was so scary Ava had to hold Stacy's mouth so she wouldn't scream.

Unlike the psycho with an axe who was chasing them previously, he at least had a human looking body; this creature looked like something straight out of a cryptid video. It looked like it was eight foot tall although it was hunched over, completely naked with no definable reproductive organs, large eyes, and pupils so big it almost completely covered its eyes. Strains of long black hair coming out of its head, and long sharp nails and teeth.

Ava's eyes widened as she was still holding Stacy's mouth. She was almost paralyzed with fear.

"Don't move, Stacy. I don't think it saw us," Ava said as she started to remove her hand from Stacy's mouth.

"Hey, you two hurry up and get under here," Cameron said, hiding under a table.

Ava and Stacy both ran under the table with Cameron, still looking at the creature as it was standing there just looking around.

"So I'm NOT even going to ask what the fuck that thing is, but I'm glad you two are okay," Cameron said to them.

"I'm glad you're okay too...where are Eugene and Brad?" Stacy asked him.

Cameron looked at them while also trying to keep an eye on the creature. "Well after you guys walked to the store, we started to do the same until we heard that thing walking around and when we saw what it looked like we decided to hide in different spots."

"This probably isn't the best time, but we saw writing on a wall that told us not to take an exit. I don't think we're the first ones here, Cameron," Ava said to him.

As the three of them stayed under the table to ponder what to do next, the sound of a can fell not too far away from them. It alerted the creature who started to make a mad dash in odd fashion towards the three which caused them to freeze in a panic, but before the creature could get any closer a loud bang could be heard coming from the side of them and the creature immediately fell to the floor.

A person wearing what looked to be night vision goggles and a bullet proof vest armed with a double-barrel shotgun stood on a nearby table. "Come with me if you guys don't want to end up as a scratching post for that thing."

Without a second thought, Cameron, Stacy, and Ava ran out from under the table to see the person wearing the makeshift body armor. The person jumped off the table and looked at them for a couple of seconds.

"Let's blow this popsicle stand...oh and don't worry about your friends, they're safe," The unknown person said pointing to some stairs.

"Well you're the one with the gun, so I'm following you," Ava said.

As the group ran up the stairs the unknown person directed them to another flight of stairs leading onto the third floor. The unknown person pointed to a store that had wedding dresses in the windows, as the group got closer the gate opened and a kid wearing an orange backpack and blue flannel shirt with large curly hair opened it.

"Took you long enough I almost thought you kicked the bucket," The unknown individual said.

"Nope not kicking any buckets yet," The other unknown person said back to him.

"Fuck me I thought you guys were as good as dead," Eugene said running to aid his friends.

"It's good to see you're okay too," Ava said back to him.

Cameron looked at the two people for a second. "Thanks for saving us, but who are you guys and how the hell did you get here?"

The person with the night vision goggles started to take off the goggles and bullet proof vest revealing a frizzy red-haired girl, "My name is Isabella, and this is Alex and welcome to the shittiest mall you'll never want to visit---that actually sounded much cooler in my head. Also don't worry about that barf bag out there it's blind, so unless we're close it shouldn't be a threat."

Alex looked at Isabella with an awkward glance and then looked back at the gang, "Yeah sorry if this is a bit overwhelming for you guys, it's only been the two of us trapped in here for some time."

The gang paused and looked at their rescuers. Then Stacy asked, "Um...just how long have you guys been here?"

Isabella paused and started counting on her fingers, "Not too sure, but I know it's totally been over a thousand days---at least in here."

Brad looked at Isabella. "Oh I get it you were trying to tell a joke because we're in a time loop. I get it...it's a joke, right?"

Alex started to take his backpack off. "Well yes and no...it's true we're in some weird time loop and jokes help pass the time, but uh...this might give you an idea of how long we've been here."

Ava took the worn-out notebook and opened it. "Shit no wonder you guys know how to fight against that thing," Ava said with shock as she showed the others the notebook.

"Every tally mark was every time we died, and we have 7 other notebooks just like it---some died more than others," Alex said.

Cameron looked at it. "This is insane this whole notebook is filled with tally marks even on the back of it."

Stacy looked at Cameron with a worrisome look, "So is there really no way to escape this place? Are we really gonna be trapped here forever?"

Cameron looked at her, "I know we'll find a way out of here. Even if it doesn't look like we will. I promise we'll get out of here."

"Well this is gonna sound strange, but we kinda thought somebody was gonna show up sooner or later I just wasn't expecting more than one." Alex said.

"I knew Steve was on to something, he was right about it all along" Isabella said.

Ava looked at Isabella and Alex, "So what exactly did Steve figure out?"

"You guys are going to want to sit down for this one. I'm about to tell you some crazy shit," Isabella said.

"So I can't remember how long ago it was, but back then it was me, Steve, Ruby, and Alex who ended up trapped in this place. We were all confused about the situation, but quickly grew to an understanding when that thing out there ended up chasing us and picking us off one by one.

That's when we realized if we wanted to escape, we needed to work together and we needed to figure out where we were and how we ended up here."

She continued, "Nobody had any ideas and at first we thought we were all just dreaming, but Steve had this crazy thought that we were stuck in a time loop. Which didn't make sense until he explained it, since he was a total nerd that loved sci-fi movies and comics I guess, that's how he knew so much about it. He came to the conclusion that when we die certain things around us stay the same, so if we spray painted an area we knew, we were there before or not to go there. Since dying over and over again sucks, Steve thought it would also be a good idea to make a hideout so that freakish skinwalker thing can't get to us. Ruby came up with the idea of making a notebook to document every day we spent here... or die and it seems like time works like ours, but it doesn't get light it only stays dark."

"We escaped from this place tons of times, but no matter what we just ended up back here no matter how many exits we took. Before uh...Steve and Ruby passed they had vivid dreams about being trapped in some place and hooked up to machines. Every time Steve and Ruby died the dreams became more vivid and soon Steve was convinced that we weren't just trapped in this place by accident, but that somebody kidnapped us and forced us into this place. He was so determined to get us out he wanted to have more vivid dreams in order to help us, but one day when he died, he didn't come back and neither did Ruby after a while. Steve left his journal of notes that had a bunch of theories as to how to escape. But we never actually tried them because we didn't have enough people and after that we just decided to chill in this place until we had somewhat of an idea of how to escape. I mean there's a bunch of stuff that happened in between, but for the most part that's how we ended up here and eventually you guys showed up."

"Wow I'm sorry to hear that it sounds like you guys have been through some shit and it sounds like Steve and Ruby were good people---man is it a draft in here?" Brad said wiping his eyes.

Isabella twirled her thumbs, "Well Ruby could be a real bitch at times, but she was pretty and taught me how to speak some Italian.

She was also a really good painter and Steve was probably the nicest guy I've ever met. Also wasn't bad looking for a nerd. We even talked about trying to be together if we got out of here."

Alex looked at the group. "Steve's journal had one theory that somewhat made sense. He theorized that we're not the only ones trapped in a time loop and that there could be other time loops. He thought that if we're trapped in the same space then someone could eventually show up from another loop, but we never actually believed that would happen. He had a bunch of weird theories and even a way to escape."

"We tried that already and we just ended up here," Stacy said.

"Yeah but based off the notes we need to do things in a certain time frame to mess up the loop, like a very strict time frame. Did you guys manage to kill that thing that was chasing you in the school before you escaped?" Alex asked.

The gang all looked at each other until Eugene said, "Well that would be a fuck no."

"Alright well let's look over these notes. I think I might have an idea for how to escape this place for good and since we have more people it's possible. Whoever is behind this is going to have one shitty day when they have to deal with all of us," Isabella said.

As the group looked over Steve's notes and came up with an idea for escaping the mall of horrors, another conversation was taking place in the real world at a company known simply as The Syndicate. A red headed man with a nice comb over wearing a silver suit walked down a brightly lit hallway with many green doors and one red door at the end of the hall. The man took a deep breath and knocked on the door only for a woman with a stern voice responding, telling him to come in. The man's hand was shaking a bit, but he opened the door and sitting relaxed in a chair with a large desk accompanied by a head in a jar, was a woman who looked to be in her forties with long brown hair sided to the left of her shoulder with a serious expression across her face.

"How is Project Pathway coming along, Jerry?" The woman asked.

"It's coming along nicely, Miss Director," Jerry responded.

"You know there's been a lot of money and labor put into this project for many years right, Jerry?"

"Yes Ma'am, that's why I intend to put every ounce of effort into this and I'm working non-stop to make sure we can achieve the Dark Abyss and use it."

"Unlocking the Dark Abyss has been far more difficult than you make it seem. We have to use real people, then put them in a sleep paralysis state and then study them as they explore an area that is beyond our understanding. Then we have to hope that our top-notch scientists can figure out a way to harness more power from the place. Do you know the end goal of all this Jerry?"

"To make use of a power that can aid us in future wars, Ma'am?"

"Not just that, to control the mass media with that power of fear. And if the Dark Abyss can make nightmares come true then we harness that kind of power and use it to control most of the world through fear alone. We've only tapped into a fraction of it, so far putting it into the factories and having it polluting in the air has worked thus far. People have been controlled by fear for years and if we can tap into more of that power, we could control more than just the U.S."

The woman looked at Jerry for a few seconds. "Your deadline is about a couple months from being up, so I suggest you don't let things like teenagers wreaking havoc in the facility that my grandfather created happen. I'm telling you not to fuck up again, Jerry."

"Yes Ma'am, I understand, and I promise it won't happen again."

"You may leave now."

Jerry was scared and tense because he knew if he said the wrong thing or made The Director mad, she would have him "replaced" like she'd done to many before him. Jerry took an elevator to one of the other floors and walked into a large room with a bunch of workers wearing dress shirts.

"How long do you think it will take to figure out how to open a portal to this world?" Jerry asked one of the workers.

"Well if everything goes well, we should be ready for testing in forty-eight hours," the worker responded.

Jerry patted his shoulder, "Good if anything happens just call me. I have a yoga session in thirty minutes."

"Uh...okay sir."

As the conversations continued to happen in the real world, in the Dark Abyss the teenage group came up with a plan to escape not just the mall but break the entire loop.

"Alright I hope you dudes and dudettes understand what we're doing because everything has to go right for this to work," Isabella said putting her night goggles on.

"Who would've thought the way to break the time loop is by using time," Eugene said.

Isabella looked at Eugene, "It sounds simple, but we have about fifteen minutes to get done with everything, so one fuck up and we could end up screwing up our chance at getting out of here. That weird fucker out there can only see-through sound, so if we pull this off it shouldn't be that much of a problem for us."

"Anybody got any words of encouragement?" Alex said.

"Not really, let's just kill that fucking thing and make those assholes in suits regret trapping us in here," Brad said.

Ava shrugged her shoulders. "Close enough I guess."

Stacy asked the group, "Just to make sure we're all on the same plan. As soon as the time hits eleven forty-five we make our way to the two closest fire alarms and pull them to distract that creature then kill it and use the entrance as an exit?"

"Yeah, I'm not sure how long that thing has before it comes back to life, so we have to haul ass. Don't forget the exit doors are to reset the loop so no need to use them unless we're in a shitstorm," Isabella responded.

"Alright guys let's break this loop and get the fuck out of here," Brad said holding a hockey stick.

As soon as the gate from the store opened the teens split into two groups with Brad, Ava, Alex, and Eugene being in one group while Isabella, Stacy, and Cameron were in the second group.

"This thing must be sleeping or something cause it's been dead silent since we've left," Cameron said.

"It's probably because it can sense everyone moving and it's throwing it off." Isabella said to Cameron as they moved through the mall.

Stacy looked around and held her nose, "OMG is it just me or does something smell like a rotting corpse?"

Cameron put his sleeve over his face. "Not even gonna ask how you know what one of those smell like, but yeah I smell it too."

"Sheesh...do you guys see it?" Isabella said in a whisper.

As Isabella pointed, the group looked over to see what she was pointing at and in the distance there the creature stood facing a wall with its head leaning against it. It didn't move, but it stood as still as a statue with the lights from the stores shining just enough to see it. The only problem was that next to it was one of the fire alarms they had to pull.

"Is that thing---just staring at the wall?" Stacy asked.

"I've seen it do that a couple times before. I think it's sleeping but it sorta...sleeps with its eyes wide open," Isabella said.

Isabella let out a sigh "Sooooo we have a huge problem, guys. One of the fire alarms that we have to pull is on the left side of that thing."

"Shouldn't we just wait for the other guys to pull the alarm?" Stacy asked.

"We could do that, but the goal is to kill it and if it chases after them we risk losing it and we only have about twenty minutes to kill that thing and walk out the front entrance doors. We have about a minute to figure this out," Isabella replied while looking at her watch.

Cameron looked at the two girls. "I think I have an idea, but if it goes bad I need you to keep going."

"There's no way I can just leave," Stacy said.

"We have a chance to finally get out of here, so please Stace just keep going," Cameron said while looking at her.

Stacy paused and looked at Cameron. "Alright just make sure whatever you do, as soon as it moves, you move."

"Alright," Cameron said while nodding.

As Cameron crouched his way over by the fire alarm Isabella looked at Stacy.

162

"Don't worry if that thing decides to attack your boytoy I'll just shoot it like I did last time."

Stacy looked at her with her cheeks slightly red, "Uh what no Cameron's just--- a friend."

Isabella looked at Stacey with a smirk, "I can totally tell you guys are hooking up I mean he's hot your hot it's not a surprise. I liked Steve for the longest time...I guess when you're trapped in a time loop with someone for so long you guys just kinda...form bonds I guess."

Stacy looked back at Isabella and rolled her eyes, "Alright you got me. We just didn't know if we would ever escape or die in this time loop so we...decided we would hook up just one time. Until that one time happened over and over again."

"It looks like you think of him more than a quick hook up though. If you guys ever escape from here maybe you guys could be in a normal relationship," Isabella said.

Stacy smiled. "I guess a proper date would be pretty nice."

As the girls were talking Cameron could see the fire alarm and was inching his way toward the alarm and the creature.

"Man how the hell did I end up in this situation?" Cameron said to himself.

As Cameron made his way over by the creature the smell got stronger and Cameron was terrified by the height difference. He walked closer and with each and every step his heart was beating even faster until he was standing about two feet from it. Cameron grabbed the alarm but not before looking at the creature who was just staring at the wall and as Isabella said its eyes were wide open just looking at the blank wall. Just before pulling the alarm the other alarm ringed throughout the entire mall which alerted the creature who looked around and had its big wide eyes on Cameron.

Cameron didn't move a muscle, but the creature was staring at him and let out a scream which freaked Cameron out and caused him to fall back and cover his ears. A split second before the creature was about to attack Cameron, a shot rang through the alarm and forced the large creature to fall against the wall, Isabella starting walking towards the creature while shooting it with her shotgun. Cameron quickly stood up, pulled the other alarm, and ran away from the beast all while Isabella unloaded her double barrel shotgun into the creature, which was trying to get up. Just as she was reloading, she noticed she was running low on ammo, but she kept shooting the creature down.

"Hurry up Stacy!" Isabella shouted.

Stacy ran up to the creature and threw a Molotov at it causing it to scream in pain before it stopped moving, but before they left for the exit Isabella shot the creature two more times before leaving.

"There, it should be dead," Isabella said, putting her shotgun away.

"Are you two alright?" Cameron asked the two girls.

"I should be asking you. I thought you were going to die back there," Stacy said.

"Well aside from almost shitting myself I think I'm good," Cameron responded while smiling.

"Let's keep moving guys. I don't know how long that thing is gonna stay down," Isabella said.

As the group made their way to the entrance, they saw the other group there waiting for them.

Alex looked at Isabella and said, "We're finally gonna get out of here."

Isabella looked back at him. "Yeah, it almost doesn't feel real. I only wish Steve and Ruby could be here."

Alex touched Isabella's shoulder. "We're gonna make those fuckers pay for putting us through this."

As the group opened the door, they could see the same familiar fog from the school and Brad looked at everyone for a second.

"Alright guys hopefully this works," Brad said as they all began to walk through the fog.

Just before Alex could walk through, he heard fast approaching footsteps and before he could notice it the creature jumped on him and started clawing at him.

"ALEX!" Isabella shouted before grabbing her shotgun and shooting the beast with her remaining ammo.

The group ran back towards the noise and Brad ran at the creature with his hockey stick and hit it a couple times until the hockey stick broke. The creature finally fell and its wide eyes closed. The creature which had various bullet holes and burns had finally been killed, but not before causing one of the teens to succumb to his injury.

Alex was on the ground with large claw marks on him, but he looked at Isabella and pointed towards deeper into the fog.

"We can try again, let's just try doing this over---," Isabella said as her eyes were full of tears.

Alex looked at her and shook his head no and in that moment, Isabella knew what she had to do. Isabella looked at Alex who was now lying motionless on the ground. She closed his eyes and said, "You will not die in vain friend."

Isabella looked at the group and said in a tired tone, "Let's just get the fuck out of here."

As the group went deeper into the fog a bright flash of light occurred and everything went white. Brad opened his eyes and noticed he was in the familiar state with wires hooked up to his body, but now he was in an all-white room with the only thing in it was a white chair in a corner. The room was a lot different from the previous room he woke up in before and the room looked so clean that it seemed like it had never been used before. He quickly grasped the familiar situation he was in and got up slowly while still looking around. He got off the table and took the wires off him. He made his way to the only door in the room and opened it.

Brad was breathing heavy and was extremely nervous, but when he opened the door the first thing he noticed was the loud blaring alarm. He also noticed the lights outside the hall were flashing red, but most importantly nobody was around. Brad gathered his courage and walked outside the room and started opening the other doors that were close by and to his surprise he walked into a room that looked empty, but the room was similar to the one he was just in. Just then, Brad heard footsteps running in his direction, so he hid in the room and left the door cracked just a bit so he could still hear what's going on. The multiple footsteps ran past Brad, so Brad cracked open the door more and heard one of the guards talk about a "breach from the portal" and the guards took the stairs to another level.

"Breach from a portal? What the fuck is going on?" Brad said to himself as he walked out of the room.

"Brad?" a familiar voice said from behind a door.

Brad jumped in shock and turned around to see a friendly face, "Ava---I'm so glad to see you."

Ava looked at Brad with a look of concern, "Where the fuck are we Brad?"

"I think this is the shithole I woke up in the first time. We need to find the others and get the hell out of here."

"Yeah, I agree," Ava responded.

So Brad and Ava began to look for the others and started opening doors on the floor they were on until they walked into a room filled with different files and boxes. They were about to leave until Ava noticed it looked like the files had already been looked through and papers were scattered. Ava picked up some of the files and started looking through it. A guard armed with a gun cracked open the door to see Brad and Ava.

The guard looked at them and shouted, "What the fuck are you subjects doing here?"

Before the guard had any time to think about his next move a fire extinguisher hit him over the head and knocked him out cold. To Brad and Ava's surprise it was Stacy and Cameron who were just as surprised as they were.

"Thank goodness we found you guys," Cameron said.

As much as the gang was relieved to see one another, they knew they weren't able to celebrate long because of the current situation at hand. Ava looked at the group with one of the many files in her hand.

"Guys these files date back to 1965 that talk about something called the Other Side. I don't know who or where we are, but I think whoever these people are they might be involved with the paranormal."

The group looked at each other all with puzzled expressions, "This doesn't make any sense...where the hell is this place?" Stacy asked.

"We can ask ourselves all these questions once we find Eugene and Isabella, leave this place, and call the police," Brad said.

As the group left the room, they decided to take the stairs which is when they noticed this building had five floors and they were on the third. They decided to make their way down to the first floor before a guard came out of the door on the second floor and spotted them.

"Hey, wait, you guys," The guard said as they grabbed Ava's arm.

"Let go of me you creep," Ava screamed trying to break free from the guard's grasp.

"It's me you guys it's me," the guard responded, taking off the helmet to reveal a pale looking woman with unkempt red hair and a thin face.

"Who the hell are you supposed to...wait...Isabella is that you?" Ava said.

"Yeah. I guess I was trapped in that mall longer than I thought," Isabella said with a smile.

"Wait, that's impossible, you were the same age as we were in that loop," Brad said.

Isabella looked back at the door and then back at the group, "Listen I want answers more than any of you, but I can't explain everything right now. When I woke up I fought a guard, found the records room to gather some data, and found an exit, but---"

"But what?" Stacy asked.

Isabella let out a sigh, "Well I guess when we broke the time loop we messed something up because uhhh...I've seen some monsters walking around this place killing guards. We have to find Eugene and find another exit because I've been to the first floor and it doesn't look good."

Just then the gang heard a familiar sound that they've heard before walking up the stairs and when they looked down they saw a tall figure with an Axe walking up the stairs with a potato sack over his head. The figure looked at the group and started running up the stairs as if he somehow remembered them.

"Oh are you fucking shitting me?" Brad said.

"GET THE FUCK DOWN!" a voice said from behind the group.

As the figure ran upstairs he got blown back by a shotgun blast to the chest and hit the wall. The group turned to see the shooter was no other than Eugene.

"That's for punching me in the face back at the library asshole."

Isabella looked at Eugene. "Well fuck man, where the hell have you been?"

"I checked up the stairs like you said and didn't see any windows, not even in the director's office," Eugene said as he reloaded his gun.

"Well that only leaves us with one way out" Isabella said.

"Please don't tell me we're going to have to go through the first floor?" Ava said.

"Well I could tell you that...I'd be lying if I did though."

The gang made their way past the figure still lying on the ground and to the first floor. When Isabella opened the door, a horrible smell overwhelmed the group, and they could see blood on the walls and limbs everywhere. The group made their way through the floor until they saw a man lying on the ground covered with blood on the right side of his face near a door. The man looked like the one Brad saw before. Brad was the first to notice and the first one to run over to the man.

Brad looked at the man with a frown, "Hey fucker, you remember me?"

The man laid there for a couple seconds before opening his eyes and looking at him and started smiling, "Well isn't this ironic?"

Brad stood over the man. "Where the fuck are we and how do we escape?"

"We're all gonna die anyway. This place is crawling with nightmares everywhere. Even if I told you it's not like it would matter."

Before Brad got a chance to ask the man another question Isabella asked the man "What is the Dark Abyss and how are you guys able to access it? And why were there files of various missing kid's cases dating back to the 1940s?"

"We still aren't sure what the Dark Abyss is, but the theory we had was that it was home to everyone's worst fears, think of it as a place specifically for those monsters you were scared of when you were a little kid. Also if you must know we've had access to a fraction of the Dark Abyss since the 1930s and we use its power of fear to influence the world...through various means of pollution. We wanted to gain full access to it though, but as you can see that didn't work."

"Okay well what about the kids?"

"We had to find a better way to gain more access to it, but we didn't know how. We've been using kids from various parts of the United States to transport their minds into the Dark Abyss dimension, so we could better understand how to use it and hopefully travel there. But again, you can see how that backfired on us. I guess humans really aren't allowed to have access to certain things."

Isabella looked at him with anger and tears starting to fill her eyes, "Give me a good reason why I shouldn't torture you until you die, asshole? You know what you've put us through--how many---lives you've taken?"

"I don't mind being called an asshole, but I'd prefer Jerry and I'm as good as dead already. There is one thing I might as well tell you guys though, just so I can get it off my chest. If you think I enjoyed doing this job I didn't, but we all had to follow orders or else we would be killed on the spot. This place is no different than the Dark Abyss; we just fear different nightmares."

Just then a voice could be heard over the walkie talkie near Jerry. It was a voice that sounded distressed.

"Jerry. Hello? Come in, Jerry."

"Yeah I'm still here."

"The nightmares are breaking through the bunker and I don't think the guards can hold them off forever. If you can do one thing for me, type in code bronze in the cell phone I gave you. It will self-destruct this building and destroy any evidence of this place."

Jerry looked at the scared teens and looked back at his phone.

"I'll do it but there is one thing I want to tell you beforehand. I hope they rip every limb off your body."

Jerry threw the walkie talkie only for the Director to be heard screaming and through the device.

"When I type in this code I need you guys to make a left at that corner and then a right through the double doors. The exit will be there, but you've only got a minute before this place blows sky high."

"Why are you helping us?" Stacy asked.

"I've decided that I should do something with my life that doesn't involve hurting others anymore. Just wish it didn't take me this long to do it."

"Yeah, no shit," Eugene said.

So the group did as he said and ran the way he told them until they found the double doors and the exit. As the group ran for the door they heard Jerry scream and before they knew it they were outside the place. The group continued to run until they heard an explosion from the building that sounded like multiple loud fireworks going off. They looked back to see the large building now burning and soon the building was completely covered in flames. It didn't take the group long to realize they were in the middle of the desert.

Eugene smiled and laughed, "We fucking did it guys."

Cameron was relieved, but tired, "So what did you see in that records room Isabella?"

"Jeez where should I start? Well um...I guess I was born in 1984, ways to keep the body alive and well while in prolonged comas, I guess some people call those monsters cryptids and they've escaped this building before, and this place was originally supposed to provide shelter for high profile people from some world changing event called Y2K."

"Y2K? What is that?" Ava asked.

"I'm not sure, but from the little I read it sounded like some sort of apocalypse. Like electronics were supposed to stop working or something."

Cameron grabbed Stacy's hand and looked at her, "Well everything out here looks fine to me. What now guys?"

Brad looked around for second, "This place looks like it's in the middle of nowhere, but maybe we can use one of these cars to drive to the nearest place and look for help"

Isabella looked back at the group "Sounds good to me. Maybe we can find out what the date is too."

The group walked towards the cars, but unbeknownst to the group most of their surroundings and the world had been destroyed.

They would later find out the date to be January 2nd, 2000.

A Bulb's Perspective

- Shriharshita Venkat Chakravadhanula

"Why Not You?" Short Story Contest Honorable Mention Winner

Today, I may look old and bald and resemble Einstein. But back in the day, I was a handsome make of glass and metal, held together in fiery solidarity. I had within me the hotheadedness of a youth, disguised in the body of an elegant case. Well, not for long, for ironically enough, this was my best quality. I could throw my beams all day, if asked. It was, however, quite unfortunate, that I was never asked. They found purpose for me, instead, out in the open, during the night.

Ah well, at least I'll be noticed now, I thought.

In this quiet corner above the world, amidst a strange amalgamation of man's buildings and nature's breath, I was plugged in, and ready to go. I had thought, a sophisticated bulb such as myself should light the night for intellectual conversations in an evening party, or aid those wearing a suit. And instead, I got the most unsophisticated of mankind: a nine-year-old child. Man, in general seemed below me, both in dignity and position. But when I first saw her, this girl was barely tall enough to see the ground from the terrace. Try as she might, no amount of bopping pigtails and hopping legs would help her accomplish this insurmountable task. She had a fascination with mud and spent much of her time rolling in it from the patch of plants.

Ugh, children.

This would happen almost every day, and I'd see it through my sleepy eyes, realize it wasn't worth my attention, and save my 60 watts for another time. (well, I guess I was inquisitive that way…) But as evening drew nearer, she would come back. This time, with a full-grown man, and a book.

A book! I knew it was my time to shine.

A large chair would be perched right below me, as I got ready to provide my warm, curious light. The man would sit with the child on one lap, and the book and is arm on another. And off they would go, into stories of the wild, and the past, of lands near, and faraway, till the child was asleep. And then, I'd be turned off, and the night would swallow them.

The next day, it would happen all over again. Night and night again, I'd see the same thing, until I suddenly realized, that while showing her the nights in my light, I had grown a little fond of her.

As time progressed, the nightly visits grew fewer and fewer, until they stopped completely. I thought, maybe she'd grown too old for me. For a while, that's how it was. But then, as if to remind me, she'd come back. This time, however, she was alone. I think she'd only remember me when the lights of the house were forbidden from serving her. In fact, I'm pretty sure she was supposed to be asleep, but I was happy to be her partner in crime. Now, she'd read books of her own, but I didn't get to hear these stories. Although some part of me was sad about this, ultimately, I decided I didn't want to know what girls in their teenage read about.

Even this routine didn't last forever, though. Turns out, my sophistication rubbed off on her, cause now she was an artist, painting the night sky with my help. Gone were the days of supervision, now it was her and the brushes. The paintings were terrible to begin with, but gradually, they got better. But these vanished as suddenly as they had appeared.

Then came words, along with contemplative sighs. I wonder how much contemplation 14-year-olds go through, but from the sights of it, quite a bit. And that's when I realized, just how much had changed. From reading children's books, to children writing in books.

And then, all of a sudden, this gradual undulating curve became a steep fall. For a few days, I was not used at all, and I kept wondering where all the angst went, when I saw a few workers taking out the tiles of the ground! I saw so much that summer and heard so much more. But my biggest complaint was, that I was not used at all! Workers only came during the day, and I was all alone during the night. I thought, how much worse can it get? I'm only rusting away. Turns out, quite a lot.

One of the days, while putting the tiles back in place, there came a splatter of substance, all over me! I was furious, but I couldn't even dissipate my energy. Dust, I was used to by now. But this! This was humiliation of a new degree. My smooth and transparent body was now, by part, rugged and impenetrable. I used to be a symbol of elegant innovation, but now I was the face of decay.

As I lay there, unable to wipe it off, waiting for it to solidify and become a part of me, I realized, that I would never see the girl again. I was an abandoned bulb, and one unable to commit to its job. The light that once shone within my soul with the brightness of the sun, now dimmed. I closed my eyes indefinitely.

And just when I thought all the light within me had drained out, the stars brought some more. While I slept, the terrace was completely done again, and one night, out of nowhere, I was awoken from this deep slumber. Unable to keep my eyes open for too long, though, I blinked several times, and then squinted, to see the familiar face of the girl, this time, much older. I was unable to contain my happiness, until I realized, I must. She had left me here, to my own devices. My face was so crusty, I didn't want her to see me either.

But just then, I saw her face. I knew that expression. I realized; my indignity didn't seem to upset her. Instead, it she was fascinated by it. The cement left a scar, which morphed into shadows. Shadows, in which she saw stories. Well, I guess there wasn't much else I could expect from a girl who thought mud was interesting. Cement is a kind of mud, isn't it?

Old age, however, got me. As much as I tried to resist it, my insides buzzed with a sound, and I knew I wouldn't last long. At last, I was taken down. I had prepared myself to be cast away, when the girl did something that made me forgive her completely. She took off my rusty metal and put me into a box. Here I met magnets, wires, and glass lenses. Ah well, retirement homes are swell.

Average Man: Just Your Average Hero

- AnnE Ford

"Why Not You?" Short Story Contest 2nd Place Winner

8:30 am on the dot. It was a Tuesday, and I had taken the morning off to stop in at the DMV. I clutched the warmth of my coffee cup closer to my body, the cardboard sleeve reading "My Cup Runneth Over," in thick black lettering—the name of the café down the street from my apartment building and my favorite place to grab a black coffee on my way to work.

"Welcome to Borden DMV, what can we do for you today?" A woman with bright red lipstick and pointed nails asks dryly.

I jerked my head up.

"Oh umm, license renewal," I explained as I handed her my license.

"Mmhm," The women remarked, glancing down at the card I had handed her.

"Looks like this expired yesterday," She commented, tapping her sharp nails on the counter.

"Well...I, you see... I was...," I stammered.

"NEXT," She shouted, jerking me backward.

She handed me back my license and a tag with a 76 written in big red letters. I was ushered toward an already packed waiting room. With a heavy sigh, I lowered myself into an empty chair and proceeded to glare at the concrete wall to pass time.

I let my mind wander to work and dreaded the days to come. The life of an accountant is not exactly one of great excitement, and I often found myself a loner among my coworkers at H and R Block. I enjoyed my job, but sometimes I did wish my days off held a bit more excitement than just trips to the DMV.

After what felt like an eternity, I got up to stretch my legs and make a quick trip to the bathroom. My license and number card still in my hand. I was passing the women's restroom and about to turn into the men's when a sturdy force knocked into my shoulder, almost throwing me off my feet.

I whipped around, looking for the source of the impact. I could have sworn I heard a deep grunt, but the hallway was empty and quiet except for the soft buzz of florescent lights. Shaking it off, I decided to forgo my trip to the bathroom and step outside for some fresh air.

I pushed open the heavy door and was greeted by a brush of cold air that blew the last bit of morning sleepiness out of my eyes.

To my surprise, I was not alone outside the back of the DMV.

A man dressed in florescent orange like a traffic cone was crouched next to the dumpster a few feet from the door I had just exited.

He had dark hair and a mustache that looked extremely out of place among his sharp features.

"Here kitty. Here kitty, kitty," the man mumbled repeatedly in the direction of the dumpster.

Slightly weirded out by the unexpected presence of this man, not to mention his peculiar behavior, I began to turn back toward the building when the man caught sight of me.

"SIR!" he jabbered in my direction.

I cringed a bit. Please no, I thought to myself. I had no interest being involved in whatever this traffic cone of a man was doing.

"Are you here with the cage?" he asked me expectantly.

This traffic cone must have lost his cat, I concluded.

"Uh, no. I'm Ro.."

"ROB NEWMAN!" he yelled at the same time I spoke.

I stared at the man, blank-faced, and tried to figure out if he knew me from somewhere. I did not recognize him at all, and he only stared back, giving no indication that he recognized me.

Thankfully, he broke our awkward stare.

"Sorry, sorry," he muttered. "I forget it freaks people out. I'm telepathic, but I can't always control when I use telepathy and when I do, I have to shout what I hear," he explained with a sigh.

Suddenly struggling to find my voice, I cleared my throat and was about to ask him to be honest and explain how he knew me when he spoke again.

"Do me a favor, Rob. Come boost me into this dumpster," he asked me matter-of-factly.

I was prepared to sputter out any excuse to avoid this situation when the door opened from behind me. There was no one there, but traffic cone seemed to think otherwise.

"CREEP" he shouted.

I startled, thinking he was addressing me, but his eyes were focused slightly to my left.

"Come help me examine this dumpster," he asked, his gaze still set off to my left.

Frozen in my place, I watched as the traffic cone dude floated off the ground and was dropped headfirst into the dumpster. Before I had a chance to fully absorb what I had just seen, a mass of grey and black blocked my vision, a long, striped tail trailing behind it.

With an earth-shattering thud, the mass landed in front of the dumpster. It was a raccoon, but not just any raccoon. This one was

180

about the size of my 2004 Toyota Sedan...and it was heading straight toward the guy in the dumpster.

Acting on pure adrenaline, I shouted "HEY!" in the raccoon's direction and instantly regretted it. The raccoon turned to me, his nose twitching as we made eye contact.

"Shoo!" I exclaimed, hoping this raccoon was as scared of me as I was of it.

The raccoon froze for a split second before barreling right toward me. I threw my hands up and dove out of the way, dropping my license and number onto the pavement.

The raccoon seized the two cards off the ground before disappearing into the alley behind the DMV.

Oh perfect, just perfect, I think to myself. What are the odds the giant raccoon has a taste for licenses?

"THERE HE WAS AND THERE HE GOES!" traffic cone man yelled as he scrambled out of the dumpster.

"ARRGHH!" I scream, my fear and unease at the situation finally poking through my shrinking adrenaline. "MY LICENSE!" I shriek. "I NEEDED THAT!" I needed to present proof of my license to get it renewed, and now it was gone. I was never going to make it into work this afternoon.

"Don't worry Rob we will get your license back," Traffic cone man states as he makes his way over to me. "I'm Obvious Spy, my partner Invisible Creep and I are working to catch the huge raccoon," he explained, "He's a danger to the public—knocking over cars, destroying dumpsters, the dang thing even knows how to open doors."

"Invisible...who?" I stammered; pretty certain we were the only two people present.

Then, I felt a hand slip into mine.

"Hii," a voice whispered into my ear.

"Ewwwll!" I shrieked as I yanked my hand back, utterly disturbed.

"Yeah, he's very friendly," said Obvious Spy with a dismissive wave of his hand. I gave myself a quick pinch. Nope, definitely not dreaming and I'm not a drug user so this must be real.

"We've named the raccoon Sidney because when he sneezes it sounds like he's saying AHHSIDNEY!" said Invisible Creep from the space next to me.

Yep. Ok, there does seem to be an invisible person. I attempt to rationalize this in my head, to no avail.

"We thought he'd been burrowing under the building to get to this dumpster," Obvious Spy explained as he waved a hand in the direction of the dumpster. "Creep was just inside the DMV checking for any signs of burrowing."

I remembered the force I ran into outside the women's bathroom and thought it best not to mention that raccoon activity might not have been the only thing Invisible Creep had been looking for.

"Right," I said, backing up slightly from the space Invisible Creep was supposedly standing. "So, you guys are cops? Or what?" I questioned, unsure of how these two lunatics were going to be able to catch that huge raccoon and get my license back.

"Cops?" Obvious Spy gave a small laugh. "No, no, we are from the A.F.A.T.S, the Academy for Almost-Talented Supers" he explained. "We are trying to catch Sidney to earn the PP Award, our public protection award, and be named real heroes."

Sounded like an insulting girl scout troop if you ask me, but at least they were acting on the orders of some authority. Although almost talented does seem like a good way to describe someone with telepathy who has to shout whatever they hear.

Before I got the chance to ask any more questions, the ground beneath my feet began to wobble and a distant boom grew louder. I turned my head just in time to see a grey blur barrel down the street past the DMV, destroying everything in its path. My license still gripped between its sharp teeth.

"SIDNEY!!" Obvious Spy yelled. "Quick! We need to follow him!" he exclaimed. "Rob, do you have a vehicle?" he asked frantically.

"Yes, that's my Sedan, but I.."

"THERE'S NO TIME!!" he shrieked, pushing me toward the driver's seat of my car.

"FOLLOW SIDNEY!" Obvious Spy yelled, pointing in the direction of the wreckage.

Taunted by the sight of my license dangling out of the raccoon's mouth, I started the car and zoomed out of the DMV parking lot. Following the trail of destruction, I sped down the street until we finally saw Sidney ahead of us. The raccoon was leaping over buildings, narrowly avoiding squishing pedestrians in the process. I pulled the car into the parking lot of a nearby McDonald's.

"So, what your plan for catching this thing?" I asked as I turned toward Obvious Spy, who was perched in my passenger's seat.

"Well we have a rope," Obvious Spy began, holding up a rope that I had somehow failed to notice before.

"You're kidding me right, you're kidding?" I argued. "You think you are going to be able to capture a school-bus sized raccoon with only a rope?" I rolled my eyes and unlocked the car door, letting the two out.

"Just please, get my license so I can get it renewed and make it to work ok?" I pleaded as they ran off after the raccoon, rope in hand.

I watched them chase the raccoon around for a bit in what looked like some sort of circus act gone wrong. My stomach grumbled, and I decided to pull my car through the McDonald's drive-through while I waited, considering whether I should abandon these weirdos and just take the bus for the next few weeks until I can retake my driver's test.

"Welcome to McDonald's what can we get for you today?"

"Hi, can I get a Big Mac?" A couple blocks away, Sidney was sprinting down the road, my license still in his mouth, after a blue Volkswagen Beetle, nearly squishing all of the pedestrians in his path as Obvious Spy chased after him, panting heavily. I sighed.

"Actually, could you make that five Big Macs?" I asked.

"Certainly, your total is $17.85, please pull to the first window." I reached for the paper bag and the car filled with the salty aroma of burgers.

I pulled out of the drive-through, the paper bag still warm in my hands. I unwrapped one of the burgers and took a bite as I drove after the mass of fur.

Up ahead, the Volkswagen pulled off the road and Sidney followed it, eventually sitting behind the small car, and rocking it with his clawed hands. I pulled up next to the stopped car and opened my door.

"Get the rope ready," I instructed to Obvious Spy and Invisible Creep, as I hopped out of the car and walked toward the Raccoon who could easily squash me like an ant.

"HEY!" I shouted toward Sidney.

The raccoon froze once again and jerked his head in my direction, giving the Volkswagen's passengers time to flee from the car. Slowly, I opened the paper bag and pulled out a Big Mac.

The raccoon dropped my license from its mouth.

Sidney's eyes were glued to my steady hand movements as I unwrapped the burger and held it up into the air. He crept stealthily toward me. I tossed the Big Mac a few feet in front of me, where it landed on the pavement with a soft thud. Sidney scurried toward the fallen burger and gulped it down greedily before locking eyes with me again. I unwrapped another burger and threw it slightly closer. Sidney moved closer and consumed the burger in a single bite.

I picked up another. Sidney's eyes were locked on the third Big Mac as I waved it around in the air. The animal's head moved along with the movements of the burger. The raccoon moved closer. And closer. The raccoon seemed to get even bigger as it approached me, its black eyes gleaming with hunger. I instantly regretted my decision to hold this burger instead of just tossing it in the same manner I had tossed the others.

Sidney ran toward me full speed and I barely had time to jump out of the way before I was knocked backward onto the hard pavement with the impact of the raccoon as it jumped.

Right. Into. My. Car.

My once beautiful silver sedan was destroyed, with a huge-raccoon-sized smash in the side. I covered my face with my hands and took a shaky inhale as I tried to keep from yelling... or crying.

When I finally removed my hands from my face, I was at least relieved to find that Sidney, the car murderer raccoon, was now thrashing against the restraints of a white rope—tethered on one side by Obvious Spy, while the other side was held firmly in mid-air, by Invisible creep.

"That a boy Sidney," Obvious Spy cooed, patting the raccoon's side.

"AHHSIDNEY!" the raccoon sneezed.

"Well, what do you know, his sneezes do sound like he's saying Sidney," I commented to no one in particular.

I retrieved my now slightly soggy license and number from the spot where Sidney had dropped it.

Before I knew it, the four of us were surrounded by reporters and police officers.

"You've done it!" a blonde reporter remarked as she held a microphone out in front of Obvious Spy. "Who do we have to thank for taming this large pest?" she asked him.

Obvious Spy grinned. "I'm Obvious Spy and this is my partner, Invisible Creep," he nodded toward the floating tether on the other side of the raccoon. "We are students from A.F.A.T.S. who have just earned our PP badges!" he exclaimed. "OH! And this is our new friend...uh, Average Man!" he motioned toward me.

Average man? I gave him a pointed glare, expressing my distaste at my assigned hero name. He gave me an apologetic shrug and smile in return.

"Incredible!" the reporter responded. "There you have it, folks, Two Super-heroes, and their average friend have just saved Borden from the huge raccoon!"

I rolled my eyes but returned Obvious Spy's smile.

Someone touched my shoulder. I jumped back and yelled in freight. "AH Invisible Creep!"

Obvious Spy broke into a fit of laughter.

I was never going to make it to work, but in a way I was glad. Despite the weirdness of the day, it was quite an unforgettable experience. And they were strange, but I think I made two new friends. Suddenly, I didn't feel so lonely anymore—and I might have a new side job as Average Man, super-hero.

But I was still not thrilled that I have to buy a new car.

A police officer approached me as Obvious Spy continued to feed burgers to Sidney.

"Rob Newman?" he asked me.

"Yes?" I responded.

He handed me a yellow slip of paper.

"Driving without a license in the state of Indiana is a $500 fine."

THE YAKSHA

- Kacey Flynn

An unrelenting afternoon sun beat down on the small town of Yasoi. The unbearable heat of summer had begun to fade, replaced instead with crisp autumn winds that crept through cracks in the walls and under doors to steal warmth from every home. Hard packed dirt roads wove throughout the entire town like the veins of a body, each filled with workers from the rice fields hurriedly making their way home or to one of the taverns bound to be better heated. Very few citizens seemed to notice the faint shiver that went through their body as the silver haired Yaksha walked by, thinking it nothing more than the chill wind kicking up. Those who did spot her quickly turned away for fear she might cut them in half, or drink their blood, or some other rumor they had heard and now recited as fact.

After years of practice Sana had gotten used to the hostility, there were very few places welcoming to those like her, people who walked hand in hand with the weirdness of the world. Ironically, she now felt more kinship with the creatures she was hired to hunt than those who hired her. And in the back of her mind each night she wondered if tomorrow would be the day they put a bounty on those like her.

Loud laughter and chatter drew her from the street toward a tavern situated along the main road. A worn sign hung just over the door, faded letters spelling out the phrase 'Nightingale' followed by the essence of what was likely a beautifully painted bird at one point in history. Pushing open the door she stepped inside, paying little mind to the stench of sweat, ale, dirt, and the faintest hint of urine.

It was clear just from her attire that she was an outsider. Most of the townsfolk dressed in loose fitting, breathable cotton clothes fit for working the fields. Sana however was clad almost entirely in armour. Much of it was made of dark leather, with her stomach and upper arms offered extra protection in the form of a thin sheet of mail. A leather bandoleer stretched across her chest which was almost entirely filled with vials, and if one looked close enough they could see the pulpy viscera floating within. Attached to her back was a wooden box decorated with seals, the faintest sound of scratching coming from within. At her side were her weapons, a long-barreled revolver on her left kept in its holster with a simple leather strap, and at her right was a slightly curved sword in an onyx sheath.

Conversation and laughter became hushed as she walked across the floor toward the counter opposite the door, once she had reached the other side of the tavern her leather boots seemed to be the loudest sound in the entire place.

Catching the eye of the middle-aged woman behind the counter, she was not surprised to see the woman's eyes flit down to the medallion pinned to her armour before returning to Sana's piercing violet eyes. The woman offered the faintest of smiles before speaking.

"What can I get you?"

"Just directions if you'd be so kind. To the lord's manor."

The woman smiled and Sana was certain there was relief in her eyes.

"Of course, it's just-"

"Yer kinds not welcome 'ere."

A gruff voice spoke from behind Sana, laced with disdain. She let out the softest of sighs before responding.

"I'm just here for directions, then I'll be on my way. Go back to your drink."

Her hands balled into fists, fighting back anger that burned in the pit of her stomach. Her eyes fell to the counter, staring intently at the wood grain there that had soaked up many years of ale.

"Yer not in charge o' me ya freak! Gods damned monsters ye' are. Drinking tha blood o' newborn babes for yer demonic powers."

Sana could not help the small chortle that escaped her lips at that statement. That was certainly the strangest falsehood she'd heard about Yaksha.

"Oh, think it's funny do ya freak!?"

"I find your lack of intelligence amusing, yes." Turning her gaze back to the woman at the bar, who had begun to twist the small towel in her hands anxiously. "The directions, please."

A meaty hand slapped down onto her shoulder, gripping with what she assumed was all his strength, though she could barely feel it through her armour.

"Think ye'll get away with tha' insult?"

The question was followed by the sound of several stools shifting on the wooden floor. Sana could hear several bodies standing up, she guessed it was no more than four individuals drunk or stupid enough to think they stood a chance against someone like her.

"I think you should remove your hand."

"Or wha?"

Without any warning Sana spun on the spot releasing the burning anger in her stomach. With her right arm she hit the man who had touched her square across the jaw with all the strength she could muster. He crumpled to the ground clutching at his jaw which bulged out to the left, clearly broken. Blood pooled from the man's mouth as he wailed in pain. She looked from the body on the floor to the three other individuals surrounding him, her violet eyes curious if they were going to be smart and sit down or choose to attack her.

They chose stupidity.

The first man rushed at her with fists raised. She grabbed the nearby stool from the bar and smashed it across his face, the wood almost completely shattered as she swung it into him, only the leg survived which she held firmly.

As the second man came toward her she raised her foot swiftly, bringing it as hard as she could between his legs. He screamed momentarily before falling to the ground and vomiting up the contents of his stomach.

Before the final individual could even consider moving toward her Sana flung the stool leg toward him as hard as she could. It collided with his nose and she heard the crunch of cartilage. Blood spurted from his face like a geyser and he fell to the floor shrieking in pain.

With a sigh of annoyance she turned to face the woman at the bar whose face had gone pale with fright.

"The directions." Sana's formerly gentle voice had been replaced with a more chill edge.

"J-just follow th-the main road un-until you s-see a stone pat-pathway." The woman's eyes were pleading, almost like she was expecting Sana to lash out at her next.

With a nod of thanks Sana fished out her coin-purse and produced a single silver coin which she set down on the bar.

"For the stool."

Taking a glance over her shoulder at the four bodies she'd left on the floor, which were now being attended to by some of the other patrons, she fished out another three and set them down next to the first.

"For the trouble."

Now armed with directions it was not difficult to find the lord's manor. Located just off the main street the dirt roads were replaced with cobblestone pathways, though several of those paths looked to have been crushed by something quite large. Sana made her way inside the walled estate and up to the manor, knocking loudly with the large heavy iron knocker in the shape of a dragon's face. Overall the estate was not as opulent as she had expected, with only two stories it was not even the largest building in town. Though the lush greenery she had walked passed in the front certainly marked it as a place of at least some wealth.

The door creaked open and a young woman poked her head out, gazing curiously up at the figure who was at least two heads taller than her.

"May I help you?"

Sana nodded and produced the writ that she had been assigned to perform the job in question. "I'm here about the job your lord requested."

The woman took a moment to look over the writ before opening the doors wide enough for Sana to enter. The entry way was about what she had expected, large yet moderate in its decadence. Small tapestries lined the front chamber detailing history of Yasoi, several of which Sana suspected had been done here in the village and passed down through the generations. At the far end was a painting in a regal golden frame, the stern looking middle aged man it depicted Sana guessed was either the lord or his father.

She was led into a smaller room off the entrance which had little more in it than a single table and a few chairs. It was the kind of room one would conduct meetings in, lacking in any frivolity that might distract from the important matters at hand.

"Can I bring you anything while you wait, miss?"

Sana almost choked at being addressed with such formality. The woman did not even seem to be forcing the words through clenched teeth either. It was rare to be addressed with the respect a regular citizen might be, rare but always appreciated.

"Just some tea, if it's no trouble."

The woman offered a nod of acknowledgement before sliding the door to the room closed and shuffling off to fetch the lord and the requested tea. Sana took this moment to unburden herself of the box on her back, resting it against the wall nearest to her. She produced a long metal pipe from her pack and began stuffing it with blue green roseweed, her eyes constantly shifting back to the box at each faint scratch made from within.

Before long, the door to the room slid open again and the woman who had greeted her was accompanied by a man whom Sana suspected was not the lord of the manor at all. He was a man of middle age, his face bearing not only the lines of age but scars to indicate he had seen at least a few battles. Though he wore a fine tunic Sana could hear the faint shifting of mail underneath his garb. He seemed to be carrying no weapons though she suspected he had at least one hidden on his person. The man eyed her curiously before engaging in a quick whispered dialogue with the attendant who had shown Sana in, after which he seated himself across from the Yaksha.

Silence filled the room, broken only by the shuffling of the attendant as she set Sana's tea in front of her before excusing herself and shutting the door behind her. Sana had already lit the pipe and was drawing heavily on it, aware that the man across from her was eyeing her intently. She exhaled the blue smoke, blowing smoke rings to entertain herself.

"You are not exactly what I pictured." The man's voice was careful, as if he had been calculating the best words to properly phrase his first statement.

Sana paused from her pull on the pipe, turning her gaze to the man and watching as he stared unflinchingly back at her. She knew exactly what that statement meant; it was not the first time she had heard it, nor did she think it would be the last.

"Well, we Yaksha come in all shapes, sizes... and genders." She took another long pull on her pipe, silently enjoying the very faint way the man squirmed from her response.

"Yes, well anyway. I am captain Byron. I command the guards here in Yasoi and serve as Lord Taloi's adviser in matters such as these. As you know from the request there has been a large beast causing havoc in the town for nearly a fortnight."

"Looks to me the rampage is mostly contained to the stone pathways outside."

The man known as Bryon raised an eyebrow at her statement. "There has also been significant damage to the outer walls of the village, and unfortunately we have lost the lives of at least three citizens."

Shifting slightly in her chair Sana tapped the ashen contents of her pipe out onto the table, ignoring the annoyed look Byron shot her. She began packing the pipe with more roseweed before speaking again.

"You mentioned in the writ that it was an ogre?"

"Yes. Well, we believe it to be from limited sightings. It is large, nearly three metres in height. And the reports we received from the unfortunate citizens caught in its path, before they passed on, were that it walked almost like an ape. And it's hands were like the size of boulders."

"That certainly sounds like an ogre."

"You seem unconvinced."

"Ogres are solitary creatures and tend to stick near their burrows... they're also only violent when provoked."

Byron scoffed at the statement, waving his hand as if it was no matter. "You call me a liar then?"

"No, but I don't think I'm hearing the full story." Taking a long pull from her pipe she blew the smoke directly toward Byron as she stared into his eyes, watching as the man squirmed uncomfortably once more.

"You have been hired to do a job, Yaksha, not to pick apart the information I have given you." He reached inside his tunic and pulled out a leather sack that jingled with coin. Tossing it across the table it opened and some of the contents spilled onto the table. The golden coins were engraved with the Imperial seal, the image of two dragons encircling a sword. "Now do what you were hired to do."

Picking up one of the golden coins Sana examined it before rolling it across her knuckles. "If you want me to get rid of this ogre I'll need some kind of assistance."

Having stood up Byron was almost to the door before he turned, staring at her quizzically. "Assistance with what?"

"Laying traps. Chances are it'll be back again by nightfall, and I won't be able to lay them all myself."

"Fine, fine. I'll have Anaise meet you when she is finished with the laundering."

"I'll be out by the pathways."

Sana was pleased to learn that Anaise was the woman who had greeted her at the door. A woman likely around the same age as herself, with long raven coloured hair held in place by a rather lovely hairpin carved from some kind of polished bone. The woman smiled politely as Sana nodded to her, and once again she was pleased to see that the woman did not recoil at the idea of meeting eyes with a Yaksha.

"Sorry to make you wait, miss."

"No apology needed, sorry to pull you away from your duties." Sana knelt by the part of the pathway that had been crushed by the ogre, she examined each piece carefully with sharp eyes.

"It's not a bother at all. Truth be told I was happy to get some sun. I'm normally inside most of the day."

Standing up Sana moved further along the pathway, examining each piece of stone thoroughly. Anaise didn't seem to mind standing around doing nothing, yet there was a curiosity bubbling in her eyes.

"Can I ask, miss, what-"

"Sana."

"What?"

"Please just call me Sana." Looking up at the young woman she smiled before returning her eyes to the stones.

"Well, Sana then. Can I ask what you're looking for? Captain Byron told me you needed assistance setting traps for the ogre."

"That's partially true. With two of us we'll be able to set them in less than two hours. But I wanted some time beforehand to examine these stones first."

"Why?" There was no judgement in Anaise's voice, just unvarnished curiosity.

"Like I told the captain, ogres are solitary creatures. For one to come out of its burrow just to cause havoc doesn't make sense."

"But... it's a monster isn't it? Monsters kill."

With a slight sigh Sana paused her examination and looked up to meet Anaise's stunning green eyes.

"Monsters, as you call them, are just animals that have been warped by magicks. There's little difference between a hellhound and an actual hound, aside from one having two heads."

"...two heads?"

Sana smiled before returning her eyes to the stones. She carefully shifted each one, prodding with her dagger to look at every side of each one of the finely cut stones.

"How long ago was this pathway put in?"

"Quite a while ago actually. Though much of the stonework has been replaced recently."

"How recently?"

"Perhaps just over a month?"

"And the attacks started almost a fortnight ago?"

"Yes mis...Sana."

Having worked her way down much of the path already Sana paused at one of the stones that seemed to be surrounded by a faint pink tinge. Putting the dagger in between she carefully began prying the stone up. Turning it in her hands she was not at all surprised to see the outlines of what looked like a face stretched in the stone. Anaise shrieked yet Sana ignored it, running her gloved fingers across the small, stretched face with a look of sadness on her own.

"What...what is that?" There was audible disgust in Anaise's voice.

"It's a baby."

"A... a baby?"

Sana held the piece of stone carefully as she stood up, shaking her head as suddenly everything began to make a bit more sense.

"Ogres reproduce asexually. They search for very specific rocks that resonate with their core, and once they find that rock it becomes a cocoon for their spawn... it takes several years for ogres to reproduce this way, and they guard these rocks with more ferocity than anything else."

Silence fell between the two until Sana let out a small sigh. "The lord must have decreed the rockspawn be made into his new pathway..."

"But it...it was just a rock."

Sana stared at Anaise for a moment, thinking about the best way to word her response.

"Every healer knows that a pregnancy cannot safely be ended after a certain month, the same is true here." She turned the stone face toward Anaise who cringed at the sight, "and this was no longer just a rock."

Silence fell between the two of them for quite a while before Anaise finally spoke.

"What are you going to do?" There was uncertainty in her voice.

Another sigh escaped Sana's lips before she spoke. "I'm going to complete the job I was hired to do. I have more than just my own reputation to uphold." Taking a look up at the sky she looked back to Anaise. "Can you go get us a pair of shovels? We better start digging these traps."

Night fell upon the town of Yasoi almost as swiftly as a hawk snatching up its prey. The chill autumn winds bit harder without the warmth of the sun to assuage it. Streets formerly filled with pedestrians were now empty, Yasoi had become like a ghost town in a manner of hours. The captain of the guard had ordered his men to relay the message that every citizen was to remain indoors tonight no matter what they might have heard, and those living in the section of town Sana and Anaise had set traps in were relocated to other abodes. Only one figure remained exempt from the order, and she remained perched on the roof of a building near the stone pathway.

No matter where the ogre entered the town Sana knew the creature had but one destination in mind. Like a bloodhound it could smell the remains of its child laying in the ground that people now walked upon without care. It still churned her stomach, yet she could not refuse the work for fear of bringing a black mark upon the guild. She checked her stock of potions almost every hour, a habit she had picked up from one of her teachers, her anxiety rising with each passing moment.

To ease the rising anxiety, she ran a string of prayer beads through her fingers, whispering a small mantra as she rotated each bead. The beads had been crafted from the bones of the first monster she'd ever slain, a perpetual reminder of how far she'd come as a warrior. There was a total of one hundred and eight beads, with each one having a specific mantra connected to it; each passed down from the Children of the Forest, the first to take the title of Yaksha.

In the early hours of the morning it began, first with the sound of boards shattering from the west side of the town. There was a feeling of tension rising in the air as Sana removed a vial from its place and swirled the contents around. Each one had a very limited span of time and needed to be consumed either during or just before some kind of engagement, and she wagered it would be difficult to consume one during confrontation with an ogre, especially one looking for its child.

THUD.

Loud stomping warned of the ogre's imminent arrival, each footfall growing increasingly louder. The occasional crash could be heard as it stumbled into buildings, followed by a growl of annoyance before it continued trudging forward. After several agonizing minutes it came into view. Standing well over three metres in height, with limbs as thick tree trunks, and skin a blend between grey and green. The creatures bulging eyes scanned for any sign of its child while it walked, and Sana noticed that one was nearly completely shut. She shifted closer on the roof until she could see the faint remains of arrow shafts sticking through the much thinner hide near its eyes, shafts which it had tried to pry out but only succeeded in digging further in.

THUD.

It moved ever closer to the traps Sana and Anaise had spent the better part of the afternoon digging, set just before the stone pathway.

THUD.

Sana's hand fell to the hilt of her blade, carefully and silently sliding it from the sheath.

THUD.

CLANG!

Iron bands snapped sharp on the ogre's foot, the teeth of which had been laced with a poison meant to dull a creature's senses. A roar of frustration shattered nearby windows. There was loud grunting accompanied by the grinding of chains as it tried to yank its stump-like foot free of the bear trap yet only succeeding in causing it to clamp down harder.

Pulling the cork of the vial out with her teeth, Sana downed the contents in a single gulp, ignoring the acrid taste and trying to put her mind beyond the pulpy viscera that was now making its way down her throat. Closing her eyes, she took a long, slow breath as the potion took effect, expanding her lungs and increasing the oxygen she could intake. She could feel her own body temperature rising and her muscles straining underneath her skin.

Opening her eyes she launched herself from the rooftop at the ogre, drawing her blade back to strike. Having seen her from the corner of its eyes the creature brought its meaty arm up to block the only way it could. She struck with all her strength, swinging the blade down hard. She could feel her blade moving through muscle like a hot knife through butter, cutting mostly through bone before feeling resistance.

The ogre swung its half-severed arm launching Sana back several feet and spattering the ground with black blood. She rolled with the momentum, ignoring the minor pain as her shoulder and side collided with hard ground. Springing back to her feet she held her blade ready to strike again just as the ogre tore the chain keeping the bear trap in place free of the walls. It turned to face her, one arm dangling, almost completely severed, the muscle fibres straining to keep it held on.

It roared at her before charging, though due to its arm being so damaged it crumpled under its own weight and fell to the ground.

Taking in another deep gulp of air Sana rushed at the creature, aiming her blade to take its head off in one clean strike, this time foiled as it twisted slightly and shot out with the boulder-sized fist still firmly attached to its body.

Leaping she twisted her body in mid-air narrowly missing the full force of the impact. She stabbed her blade down into the creature's arm to stop herself from moving toward it's snarling maw, gripping the hilt hard as it began to try and shake her free.

Placing her legs on its muscular arm she pulled her blade free as it shook, launching her up and into the air. She spun in the air to readjust herself and came down with the entire force of her momentum. Her aim was true as the blade cut cleanly through the creature's thick hide. The resistance from its spine was barely noticeable from the severe momentum of the drop. It's flailing ceased as a pool of blood slowly began to seep out from its body.

She slumped to one knee, the effects of the potion beginning to wear off. Her muscles ached and she could feel that her bones had been bruised from the initial fall, possibly even broken. It was slightly more difficult to breath and she knew it would be for the next several minutes, but she had completed her task.

It was at that moment she heard the booted footsteps of people approaching.

Half a dozen armed guards made their way toward the body of the dead ogre. Led by Byron who had replaced his modest tunic and chain with attire that very clearly marked him as captain of the men and women following him. The squadron of guards looked relieved to see the dead ogre, some even managing a relieved smile. Byron gestured to the body.

"Fetch a cart for the beasts head. We'll put it on display in front of the lord's manor, show the people who protects them."

The sudden sound of an explosion rang throughout the street, the smell of gunpowder hung heavy in the air as a lead pellet kicked up dirt less than a foot away from the approaching guards.

Sana stood on slightly shaky legs, her revolver in hand aimed at the approaching guards, whose hands instantly went to their blades. Byron looked on in utter shock.

"What in the nine hells do you think you're doing Yaksha!?" The man's face was turning red with anger and small flecks of spittle left his mouth as he shouted.

"I will not...allow you to desecrate this creature...more than you already have."

"De...desecrate!?" Some of the guards laughed at Sana's statement, yet none removed their hands from their weapons. "We have done nothing of the sort."

"You stole it's baby...probably forced it into its burrow during sunup...turned it's kin into stone." Sana was beginning to regain her strength. "And now you wish to mount it's head on display?"

Shaking her head she assumed a readied stance, aiming her gun at the figures and keeping her sword level in case any got close.

"I will not let you near this creature."

Byron's face had gone even redder from Sana's response, clearly a man who had never been told no in his life.

"You would defy your writ!?"

"Your request said nothing about letting you have your way with the body."

There was silence between the two parties.

"You would risk your life for this... this dead thing?"

Sana's lips twisted into a small smile, and the only answer Byron needed. With a wave of his hand he shook his head.

"Come on then... we'll leave these monsters be."

Sana stood ready for attack until she could no longer see the guards anymore, it was only then that she sheathed her blade and holstered her revolver. Putting her fingers to her lips she gave a soft whistle and smiled as Anaise appeared from a nearby alleyway, carrying the slab of stone they had pried up from the pathway.

"You're crazy to have gone against the guards like that."

With a shrug of her shoulders she smiled, a much more pleasant smile this time. "Sanity is overrated."

Taking the stone from the young woman Sana laid it down next to the dead ogre before Anaise handed her a pitcher of oil which she spread across the body. Standing back she lit a tindertwig and tossed it onto the bodies, watching as it erupted into a column of flame. The smell was unpleasant, but slowly the body began to burn away. Yet neither woman moved from their place.

"Thank you, Anaise."

"For what?"

Looking over at the young woman Sana saw legitimate confusion in her eyes. She either didn't understand the risks she had taken to help her or didn't care.

Shaking her head Sana smiled.

"I will admit, I didn't do it entirely out of selflessness..."

Meeting Anaise's golden eyes Sana could see the slight hint of guilt in them. She had intended to pay her for her service, there was no shame in that. With a nod Sana took hold of her coin-purse, opening it she began taking out some of the gold before the young woman spoke up.

"No not money!"

It was now Sana's turn to be confused. She looked up at the young woman who seemed to fidget under the gaze of Sana's violet eyes.

"I...I want to come with you when you leave."

The surprise on her face grew even more apparent at Anaise's declaration.

"Well I... I never really fit in here. My parents have both passed on and... I really would like to learn more of the world. Maybe I could help teach people that there's more to these creatures than they know." She gestured at the still burning corpse.

There was silence between them for a moment as Sana considered the request. After a few moments she put her hand out and the smile returned to her face.

"I'd be glad to have you travel with me."

The two of them shook hands, each smiling as the corpse of the ogre burned behind them. The sun had begun to hint at rising on the horizon, and the chill of autumn began to lift ever so slightly.

WHISKEY SAID THE MOON

- Grant DeArmitt

"Why Not You?" Short Story Contest Honorable Mention Winner

The bar (or saloon as they said then) was called Zeke's, after its owner. He was kind and funny, good at making a customer feel like a friend. But Zeke, admitted those customers, was not the main reason to visit his establishment in Blue Rose, Montana. That was the whiskey.

It was whiskey that brought the moon to Earth. Whiskey, that made sad songs sweet, that warmed travelers and cooled hot nights. That sparkled in the candlelight as if to remind her of the sunrise she always missed. From her perch above the world, she had watched the first batch ever distilled. As the centuries went on and whiskey made its way around the world, her desire to try it became a need. So one night, when she wasn't needed in the sky, she went to Zeke's.

The patrons noticed her dress first, shining as it did all by itself. Soon enough, they put together that it was only the gas lamps reflecting off the silk, but this did not stop them from staring. And though her human disguise was perfect, the drunkest among them could tell exactly what she was. The thought made them sleepy. Across the room, the piano player had noticed people were no longer listening to him. When he turned to see what had distracted them, he stopped playing.

"Good evening," she said to Zeke.

"Ma'am," said Zeke reverently.

"Whiskey," she told him, and abruptness of it caught him off guard. She meant no offense, but the English language seemed to her a blunt thing, so she thought her order better match it. Zeke brought her a glass.

She lifted the drink to her lips and the smell surprised her. She had tried honey thousands of years ago, and because of the color, she had expected this to be similar. Still, she liked the bite. It was exciting, mortal. She upped the glass and swallowed the portion whole. A warmth spread from her throat to her shoulders, then across her arms even as it dipped into her stomach. On her previous visits to Earth, she was annoyed by the uncomfortable necessity of having a body. This drink made the experience worthwhile.

"Another," she smiled at Zeke, who obliged. By then, the other bar patrons had remembered their manners. Keeping their mouths almost all the way closed, they did their best to act like they weren't staring. But Sheriff Claybell, who had been playing poker, did not act. He stared at her, doe-eyed, and ceased caring about anything else.

Since his youth, Martin Claybell had been told he was a hero. First by his younger brothers, then by the Union Army, then by the people of Blue Rose. As Sheriff, he hadn't done much that was actually heroic, but he was big and blonde and was seen every Sunday in church. For a town that hadn't seen much action, that was as good as knighthood. Claybell shared their belief, and that night, he thought that the girl at the bar with the silver dress should know it.

Having rushed down her first glass, she decided to savor the next. She inhaled again, the sharpness touching her nose and making her lips curl up. When she sipped, she let the heat stay on her tongue.

When she couldn't bear the ache of flavor, she swallowed. The warmth returned, just as the large man with his silly mustache attended the bar next to her.

"Hello," he grinned. "My name is Martin Claybell, I'm the Sheriff here. If you need anything, Miss, ask for me." It was an invitation to fall in love, one Claybell had used before.

"Thank you," she said pleasantly, not looking away from her glass. If she held it just high enough, she could watch the gas lamps burn goldenly through the liquid. It made her happy.

When no further response came, Claybell said, "Is this your first time in Blue Rose? I can't remember seeing you here before, and you're the kind of person I'd call unforgettable." Another honey-trap, a surefire ticket down the aisle.

"Yes," she said. Claybell blinked.

"Well, what brings you around? Don't tell me you came to our lovely town to sit at a bar alone."

Could she hear him? She seemed upset. No, wait, distracted. Was she drunk already?

"Whiskey," she said.

Zeke, having caught on to her manner of speech, thought the comment was for him. He came over and waited for her to present her glass, but when he saw it was still full, put the bottle down. He nodded at Claybell.

"Game going alright?"

"Oh fine," said Claybell, in Zeke's direction but for the hearing of the girl. "Teddy's going to have me cleared out by the end of the night, but I always was a lousy card player." Claybell believed humility worked on some women, but he used it sparingly.

"Have you been introduced to Zeke?" Claybell asked the girl.

"No."

"Well Zeke," Claybell said, "I've never known you to be a stranger!" Zeke apologized and told her his name. She smiled, because the way his balding head gleamed through the glass gave the appearance of a halo. She took another sip.

Claybell was lost. To be sure, he thought, anyone would have been. A less confident man couldn't have strung a sentence together for her. He could at least talk to her, but a response seemed impossible. A memory of his childhood came to him then, of his father telling him about all the "types" of women. The silent type, if Claybell remembered correctly, was on that list.

"Well Zeke, I'd say she's got the right idea anyway. How about one of those for me?" Claybell pulled up a chair and looked at her. "You don't mind, do you?"

"No," she said.

So there it was, thought the Sheriff, a game of patience. Well, that's a game he could play. He would sit as silently as she and sip whiskey of his own, for as long as it takes for her to crack. Eventually, she'd give him an eye and let him know he passed her test. Eventually.

But two glasses later, she had still said nothing. In fact, she had forgotten about the man altogether, so focused was she on the whiskey. With each sip she found something new to love, some sight or smell or taste that charmed her. Near the end of the third glass, she even began to feel... well, she didn't know what. She knew drunkenness, but this wasn't that. The drunks she remembered were loud, clomping and staggering and breaking out into fits of violence or laughter. No, she felt quiet, like she was keeping a secret. She began her fourth glass.

When it was time to close, Zeke told her what she owed. As a response, she handed him the five finest coins he'd ever seen. They shone to make his world unreal, the only clear image in a blurry photograph. He stared at them at length, wondering what they were. Had he lived as long as she, he'd have recognized the ancient queen on their faces, read the runes on their behinds. But Zeke had lived much less, so he only thanked her for her generous contribution.

Claybell was embarrassed. He hadn't gotten so much as a smile out of the girl. The Sheriff tried to quell his shame with drink, but the two only fed each other. By the time the girl was handing Zeke her silver, he felt he had to change his situation.

When she started toward the door, Claybell got off his seat. His legs were untrustworthy, so she had gotten a few strides away before he was on them properly. As a result, the smooth approach he planned was more of a lunge. What he might've meant as a tug on the elbow was a hard grip, like a parent puts on an unruly child. The girl merely studied the grip on her arm, uncurious and unsurprised.

"Hold on," he slurred. "You're not leaving alone now, are you? At this time of night?"

"Yes," she responded coolly, removing her arm from his grasp. Again, she made to go.

"Now wait just a minute," said the Sheriff, puffing his chest up and smiling in a big, sly way.

"You are the prettiest girl I've ever seen in this town. And I will be damned if I let you leave without a kiss."

He pulled her in toward him. His poker-playing chums, the only other patrons left, made whoops and laughs. Here was Courageous

Claybell, they thought, making a move they never would have dared, sober or drunk. They toasted him. Zeke looked away, ashamed but quiet.

Claybell's kiss was cruel. His hand gripped her arm tight enough to hurt. His mouth was open and he was laughing. This was a message he needed to send, that he was strong, and she was not. That she had not gotten the best of him. The ugly kiss lasted for as long as he could hold her, so long that even his poker buddies shifted in their chairs.

When she finally wriggled free, he guffawed. He had won. She could piss off now, for all he cared. She was probably a poor lay anyway, he planned on telling the boys, the "delicate" ones always were. Before he started back toward them, Claybell decided he had time for a gloat. Something like, 'Pleasure meeting you,' or 'You come back anytime,' but when he saw her, his voice failed.

She was glowing. No, burning. No, changing, changing shades of white to become harsher and purer with each second. Hers was a light that you could hear, and it got louder and louder until it was the only sound in the saloon. It bored into the eyes of Martin Claybell and his friends, but for all that it pained them, they couldn't look away. Something in their brains wouldn't let them.

The sound of her light changed then, rising in pitch and intensity. A scream. The men felt a pressure against them then, a scalding breath that forced them down to the floor. Around them, the walls and ceiling of the bar began to fade. Darkness and stars and the gleaming sands of the outside were soon all they could see. Night, True Night, had entered Zeke's, and her Daughters were not far behind.

"You," said the girl to Martin Claybell, her voice booming over and mixing with the sound of her light, "Do you know what you have done? You belly-crawler, slobberer, mold-gatherer. You want a kiss? Have one."

At her words Claybell rose, slouching toward the gleaming figure. His body, not under his own control, became intertwined with hers, searing the fabric of his clothing onto his bubbling skin. Claybell's lips began to part, and for a moment he believed she was actually trying to kiss him. But his lips kept parting. His mouth opened wide, comically wide, and when it reached the widest it could go, it opened wider.

CRACK.

Martin Claybell slumped to the ground, his famous smile split forever. The girl turned to his fellows. "And you," she said, as they shook and cried and urinated, "you have kept poor company. I shall grant you better friends." She motioned behind herself and, finally, the men were able to avert their eyes, just in time to see the Daughters of Night arriving in Blue Rose.

Angrily they marched in, the coyotes, owls, snakes, and wolves. The shadows, fairies, poltergeists, and banshees. The cold winds and distant howls, the creaking of floorboards in empty houses, the certainty of being watched. The twins, Dream and Nightmare, the darkness that billowed as a cloak at their backs. The crows, the dead, the forgotten, the still to be. All come to avenge their eldest sister, caught up in thoughts of blood and retribution.

It was at that moment Zeke emerged from behind the bar. His shameful look down had saved him from being trapped by the sight of her, and he had taken cover when the walls started to disappear. But when he decided the little counter wouldn't protect him from what was coming, his only choice was to act.

"Wait!" he cried. "Please, I wasn't like them. I didn't laugh. Let me go."

"Laughter, silence," she said, "It sounded the same to him."

Zeke knew then that he was to die. He looked at the stars being blotted out by the encroaching horde and thought suddenly of his wife, of how he'd never see her again. A bitterness welled up inside him; how many late nights had he spent here, instead of with her? How many times had he stayed open just an hour longer, to make just a little more money, instead of going home to her? She was better than what was here.

And with that, Zeke understood what could save him.

"The whiskey!" he cried, leaping to his feet. "You can have as much as you want. The whole of it! Just let me go, and you can have the whole of it."

The girl cocked her head, curious. She motioned to the floor, where her sisters had already begun their work on the poker players. Broken screams bubbled from bloodied throats.

"When my sisters are done with them, they will come for you. Perhaps, bartender, for this entire town. How, then, do I not already have your whiskey?"

Zeke's mind raced. "I'll make more!" he declared. "There are only two bottles left behind the bar. Some six barrels in the back. Drinking as you've done tonight..."

He stammered. She smiled.

"No disrespect meant, of course, ma'am. But it's just that, well, what I have now, it'll only last…it won't be long. You'll be in want of it, before the year's out."

The girl considered this. It was true, she had drunk her share. She probably would have even had more, had Zeke not announced the saloon was closing. Still, another thirst clawed at her. She wanted revenge, wanted it in the way that a higher being wants it from one lower. Like the revenge we might wish on a fly who has landed in our soup. A cruel revenge, a total one.

"And what about when you are gone, mortal man? You approach your evening years. What will happen when I am thirsty but there is no one to fix me a drink?"

"I'll teach my children," said Zeke.

"And they'll teach theirs. You'll have it for…" Zeke realized he didn't know how long he should say. A hundred years? A thousand? It dawned on him that he had no idea what this girl was, much less how long she'd live. "…as long as you like," he finished.

The girl did not respond and Zeke's mind whirled. She had granted him the chance to bargain, and he needed to make the best of it. A final idea came to him then, an offer so bold that, even in his current danger, he considered not making it.

"And it won't be for no one else."

The determination on the girl's face softened. The little man had surprised her. She called her sisters back from the mess they had made of the poker players and, seeing that the front lines had stopped, the rest of the Night's Daughters paused their march. All things were still as the girl pondered. Finally, she spoke.

"Zeke," she said, "That is not your real name."

"No, ma'am. It's Ezekiel. Ezekiel Pudge." She laughed, not unkindly, at the name.

"Well, Ezekiel Pudge, that is an excellent offer, and I will accept it."

Zeke's heart rose, elated at the news, at the thought of seeing his wife.

"But Ezekiel Pudge, know this. I am always watching. There is nothing I do not see, even on the nights you do not see me." Here Zeke realized what she was. His knees shook. She continued. "If you are untrue," here she motioned to her sisters, "we will return. And we will finish what we started." She pointed to the poker players then, or rather, the mound of liquids and solids that was the poker players. "Are we agreed?"

Zeke couldn't imagine a handshake was appropriate, so he bowed, very deliberately and very slowly, showing he meant her only respect. He looked silly, and she laughed again.

"That is good," she said, then turned toward her sisters. "Now, we will go."

On her command, her sisters retreated, dissipating into the wild and the air and the dreams from which they had come. Night herself took leave from Zeke's, returning the walls and ceilings to where they belonged. There was just a girl left, still beaming softly. Zeke went behind the bar and fetched the two bottles he had left.

"The rest is in the back, I'll go -" the girl held up a hand and Zeke stopped talking.

"This is enough for now. I will come back for the rest."

"When?" said Zeke.

"Every night that I am not there," she pointed up. Then, without a goodbye, she left.

216

Zeke buried Martin Claybell and his friends behind the saloon. Their graves were unmarked, because soon enough there would be a new Sheriff, and the new Sheriff might be suspicious. Zeke finished cleaning up, locked the place that bore his name but no longer his product, and went home. He crawled into his bed, next to his sleeping wife.

There were other strange nights in store for Zeke, who spent his remaining years watching the moon. But the rest of this one was familiar. The wind, no longer angry, was soft outside. The coyotes howled, but from far away. The only difference between this night and all others was that five stars were missing from the sky, softly glinting as they were in Zeke's pocket.

THE SPECTER DANCES

- Ian Tigomain

"Why Not You?" Short Story Contest Honorable Mention Winner

A soft glow came from a distant room, it illuminated the dark hallway. Walls in the corridor faintly echoed music till it faded. Cigarette stench permeated the hall and a dense cloud of smoke welcomed anyone who dared enter the next room.

Passed the fumes and into the light, an elegant ballroom was revealed. Close to empty; still, it was a marvel. White marble floor stretched out the length of the room. Walls as white as the floor broke up by gold trim. There were royal red curtains that denied access to any outside light. Floor to ceiling ornate pillars helped add a touch more majesty to the ballroom. Light radiated from a glittering chandelier, it was gold, like the trim, and it appeared to have thousands of tiered lights. Each tier had crystals that made the chandelier even more awe-inspiring.

Centered between two pillars was a black grand piano. A clean-shaven man in a tuxedo sat on the piano bench. He peered out at the ballroom. Placed on top of the piano was an ashtray, cigarettes, a decanter filled with scotch and a vial that had a picture on the label.

The man pulled a cigarette and matches from the pack; he struggled to light his smoke as his hands trembled. Once lit he discarded the match into the ashtray, it dropped next to a cigarette that still burned. One long drag from the cigarette and then he picked up the vial that had a label which resembled a pirate flag, black with a white skull and crossbones. Tears grew in his eyes. He

218

slammed down the vial and picked up the decanter. He stared at the decanter, swirled the scotch, and took a swig.

While fixated on the piano he put the scotch back down and placed the cigarette in the ashtray. He sat up straight, wiped away some tears and then played. The piece started off slow, but that did not take away from how exquisite he performed. When the pace picked up his hands fluttered like hummingbirds across the keys, it was as if he and the piano were one. He had played that piece more than any other, that night alone he was on his tenth performance. Focused on the ballroom floor, he did not even blink. And then it happened.

Through the smoke, something appeared across the room. It started out small but within a second or two it was full size, a vaporous figure that moved gracefully. A woman, his beloved, danced to the music. No longer human, more of a ghost, a luminous mixture of sky blue and white. As the specter danced, he noticed she did not cast a shadow. His beloved twirled around in her beautiful evening gown. It brought a smile to his face. She glanced at him as he came to the end of the piece; he detested that part. Not only had a noose materialized around her neck, but she also waved for him to come over. Yet every time he stopped and stood up, she vanished. He was left alone.

Yesterday was the last time he screamed out in anger. Today was the fifth day, and that could have been the hundredth time he played their song. When she evaporated he consumed more scotch and wept, amazed there were any tears left in him. Could hell be worse, he wondered?

Vial with the skull and crossbones stared at him. In his mind, it taunted him. Contents of the bottle, poison used for rats. Upon purchase they had told him if someone drank it they could perish. He gripped the vial in his hand for a minute and then placed it back on the piano.

A few drags from his cigarette, and then he continued to play. Like before she materialized as he was a few notes into their piece, and like before as he concluded she gestured for him to come over and then vanished. He let out a disturbed laugh. It was now obvious that hell had to be better. In fact, he welcomed hell.

An internal conflict had him argue with himself till he snatched up the poison and drank the entire bottle. The horrid aftertaste of the liquid death made him reach for the decanter. He guzzled a mouthful of scotch. Only seconds had passed, yet he felt nauseous, did the poison work that quick. He clutched what may be his final cigarette and took a drag.

Poisoned and drunk he started his next performance, a smoke dangled from his lips, his play was still brilliant. Like every time before, the specter appeared and danced. His eyes grew heavy, and the room started to go out of focus as he watched her dance. Hands that had been so superb now struggled to play their composition. A moment later he collapsed.

His head snapped up. No longer nauseous, something was strange. He felt airy, like his weight was gone. It took a minute for his eyes to adjust, and there, on the floor, he saw himself, dead. Anxiety overtook him until a familiar hand grabbed his; a sense of calm washed over him as he turned to his love. They embraced, then they kissed, and as they kissed the two specters glowed to the point of blindness. The chandelier lights exploded when the two lovers were at their brightest.

Glow in the room faded, darkness ensued. The only light and sound came from a cigarette. The bright amber glowed as the cigarette cannibalized itself. Within minutes, even that tired.

Steps echoed through the hallway. A light switch got flipped, which brought the chandelier to life. A vast empty room presented itself to the couple that stood in the doorway.

"Honey, I swear I heard a piano playing," the man said, "I also smell cigarettes."

"This is our fifth day here, and it feels like the hundredth time we have gotten up," the woman responded. "We do not own a piano, and I do not smell anything. In a few months I want to get a piano so I can listen to you play the composition you wrote for us. Please, let us go back to bed," she said.

"Okay, maybe I am going mad," he joked.

KEEM

- Nick Couture

They said I need to keep this journal. To write everything down. They said this will help me cope. They said that this might be "cathartic." They said most kids don't have to deal with stuff like this, but in my experience we see people dead a lot. As I retell this, a lot of it is hard to put into words, everything feels too fresh, and maybe some of it doesn't make sense, but the episode of Darkwing Duck I'm watching I've already seen at least 8 times, so I got time.

-1-

Around 2PM we walk through the blown-out window into Kim's General Store. Kim's sits at the end of a strip mall, and not a particularly nice one, if strip malls can ever be nice. I try not to step on too much glass. I'm wearing my new sneakers I don't want to wreak, especially if I'm trying to ball on Eduardo tomorrow.

Eduardo is my best friend. We both suck at math and failed out of the same class. When we failed out they still let us get credit if we stayed after school, working on math worksheets. Neither of us tried very hard, but heck, I'm just glad I didn't have to retake the class or get held back. We all knew a kid that got held back, kind of turned them into a pariah, marked for life.

I got these new sneakers specifically to ball on Eduardo. When Mom took me to Sears to buy a few things, they were on sale, just sitting there all shiny and white. They're off-brand but still dope as hell. Eduardo thinks he can dunk, but he really can't even jump 2 feet. For real though, he has a knee condition I think. Once when we were playing snake in the grass during gym he fell right on his face, like one of those plastic drinking birds.

As I follow Tony through the store he says he's been here before. Him and some friends bought some really hot spices to pull a prank on a girl they said was a slut. They rubbed it all over her glasses, locker, books, and everything she touched throughout the day. Apparently it was so bad that she had to go home early.

A lot of stuff in Kim's has already been taken. Shit is everywhere. I wonder if people even wanted to take anything, or if they just wanted to fuck shit up. It's hard to fault them for that, especially around here. We're from the neighborhoods the white people don't come to.

We walk to the coolers in the back of the store. I look around but the store seems totally empty. I feel paranoid someone could be around but don't want Tony to call me a pussy. Pussy was his favorite word.

This is how I remember everything going down:

Me - "C'mon, let's bounce."

Tony - "Nah hold up, I see it."

Tony walks over to the glass of the cooler, pointing on the glass.

Tony - "There it is Keemy Boy. Javier's Raw Coconut Drink. You got to try some."

He hands me one, shoving 8 more in his backpack.

Tony - "Here try this."

I read the label. It looks to be imported from China or Japan or Thailand or Mexico or someplace foreign I've never been. Half of the words on the back are in a different language, but Tony forces it on me, so I crack it open and swallow some.

Tony - "Shit's good huh?"

It tastes like grandma's coconut cream pie melted down into a drink.

Me - "Alright it's pretty good."

The back of the can reads 64g Sugar, 170 mg Caffeine. I think that's (is there supposed to be a word here?)

Tony - "Ya buddy. When have I steered you wrong?"

This is when everything gets a little muddled.

"MY STORE! GET OUT OF MY STORE!"

My head turns like a top so fast. I'm spinning.

Tony - "Oh fuck."

Tony says it with a straight face. Like he's just waiting for a sack from Lawrence Taylor.

Does anyone else get a stomachache when you're feeling nervous? Like you might explode. Like all the shit in my stomach will rip me open. Like the little baby alien popping out of that dude's chest in Alien. I tried explaining this to Eduardo one time. He said he could feel me on some level but then he just wanted to get right back to talking about Mortal Kombat.

Robocop changed my life. Dad took me to it. He would always show up early on Saturdays in his ruby red Cutlass. We'd be the only ones in the theater. The dudes working wouldn't even have the popcorn made up yet. Didn't matter though, Dad used to say, "Movie theater popcorn is expensive, it's over-rated, we got some at home." Sometimes I would grab a bag just sitting on the top of a trash and go get a free refill.

Dad used to think of himself as a comedian. He'd often take on the spotlight of a block party or barbeque and get the whole crowd rolling. I never thought he was that funny, but I always smiled when he'd turn to me after telling one of his jokes. Mom and Auntie Nae would always get so mad at him for telling raunchy jokes in front of me. I never paid attention, but they sure did. I guess he sorta tried to censor himself when he was around them (to the best of his ability). He used to call them stuffy old grandmas, which would then get Grandma Jo pissed if she was around. Man, they would turn on him so quick. It wasn't until all the girls in the room had left that he could really let loose. Him and Uncle Jeff would talk about some stuff I'm still not fully aware of.

I remember he started performing at a comedy club called Mikey's. It was mostly a bar, but the back had a stage. One time Mom, me, and Tony, surprised him. He didn't see us in the crowd until he was up there on the stage. God did he bomb so hard. We didn't think nothing of it, he was our goofy Dad. Looking back I think he took it pretty hard though. I think he thought we might look at him differently now, realizing he wasn't actually the next Pryor or Murphy. Mom and him had a huge fight that night and that was around the time he stopped sleeping at our house.

Not long after all that was when he took me to see Robocop. Peter Weller getting his shit rocked in the first act, bullet after bullet fucking shredding him, made me feel something I can't describe. It didn't feel like the kid shit I used to watch. Kid shit was the other things kids in my class were into. Even something like House Party felt like kid shit, mostly because Eduardo still loved it and he's my judge for whether something is hitting with the masses.

A few months prior I started getting those panic attacks. One second I would feel great, the next I thought I was dying. Had Mom take me to the emergency room the first time it happened.

My heart was beating out my chest. My vision narrowed to a focus. I was in a daze. Mom had to miss her shift so when the doc came in and told me I was fine, you already know she wasn't happy. Nobody knew why I was fucked up. Doctor said maybe it was caffeine. Too much sugar. Not enough sleep. All-in-all it was brushed off and ruled not a problem. But it kept happening. One time I was sitting in Mrs. Emmerson's science class and one hit me. One minute I was Bunsen burning with Carlos, the next I felt fucked. Told Mrs. Emmerson I had to use the bathroom. Paced around for a good 20 minutes before I felt ok enough to function as a normal human again.

Watching Robocop almost felt like a panic attack, but it wasn't all negative like, like I didn't feel I was going to die, but it gave me a big rush of feeling, and that feeling has kind of been what I've been wanting every time I go back to the movies.

It started to be all I ever wanted to do with Dad. Most every Saturday he would pick me and Tony up and take us to the movies. Sometimes we would drop Tony off at his friend Rocco's house. After the movie we'd pick him up smelling like weed but we never said nothing. My Dad used to say, "As long as you aren't out here robbing and stealing." Tony would say he just got done robbing but not stealing so it was alright.

It was the loudest thing I'd ever heard. The shot Mr. Kim had fired from his shotgun totally shredded through Tony's shoulder and the side of his ribs. A dead-on shot would likely have killed him right there on the spot. When Mr. Kim fired the shot I'm not sure he realized the power he held in his hands. I remember immediately hitting the floor, thinking I had just died. I was just lying there with my hands on my ears. Then I look over and see Tony on his back holding his shoulder. Mr. Kim was now on top of us, barking. In Vietnamese or Chinese or Japanese or whatever the fuck. In disbelief Tony removes his hand from his shoulder. His hand was covered in blood, bright red, I'll never forget it. He spits up more blood.

I don't know what it was, maybe it was all the movies, or the horror stories Mom would tell me from her years at the ER, but I knew I needed to act quick. I jumped to my feet and laid a shoulder into Mr. Kim, knocking him to the ground. More importantly, he dropped his gun. When I jumped on the gun pure adrenaline had taken over. I scramble, picked it up and pointed it at Mr. Kim. All I remember yelling was "motherfucker help."

Mr. Kim helps me load Tony into a shopping cart. One that Mr. Kim assured me had the best wheels in the whole place. He is barely awake at this point and losing a lot of blood. As we leave Kim's, new fires have sprung up, and the ones that were there already are twice their size. I'm running as fast as I can as I head onto the road. The road has essentially been barricaded at this point. Everyone who is out today is already too pissed to care about me and Tony. So I just go in the direction I'm pretty sure the hospital is and pray to God we get to hang one more time.

229

Funny to think this is all because of Rodney King. One dude. I'm sure everyone has heard about it at this point. It's hard not to be upset about it. He got beat to a pulp.

But I can't help but feel so fucking angry at him.

That this was his fault.

What was the point?

Tony was born on Easter. My Mom never lets us forget that. She said her and Dad were in church on Easter Sunday when her water broke. That always threw me off because I cannot imagine Dad in a church. I guess back then when you got pregnant young and not married, you really had to prove to people that you weren't a godless heathen.

Mom said she was pissed because she missed Grandma's Easter dinner that year. Grandma's Easter dinner was something totally unmissable and the highlight of everyone's year no doubt. Of all the amazing dishes, Grandma's mac and cheese was by far the #1 top dollar dish. Of course Tony would usually eat most of it, even stealing extra portions to bring home. Bro, he could eat. It was his birthday so he could get away with it. The wild thing no one can explain is that you can reheat that shit! Everyone knows mac n cheese is crap after it's fresh. Not Grandma's. Hers is so creamy, cheesy, pure amazing.

Tony usually always wore a sports shirt. Never an LA team though. His favorite team was the Cleveland Browns, mostly because that was dad's favorite team. Dad used to talk about how good they were in the late 60s/early 70s. When they got good again, Tony and Dad would yell in the living room watching playoff games. I think Tony just liked that the Browns were different. Out here the Raiders are king. The Raiders are dope and if you wear Raiders shit you are dope. The Browns are just a color. That was Tony's style though.

His shoes had to be Nikes. He would never be caught dead wearing anything else. We went bowling one time and he refused to put on bowling shoes. He was committed. I guess that's one thing that I always liked about Tony, he always stuck to his guns. He always went in headfirst. For me, I have a hard time committing. I can wear anything from a corny ass Sonics shirt to a Houston Oilers shirt. It's sports, it makes no difference to me. It's just stuff. Things. Tony would be clowning on me for this.

-5-

With Tony bleeding out in the cart, I headed in what I think is the right direction. I've never been too good at navigating, with my head always in a book or off thinking about something else anytime I'm in a car. I can't get over how Tony felt so damn heavy in that cart, it made me wish he ate a little less of Grandma's mac and cheese and a few less cans of that weird ass coconut drink. I could barely control my breathing, just repeating to myself "fuck,fuck,fuck, shit,shit,fuck,fuck" over and over and over. When I finally get the courage to look down at Tony I notice his breathing is light, almost not there at all.

As I round a corner I finally see some other looters standing near the front of a convenience store. Just seeing someone else feels like an oasis. I run over yelling my ass off, my voice cracking. It's two dudes. One short with a scruffy beard and reminds me of my bum ass Uncle James. The other is tall with a bald shiny head. They're caught off guard.

I remember our exchange going something like this:

Me - HEY! HEY! Help me please! My brother's been shot!

The bum ass Uncle James doppelganger drops two duffel bags of stuff and comes over to look at my brother in the cart.

Uncle James v2 - Oh shit. He's really hurt. Cops got him?

Me - No Mr. Kim. We were in his shop looking around. He caught him on the side with a shotgun.

Uncle James v2 - Oh fuck. Fucking gooks.

He reaches down to Tony, examining the blood on his side. He's almost afraid to touch him.

Me - I promise he doesn't have AIDS or nothing. He's really hurt. We need a ride to the hospital. Do you have a car? Please sir, please.

I remember putting my hands out like I was praying to this man.

He looks back into the 7/11.

Uncle James v2 - Uhhh, Jay! This kids really hurt here. They need a ride to the hospital. You got the keys?

I sit with Tony in the back seat of their Oldsmobile. Tony is laid out on his back with his head in my lap. Their car smelled like stale beer and weed. There's one of those good smelling trees hanging from the rear-view window, but it must not have been working.

Shiny Bald Head - Shit. He's bleeding pretty bad isn't he? Shit. I knew we should have laid a tarp down.

Uncle James v2 - Tarp? You got a tarp? That kid is dying Jay. We got no time for tarps. Pffft. Tarps.

As they continue to bicker on, this is around when Tony starts to cough. I remember being so excited just to hear something from him, "any news is good news" and all that.

Me - Tony. Tony. You there?

Crickets.

I don't remember exactly but I'm pretty sure this is when Tony died.

I snap back to reality when the guy with the beard reaches back and shakes my shoulder. He tells me there's no way through, that the roads are blocked, and he wishes he could help more but this as far as they can take us.

I yell and tell them to find a way. There had to be a way through I'm sure. I'm sure they were just lazy. I'm sure they didn't want to run into any cops, with all the shit they stole sitting in duffel bags in their car. I just didn't make sense, but I was in their car and I guess they had already helped me. If only they had stole some secret life saving medicine from that 7/11 instead of Twizzlers and caffeine pills.

They drop us off at a grocery store parking lot. They help me load Tony into a cart, then speed the hell off. I can't muster any courage to look at Tony. I know he's gone. I know the nearest hospital is too damn far. I know I don't even know where that is. This city is on fire. No one is listening.

I head out anyway, not to the hospital, but to the theater. The cheap dollar movie theater. The one where this whole damn trip was supposed to be headed. When I make that choice I feel calm. I feel strong. I feel in control in a way I don't think I have ever felt. And then I hear something weird:

"Hey...Hey Keem"

I look behind me but it's no one. I press on thinking it's the adrenaline/fear/everything making me crazy.

"Keem. Look here boy"

I remember whose voice it is. It's Dad's. It's fucking Dad.

I should probably mention this: Dad died 2 months back. He had decided to move to Florida for a job, promising to visit us often, but that the money was too hard to pass up. He said all that extra money would mean more dope shit for me and Tony. I said he better always get us the newest game consoles right when they come out. After some jokes that girls don't like nerds who play video games, he agreed.

He started his new job and not a week later he was dead. He went into the hospital for a headache. They diagnosed him with an aggressive brain tumor. And that was that. We found out he was dead when his sister, Auntie Grace, called Mom. It was one of those rare times we were all home watching TV on the couch together. We were watching Jeopardy because Mom always liked to answer the questions before the contestants. I thought it was boring, but she was smart like that, so it was fun to watch. She got the news and just immediately started bawling. We all knew right away it was Dad.

I look over to see Dad right there. Clear as day. He was right there running beside me as I pushed Tony. I remember blinking and rubbing my eyes about a million times to make sure what I was seeing was real. But it was, he didn't go away. Dad put his arm around me, and we just kept running. I'm not sure why but I never got the urge to say anything or reach out to touch him. Everything just felt alright, like a big wild cosmic force, like Galactus giving me the power cosmic. I was Norrin Radd, the Silver Surfer, sailing through space, soaring, cutting through the streets like a knife through butter.

When we get to the theater, I head around the back. Something me and Tony discovered a few weeks back is that they keep the back door unlocked. We noticed when the employees would take smoke breaks they would just open and close the door freely. On more than one occasion we would exploit that to watch a couple free movies.

Dad helps me lift Tony out of the shopping cart. We bust through the back door, heading straight for the nearest screen. But the place looks empty. I didn't even see an employee sweeping the floors.

When I enter screen #3, I hear a familiar sound.

"You probably don't think I'm a very nice guy, do ya?"

"Buddy, I think you're slime."

It's Robocop. We plop Tony down in the middle seat (best seat in the house) and sit down next to him. I could breathe. I was transfixed, oblivious to all the other shit.

Dad even ran up to grab the popcorn.

BLACK MASKS

By Toren Chenault

"From the city where niggas get hit for shit that they brother did"

One more pothole. George thought he was going to throw up. The young man across from him had already done it twice. Three times now. And four. Speed bump this time. The jolt made George keel over. He felt the acid and heat swishing around in his throat. He wished it would just come out already. Then, someone hit his knee.

"Nah, not in here. Don't do that shit next to me," the person next to him said.

George looked at the young man across from him. He was wiping bits of food from his mouth. His black clothes were brightened with vomit. So was his assault rifle. It took all of George's focus to not throw up. Grumpy dude next to him be damned.

Sixteen of them crammed into the back of the van. Heading sixty miles an hour down a highway. Thirty down a suburban street. Now twenty, creeping like hungry raccoons in the night. Their rifles rattled on the bed of the van, the clicking and shifting sounded as nervous as they looked. George was sure he was going to throw up soon. He closed his eyes as the acid worked its way to his lips.

"Don't be such a bitch ass nigga," the grumpy dude next to him said.

"I'm sorry," George muttered. "Are we almost there?"

237

The young man looked at the tiny window as if to know their exact location. He had it all mapped out, in his mind anyways. Looked back at George with confidence.

"Shouldn't be much longer."

Across from George, the other young man was vomiting again. How is it okay to take your mask off so much? George couldn't remember the last time he saw someone's real face during a raid. And *never* before one. But here this guy was, vomiting his brains out, letting everyone in the van see his real face.

He was Black, just like everyone in the van was. Always was. George could tell he was probably the same age as him, nineteen if he had to guess. Maybe twenty. There was a fear on the young man's face. A vulnerability that most didn't have on their face. Everyone with their skull-like masks on. Emotion wasn't popular in these vans. But why was it being allowed now? It was completely against the code. Against everything they had been taught over the last year. George wanted to slap this nigga. Wanted to break his nose for even disrespecting the OG's like that. His heart began to sink at the possibility.

George almost dropped his rifle as they came to an abrupt start. The young man across from him stiffened like a board. Put his mask back on. Straightened up like a good soldier. Like he hadn't just shown some of the worst weakness George had ever seen in his short life.

"Don't act brand new now, nigga," the words flowed from George's mouth. He couldn't see the vomiter's eyes, but he could feel the contempt. Or maybe it was embarrassment.

Someone tapped on the door four times.

In the middle of the street, a man stood. Solitary. Like he had been there for years. Waiting, just doing his thing. Preparing for this moment. His time to shine. He greeted George and crew with a smile.

"Welcome to Detroit," the man said. "My name is Javon."

They all knew that name. Knew that this nigga wasn't nothing to fuck with. But here he was, acting all cordial before a raid, before...the slaughter. They saluted Javon as he continued talking.

"I was born here. Feels right coming back, ya know what I'm sayin'?"

Javon spun around in place, his arms out. Twirling around like a white girl in a music video. He smiled. Then he stopped. Looked up. The streetlight shined bright on him. He was the only person who mattered in this quiet neighborhood. The only person who's opinion mattered in all of Detroit.

"I'm not a true Detroit nigga, though," he continued. "This city. Y'all know this city, right?"

Nothing. They just stood there.

"Of course not. You little niggas couldn't know Detroit."

Javon was wearing basically the same gear as the rest of them. Combat boots, a lightweight jacket, a body vest, a Black mask hanging around his neck, acting as a bandana. George always wanted to wear one of those. Breathing through the masks they had to wear was difficult. His throat tightened just thinking about it.

This was George's first time doing a raid with someone like Javon. Usually, it was just some experienced nigga from the block. Someone who had put in enough work to be considered good enough to lead a squad. This neighborhood, this city, it all seemed above someone in Javon's position. But George wasn't going to say shit.

"I don't know Detroit. My grandpa used to tell me stories about that shit. How rough it was for him and his boys growing up here. This whole block used to be nothing but crack houses. You believe that shit?"

Javon didn't have an assault rifle either. As he lamented the old Detroit, he waved a golden pistol in the air. He pointed it at the suburban houses covering the streets. It was early evening; the sun had just gone down. And George could see inside one of the nearby houses.

A white couple was sitting on the couch. They both looked normal enough. Normal white people clothes and hairstyles. Two kids sat on the floor. One was reading a comic book, the other playing on a tablet. A sitcom was playing on the sixty-inch flatscreen. America's version of happiness. Javon spit in the house's direction as he spoke.

"There's stories of what this city used to be. What it used to represent. But we'll never know that, will we?"

He put the pistol down at his side and looked down at the ground. George could hear him fighting tears.

"This shit is personal for me. As personal as it gets."

This was it. George couldn't do this. He was going to throw up. He looked for Mr. Vomit, but everyone was blending in with the blackness of the street. They could sense Javon ready to give the order. Reaching the climax of his emotions.

"Tonight isn't a normal raid, men. Tonight, we aren't just scouring through houses for supplies and money. We aren't looking for something covert, this isn't some recon shit."

He walked up to the house with the basic white family in it. They followed him. He was standing outside the window, pressed the pistol up to glass. No one inside noticed.

"Tonight isn't just about killing white people in the name of identity and freedom."

"Kill who you want. Take what you want. Do as you have been trained."

"But tonight?"

He pulled the trigger. The bullet went through the glass with extreme precision. It hit the white woman in the neck. The blood drenched the child reading the comic book. A black and white page. Drowning in a sea of mediocrity.

"Tonight, we take back Detroit," Javon said.

***

The Oldest City

"You know, my first assumption was that you were projecting your anger you have towards yourself to society. Or white people. But now, I'm not so sure. I do think you have insecurity that stems from failed relationships with your mother and father though. Let's explore that, shall we?"

Antwan only liked coming to therapy because the couch was comfy. The type of shit that sunk real slow the first time you sat down. The type of couch he'd see on those influencers' house tours. And for a price he stopped caring about a long time ago, he got to lay on it.

Sometimes he would talk to the therapist. Couldn't remember his name though. John? Jameson? Something with a J. Today though,

Antwan let his body slump in the couch and his back and shoulders thanked him. John (or Jameson) kept talking.

"You started your job as a defense lawyer five years ago, right? Did your father work? Your mother?"

Jameson was always doing this. Always forgetting every aspect of his life, reminding him of how low he truly was. And this obsession with his parents. Truth be told Antwan didn't know his father that well. Died on the job as a construction worker. And his mother died in a freak car crash. He was fourteen. Antwan had great relationships with them before they both died. But he didn't *know* them that well. Two of the strongest, hardworking people he had ever known. But John was obsessed with making Antwan hate who he was.

The couch was starting to become less comfy. He sat up.

"You hear about what happened last night?" Antwan asked. Johnson looked confused for a second. His lips pursed slightly and his nose wrinkled. 'This nigger just interrupted me' was written all over his expensive glasses. But Antwan didn't plan on being here much longer. And if he was paying, this 'licensed professional' was going to listen.

"I—I had head there was some criminal activity, yes," Jameson said.

"The Black Masks were in a nearby suburb," Antwan said. He stood up now and stretched his back, bending down to touch his toes. "They killed everyone in the neighborhood. Killed the cops that were on the scene too. Then they were gone in less than an hour."

"Did they take anything?"

"What do you think? It was textbook. Any house that had valuable stuff was destroyed. And all of that stuff is probably circulating the black market now."

"Heh," John said. "Black Masks using the black market. Never thought of that."

Antwan didn't say anything. Just stared at him.

"Sorry."

Antwan walked over to the window of Jameson's office. Seventy floors up. Stopped seeing any black people past the fifth floor. Unless they were janitors. They even fired the black receptionist. Antwan could see the city below him. It was the middle of the day so there was palpable buzz on the street. He felt good, towering among them.

"What I don't get," Antwan said still looking out the window, "Is why they attacked a white city like Detroit?"

He sighed and turned to face the therapist. Hoping the asshole would have some sort of answer.

"Well, that is an interesting proposition. Because traditionally, the Black Masks stick to cities that are more rundown, more socioeconomic problems. Easier for them to make money, gain influence, etc. But Detroit hasn't been that city in over a hundred years. None of the Black Masks were alive back then."

Johnny had a point.

Antwan thought back to law school and his study of Detroit Law. Before it became the city of beautiful ads and coffee, it was known as a struggling city. A city always on the cusp of greatness but never one that realized it. Corruption, drugs, crime.

It was a black city back then too. A city that was the butt of the joke in America. No one ever gave it a second thought. Once the mecca of culture for his people, Antwan now was the only black man in the biggest building in the heart of downtown. Maybe the Black Masks had recognized that. It was possible. Possible that America's biggest 'terrorist organization' felt tethered to the city. Never fully connected, but never full apart either.

"It's pretty romantic, if you ask me," Antwan said quietly. Jameson was more confused than before. He wanted so badly to say something relevant, something that gave his six-figure salary meaning. Trails of sweat were starting to roll down his face. And when Antwan turned to look out the window again, John finally spoke.

"It's pretty crazy. You know, my wife and I went down to the Ledge last weekend---speaking of romance, that is."

Antwan chuckled. Wished the comfiness of the couch had lasted longer. Wish he didn't have to live in this city. Even if he wanted a black therapist, they weren't allowed to practice anymore. Still, Antwan liked to imagine that this idiot understood even the smallest thing that was going on in his mind. He sighed as he turned for the door.

"See you next---,"

"No the fuck you won't," Antwan said. "No the fuck you won't."

Outside, the smell of cookie batter and white women hit Antwan like a truck. It was also the middle of the day and the sun was burning the skins of the white people around him. None of them were complaining though. They looked at him like most did here in Detroit. Scorn, disgust, the occasional guilty look from a white-passing mixed girl. Who wanted so desperately to "try" Antwan on for a night at a hotel. The thrill of the game, thrill of risk, a higher high than ecstasy. What was once a rite of passage for white women was now social life suicide. So, most white women avoided him like an expensive coffee shop. In that sense, Detroit wasn't all bad.

Ad square was his least favorite part of the city. But it was unavoidable on his way back to work. It had a fancier name that he could never remember. Named after a famous influencer or maybe a content creator. Local esports team? A development company based in Lansing? He couldn't remember. Antwan typically tried his best to black out when walking through the square.

It wasn't the football field length ads or their unbearable neon color combinations. Each ad sexier and more put together than the next. Some new vegan ice cream. The newest hip-hop track, the only other nigga in the square with Anthony. A new flavor for America's favorite dark pop. And a poster for the latest superhero movie. In and out of rotation faster than a short man playing basketball.

What always bothered Antwan the most was the people. Not the amount. Not even the fact they were white. He didn't mind people of any race, really. But he could never put his finger on it, could never find the right words for what he felt and saw in the square. But when he bumped into a young man underneath a hip-hop ad, that feeling returned.

"Nah I saw it, man. I swear!"

"That's cap. Cap all day."

"On God, bruh. Why would I be cappin'? The fuck I need to cap for?"

His stomach tightened from the smell of a strong cologne and mass-produced aftershave. He got turned around and stumbled into a woman talking with a young man underneath a condom ad.

"Ayo mamma, let me blow your back out tonight."

"Boy, bye. Get the fuck out my face right now."

"I know you a thot. You be givin' that sloppy toppy. Now you too good for me?"

The woman winked at Antwan as she left the young man. Bold. She clearly didn't care about her social status. The condom ad changed into another hip-hop sign.

Antwan trudged his way through the square. He could see his building not too far away. But then, the star-spangled neon of a superhero show nearly blinded him. He covered his eyes, his ears and brain still taking in the noise of the city.

"I woke up and chose violence today."

"Drip, drip, drip."

"Boy, that shit lives rent free in my head. Rent free!"

He persevered and came to a final ad that was lower on the ground. This one hung just slightly above a streetlight, and it was one of the duller ones on the block. Underneath it was a bus stop. Antwan couldn't make out the ad, couldn't make out what exactly it was trying to say. One second it was food, the next it was toilet paper, then a crime television show. He was too tired for this. At the bus station, three younger white men stood in the ominous glow of the food, toilet paper, and crime. They were smoking some weed. Antwan only got a glimpse of them before he heard a loud crack in the air behind him.

Except it wasn't behind him, and it wasn't just one crack. Ripples of sound pierced the air and Antwan knew what they were. Bullets. All aimed at the three weed smokers by the bus stop. Everyone scattered when that first pop was heard. Antwan wished he was imagining people yelling 'Worldstar!' at the top of their lungs as the shots went off. But they were killed before they could get their smart phones out. Antwan ducked underneath one of the massive ads. He clasped his hands over his head and tried to remember the last time this happened. If it ever happened, here in Detroit.

The three weed smokers never stood a chance. One of them tried their best to pull out their weapon when the car drove past but it was futile. Antwan looked up, even though he didn't need a confirmation on what was happening. Or who was shooting.

Two men sat on the back of a black convertible. Its rims were gold and the tires were suitable for a truck. The men held assault rifles and dawned the famous Black Masks. So did the driver and the man in the passenger seat. They slowed to a crawl once they got close to where Antwan was. One of the men noticed him. There was an awkward pause. But Antwan didn't fear for his life. Instead, he made eye contact with the bigger man in the backseat. The bigger man pointed his assault rifle up to one of the ads floating above Antwan's head.

Another hip-hop track. A dead rapper this time. It was an ad promoting his posthumous album.

Bullets flew from the assault rifle, lighting the afternoon sky as glass from the billboard fell and hit the bodies of dead white people. When he finished, the bigger man acknowledged Antwan, nodded at him. And they sped through the city, gold rims and all.

Antwan got to his feet. Weed, blood, and white women. The cake batter was gone now. He closed his eyes and rubbed his head, took a deep sigh. He trudged his way back to his office. Sad from the death he had just seen, but relieved that he could hear himself think. Amazed at the efficiency of the Black Masks, but terrified at the spectacle of...well, whatever the fuck this all was. He could finally see the front door to his building.

At least he didn't have to hear anyone say 'cap' anymore.

***

Initiation

Antwan didn't like driving too often. But after the day that was the third highest trending topic on social media, he needed a good drive. He turned on the radio as he left the city and as the sun set on Detroit.

"I'm just saying, what if this is it? What if we should have listened to them? Huh? The greats. Like Shapiro, Limbaugh, Spencer even. What if they were right about the ideas that people a hundred years ago were too damn soft to listen to. I swear, I swear. Sometimes I listen to what some of my people went through back then and I weep. Like fucking Jesus, I weep."

For life of him Antwan didn't remember leaving his radio on--- this station. But he was intrigued.

"They used to call it cancel culture. Ruined too many careers. Took too many of us out of good positions that *we* earned. I tell you what, I wish they would try and cancel me today. You hear me, you fucking monkeys. I wish you would try me...I'm Rocky Jones, we'll be right back."

Antwan let his brain drift as an ad played on the radio. The man's voice greeted Antwan like a rusty nail to the foot.

"Pete Sampson here of Pete Sampson's hunting service. I know you're afraid nowadays. So much going on, people dying all around you. Do you want a solution?"

248

The man paused for a moment, letting the listeners answer their own question. Let them drown in their own fears and insecurity. It was working well. Antwan had never heard of this man before. Once again, he was intrigued.

"Friends, I have the perfect solution for you. My company HUNT-A-NIGGER will take care of all your nigger needs. A nigger bothering you at work? Talking to your sister on the internet? Are they just plain existing and you just want it to stop? HUNT-A-NIGGER is here for you."

"Low on cash? No problem! Bad credit? No problem! There isn't a nigger alive we can't catch. And for an extra fee, you can even keep them alive and---,"

"Alright, that's enough," Antwan said as he turned the radio off.

A police car flashed its lights as Antwan stopped at a stop sign. It was bold, a police car being out this far from the city. Antwan desperately wanted whoever was in that car to pull him over. He would love nothing more to show the policeman his credentials, and to show the cop who he knew. The thought of the cop shaking in his uniform, sweat running down the side of his face, amused Antwan. He slowed down, hoping the car would turn its siren on.

Nothing. He sighed. The smile left his face. He drove on.

Debris and trash covered the street. Antwan was forced to do his usual maneuvers through the war-torn neighborhood. In the nearby homes he could see lights on. In one home he saw a family playing a board game. A child playing video games in another. When he reached a stoplight, something caught his eye. In the middle of the road was a hole the side of a few vans. Mortar rounds. Or maybe, a small missile. That wasn't surprising though. On the edge of the hole, was a child. As the red light turned green, Antwan could see the blood on the child's clothes.

He rushed out of his car, the summer air greeting him. He almost vomited at the smell. The child was hanging onto the edge of the hole. Like it had crawled its way to freedom. Only to lose the final battle here, underneath the streetlight. Antwan pleaded with the child, hoping for a miracle. Gently nudging him hoping for something, anything. He found himself tearing up at the sight. This child, this young boy. Reminded Antwan of his brother. Of his cousins. Dead under a streetlight, smoke and lead enveloping the street like a warm blanket. Antwan didn't know this child's story. But he desperately wanted to. He wept as a car stopped next to him and the child.

"You're going to want to come with us," a young man said. It was hard to hear him. He must have still been getting used to the mask.

Antwan, tears and blood soaking his clothes, looked up. He didn't want to argue. Wasn't in the mood. He told the men he'd follow them wherever they wanted to go. Even though he knew where he was going. They knew too. But this group loved their customs. Their culture. The child laid there on the street, the streetlight illuminating his body.

They arrived at a building not too far from the streetlight. He couldn't get the child out of his mind. The young man in the mask opened his car door for him. Antwan nodded at him.

"Appreciate you," Antwan said. He was led by two other masked men to a building that looked like a warehouse. There were office buildings and a factory close by. And not too far down the road, the neighborhood houses could be seen. This portion of the town wasn't as covered in mess. But Antwan did notice an abnormal amount of bullet casings on the ground. More than usual.

"What happened here?" Antwan asked, the young man being closest to him. The young man didn't answer.

"New guy, I'm guessing," Antwan said. He turned to a taller man behind him. "You going to tell me what happened?"

"Bitch ass cop thought shit was sweet. Ima just leave it at that."

Antwan remembered the cop flashing his lights from a few miles ago.

"Fair enough."

As they approached the door, two more masked men exited the building. They gestured for Antwan to spread his arms out.

"More new guys. I'm a lawyer, I never have weapons on me."

"Not really a good lawyer then," the masked man exiting the building said.

Ah shit.

The taller man behind Antwan leapt into action. He first punched the talker, knocking his mask off. The talker tried to frantically grab it, but the taller man punched him in the chest. From the aggression and power, Antwan knew who that was.

"Damion, it's alright, for real," Antwan pleaded.

"Nah fuck that. You know the rules. But more importantly, this lil' nigga knows the rules."

Damion tripped the young man and caused him to fall back on his butt. A swift knee and the young man was flat on his back. Damion raised his foot before yelling at the young man.

"No talking before initiation!" His foot came down and the young man spit blood high in the air. He rolled over in pain, coughing and wheezing as they walked past him and inside the building.

"Sleep out here tonight. Kill any white person you see. You survive, you get to start the process over."

Antwan wasn't religious but he prayed that the recruit wouldn't speak. He had seen enough blood for one day. The recruit put his head down, picked up his mask, and curled against the building, still struggling to catch his breath. Antwan could hear him crying as the door shut behind them.

***

Brunch is Expensive

This building was new for the Black Masks. Antwan knew they didn't like to operate too close to the cities. Too many police, too many chances for an altercation. Violence was their love language, but they liked it on their terms. Cities sometimes changed those terms, causing chaos. But Antwan was in ad square that afternoon. It was the only thing the world was talking about. The city of Detroit had declared war on the Black Masks, the 'Radical Black Terrorist Organization' which to the Black Masks responded the only way they knew how.

"If the shoe fits, bitch ass nigga."

He heard different members saying it as he passed rooms with the men escorting him. A popular phrase. One that was basically sung around the organization whenever 'fun' times were ahead. The energy in this new building was menacing. Antwan let out a small sigh when they reached the room he knew he was supposed to be in.

"I got it from here," he said to the men. They stood still for a moment before remembering who they were talking to. Antwan walked into the room and was greeted by the usual smell of the best weed in the world.

"Hard at work, I see," Antwan said.

A bigger man was sitting in an office chair smoking when Antwan walked in. He started coughing when he saw his old friend.

"This nigga," the coughing man said. "Took you long enough to come out this way. Out there working with them white folks."

"Shut up, Dre. You know damn well I don't work *with* any white people."

Dre bellowed. Smoke came from him nose as he did. He gestured for Antwan to sit down near the desk.

"What brings you in today?" Dre said. He offered the weed to Antwan.

"Thanks." Antwan inhaled and let it take over. "You never have told me. Where do you guys get this shit?"

"First thing my grandfather did when he founded the organization," Dre said. He gestured for the weed back and took a deep inhale. He blew three smoke rings into the air.

"Marijuana for the longest time was a white man's game. But you know that. And for years, they locked us up like savages for smoking the stuff. And when it became legal, it was white people who reaped those profits. Billions."

"My grandfather told me about this place on the corner of his street. Best shit he ever had. Black neighborhood, all that. Not one black employee," Antwan said.

Dre handed the weed back to Antwan.

"White Peppermint Tears," Dre said. He smiled wide. His diamond fronts shined bright.

"Anyways, when he founded this place, marijuana was one of the first areas he focused on. As a way of liberation, but also a way to fund the organization. Raided the best farms in America. And we developed our own shit. Better. Purer."

"You ain't lying," Antwan said, coughing.

"Didn't answer my question, Ant. Why you here?" Dre's fronts disappeared behind the smoke. His tone was stern. They were always friendly, but this was where the two friends started to divert.

"I was in ad square today," Antwan said quietly. There was no one in the dark office, but he didn't want anyone to overhear their conversation. Even though subordinates wouldn't dare do such a thing.

"Huh. Sorry so you had to see that. Hope the boys didn't scare you too much," Dre said.

"Dre," Antwan said. "This shit has gone too far. You listening to the news? They want to start nuking you."

"And who's to say we don't have our own nukes?"

"Are you---you can't be serious. Dre, what the fuck, man? Nuclear war? That isn't what this is supposed to be about?"

Dre stood up. He always wore a nice suit, nicer ones than Antwan. He put his hands on the desk and leaned forward, gestured for the weed again.

"What's the alternative, Ant? Black people's history in this country is nothing but pain. Nothing but war. We have been pushed for so long. Why shouldn't we fight back?"

"We are fighting back. What we're doing, that's fighting. What you do, sometimes---"

"Don't start with me, nigga. Don't. You play lawyer in that fancy city all day, but you still bail my boys out of jail. You still represent our cases."

"No one else will."

"And why the fuck you think that is? Doesn't matter if we shoot a white woman named Deb or rob a grocery store for condoms. The punishment has always been the same. You know that."

Antwan got up from the chair. He had heard enough. On the far wall of the room, he noticed a television. But it was black. Wasn't on.

"Do you even know what is going on out there?" Antwan asked. "Do you even know what the world is anymore, Dre?"

Dre scoffed.

"Don't bring that lawyer stuff up in here, man. We do this every other week, you know. Get high, reminisce about the good ole days, then debate the finer points of the movement."

"Yeah. I know."

"I love you bro."

"I love you too, man. But---I don't know. That shit happened right after therapy. Fucked me up."

"You ever learn that white dude's name?"

"They been fuckin' our names up for years, he'll be alright."

They stood there for a moment. Their intense greeting done.

A couch sat near a wall in Dre's office. It wasn't near the comfort level of Johan's couch, but it was peaceful. Antwan sat down, Dre joined him, pulled out another rolled blunt. He lit it up and coughed a bit as the smoke hit his lungs.

"Pink Toe," Dre said. He passed the weed to Antwan. When he inhaled, Antwan concurred with a cough.

"Sweet like a white girl," Antwan said laughing.

He sighed. Handed the blunt back to his friend.

"I heard an ad for a black people hunting service, man."

"Yeah, that nigga Sampson. We got his wife locked up on the south side. Killed his daughter last year," Dre said.

Antwan sat up. Look at his friend with disbelief.

"Chill," Dre continued. "He lynched a little girl from Florida few years back. And another in Cali. They ruled both suicides."

"Shit, that was him? How---how'd you find that out?"

"Lil' nigga's cousin was bragging about it. Got some people in the force who heard him talking about it," Dre said.

"In—in the force?" Antwan had to catch his breath.

Everything was moving so fast, a tornado of emotions in his chest cavity. He struggled to breathe. Inhale. Exhale. One more time.

"How deep does this go, Dre? This...I don't even know how to describe it."

"War. That's the word you're looking for."

"I saw a child in the street on my way here. And a hole in the ground the size of a bus."

Dre pointed to the ceiling. The end of the blunt lit up. He pulled it out and blew smoke as he talked.

"They started dropping bombs. Five days ago."

"Fuck. There's been nothing about it in the news."

"You aren't stupid," Dre said. "So, Ima let that slide."

Antwan rubbed his hair, it was nappy. He hadn't washed it in a while. His hair ripped and broke as he ran his fingers through it.

"It wasn't cops," Dre continued. "Don't know what they callin' themselves, but these niggas want us dead, Ant. But the fucked up

256

thing is they always have. Now, they have the rest of society behind them."

They sat there for five minutes, passing the weed back and forth to each other. Each exhale sounding more and more laborious.

"This shit is never going to stop, is it?" Antwan asked.

"I don't know," Dre said. "I really don't know."

The blunt was gone now and Dre stood up. He wiped the dust from his suit and walked towards the door. He opened it and Antwan followed.

"That favor you owe me," Antwan said before Dre opened the door.

Dre's eyebrow raised.

"You serious?"

"Yeah. I think so."

Antwan hated being in the vans. He remembered talking with Dre when he took over the group. Dre's grandfather was obsessed with vans. With vehicles that held a crazy amount of people, really. And for the longest time, vans meant a few things in society. A pedophile trying to blend in, a struggling painter trying to make rent, a church group. The Black Masks were all about power, getting it back, redistributing it. And Dre's grandfather saw no better metaphor than vans. You see a van nowadays and you knew who was in it and you knew what was about to happen. Except today.

Today, it was Antwan in the back of a signature van with two other people. He couldn't see their faces. The one was a recruit, his body looked lean, young. Almost too young. The other looked like a young woman. She wasn't sporting the mask though. There was a brown bag over her head. Antwan also noticed how heavy her breathing was. But she didn't move, and neither did the recruit. Antwan just sat there, staring at them both, hoping something good could come out of this. The van came to a stop.

The recruit and the young woman left the van first. The recruit drew his weapon and rapidly began scanning the area for threats. He pushed the young lady to the ground as he left the van.

"Take it easy," Antwan said. "Nothing out here but forest."

Before Antwan could finish his words, he was greeted by the chirping of birds. The smell of grass. A sunset too. No noise pollution, no noise at all. Peace. He inhaled as the van drove off, ruining the moment.

The recruit looked back at Antwan confused. As confused as one could look in a mask.

"Just follow me," Antwan said. "And don't push her like that again."

About an hour later and the sun was at its lowest point. A chill had hit the forest. Antwan found a clear spot and figured this was a good place.

"You know how to make a fire?" Antwan asked the recruit. The recruit answered with a slight nod.

"Get to it then."

Two hours later and nighttime had blanketed the forest. The recruit's fire was the loudest sound for miles. As it crackled, Antwan watched the pair of young people's face coverings glisten, even though they were black and brown.

Antwan sighed.

"From Detroit to Buffalo, we love to smuggle blow," Antwan said. The recruit cupped the end of his mask instantly. He removed it and removed the hood from the young woman as well. Antwan wanted to let out a sigh of relief, but the fire revealed just how young these two were. The young woman had a maniacal smile across her face. She then burst out into laughter. The recruit stood up, flashing his weapon at her. Antwan gestured for him to wait.

"What's funny?" Antwan asked.

"You niggas with your codes. Archaic as fuck," the young woman said. She sounded even younger than she looked.

Antwan realized he might have made a mistake in doing this. But he was committed. He knew this was going to be difficult. He could see the rage in the young man's eyes.

"You heard me say the code. Dre has given me full authority here."

The young man's eyes were frantic. Darting back and forth between Antwan and the young woman. For just a moment, Antwan thought he might die. Thought the uptick in brutality he had heard about recently within the group was true. He let those—unrealistic ideas die though. The young man sat down. Farther from the young woman this time. His eyes firmly on Antwan.

"Let's start with your names," Antwan said.

Neither one of them spoke.

"Fine. I'm Antwan. Defense lawyer. I help just about everyone in need and try my best to of service to those who need it."

The young man scoffed.

"I grew up down the street from the Detroit and hated that there weren't any Black defense lawyers in the city. So, I put my head down, studied and here I am."

Silence. The fire crackled again suggesting its own impatience with the young people.

"I'm George," the young man said.

"Sierra," the young woman said.

Antwan smiled. Happy to finally have some type of progress.

"George, do you know who I am?"

"Yeah, nigga. I know who you are," George said.

"You have a problem with me?"

George's anger was intoxicating in the worst way. There was an aura, a force around him. The fire illuminated as he spoke.

"You a sellout, man. Only reason you even get to come around is Dre. But we all know what you about."

Antwan chuckled.

"So, you don't like me because I sometimes help white people. Am I getting that right?"

George didn't say anything. Sierra wanted her turn to speak.

"He's right, you know," her voice was soft when she spoke.

Antwan looked at her, but George kept his eyes firmly on Antwan.

"What's going on here, anyway?" Antwan asked, looking at George. "What is this?"

Sierra cackled. Loud as hell. She stood up. George tried to raise his fist to her but Antwan spoke up.

"You touch her, and I will beat your ass in front of Dre, you understand? You ain't tough, nigga."

He wished his anger didn't get the better of him. Wished that his attempt to save this young man from being a Black Mask was going better. But he couldn't believe what he was seeing. He wanted desperately for this young man to want a way out. To understand what was happening here the moment Antwan said the outdated code. But he didn't. All George saw was an outsider. A white sympathizer.

"You don't know about the Brunch Crew?" George asked. "You really have been in the city too long."

The anger, or the pettiness, was gone from George's voice. He was truly shocked Antwan didn't know about whoever Sierra was supposed to represent. Antwan had become one of the old niggas he hated when he was their age. Oblivious to something changing the landscape of the culture he loved more than anything. He sat back and looked at Sierra. The floor was hers.

"The Blueprints," Sierra said under her breath. Why now, was she choosing to be meek? It wasn't embarrassment on her face. But what was it then? A lack of conviction? Fear? Antwan asked her to repeat herself.

"The Blueprints," she reiterated. More stern this time. Her brown eyes looked soft in the light of the fire.

"They call us that derogatory term because they can't handle the truth," Sierra said. The piercing pride in her voice returned. The voice of a young woman who was determined to make the world bend to her will.

"How old are you?" Antwan asked.

"Just turned twenty. Anyways, like I was saying, these dusty niggas are just that. Dusty niggas. Afraid of everything. They see their own shadow and start shooting."

The fire popped. Antwan was forced to move closer to the pair of rebels as small pieces of hot wood and stone flung its way at him. George's leg was shaking. And he finally turned that death stare from Antwan to Sierra. She was just getting started.

"History tells us one thing and one thing only. Capital. It's the root of--- all of this shit. If you have it, if you control it, you can do unimaginable things in life. Cure diseases before they happen. Stop wars without weapons. Start them without weapons."

She was staring into George's soul now.

"What niggas like this fail to understand is that there's nothing, not a fucking thing, wrong with money. The Blueprints believe in a world where black people control our own future."

"I see," Antwan said. He could tell Sierra's passion was real. Just like George's anger, it did exist. Just like the forest, or the fire existed. But Antwan wasn't sure either of them believed the words of their respective groups.

"You two, your groups that is," Antwan said, "you're like oil and water. Complete opposites of each other."

Neither one of them said anything.

"Then explain why she's here, George. Why did Dre or whoever instruct you to abduct this young woman?"

"Nigga," George said under his breath. "You know why."

Antwan's skin went cold. The fire dimmed, the forest greeting them with it's cold embrace. Antwan cursed Dre in his head. He couldn't believe his friend, his best friend, his only friend, would do this. Antwan couldn't hold back the tears forming in his eyes. But he did. Wasn't the time to cry. Show weakness. He composed himself, spoke softly.

"You don't have to do this---I---I know you feel lost. Confused. But George. Think."

George had his head down. The fire was dim enough now that Antwan couldn't see his angry eyes. Couldn't sense the rage anymore. Sierra smiled. The type of smile--- Antwan couldn't put his finger on it. He hadn't been out here that long with these two, but he couldn't remember his life before this. Everything about *this* moment felt too important to him. And all he could do was listen.

"It doesn't matter what happens to me. Because you know what happens tomorrow?"

Sierra leaned in. Her face practically touching the fire.

"Niggas die."

The snap of old sticks and pinecones caught their attention. There wasn't any rustling, no anticipation. Like those damn ads in the square, they just appeared. Two white people. Wide-eyed, deer in annoying LED headlights. They tried to back up, slowly. Antwan wished he could stop time.

Sierra stood up and to maybe even her own surprise, she was free of her restraints. That same wild look was on her face. Like all the hours she spent training on how to escape a captor had paid off. She was carrying a knife. A nice sized one. She waved it around.

"Speak of the devil," Sierra said smiling.

"P-Please. We—we don't want trouble," the man said.

"Hikers, huh? Must be nice," Sierra said. She yanked the woman down to the ground; pieces of the white woman's hair fell as Sierra grabbed her. The man just stood there. Flaccid but filled with fear.

"You kill them and you're being exactly what they think we are," Antwan said. "I've seen too much blood today. Too fucking much. Put it down and let's figure this out."

"Did you hear what I said?" Sierra said. She gestured for the man to join the woman on the ground. He complied without hesitation.

"Yeah, I heard your psychotic ass. 'Niggas die' but you have a fucking choice. You don't have to kill them," Antwan said, his voice raising now.

"This is the most power we've ever had. In all human history. They fear us now. Hehe, I actually feel safe walking in my own motherfucking neighborhood!" Sierra yelled. She cackled for a few seconds before raising the knife to the man's neck. He yelped as she did.

"Don't kill him," the woman said. "Please, for the love of God. We got lost on our way from---,"

Sierra swiped with efficiency. Antwan felt like he was watching a superhero move. The blood sputtered from the white man's neck. A good amount landed in the fire. The ripe smell of copper penetrated the forest. The man slumped. Sierra slashed his face for good measure.

"I don't give a fuck," she whispered.

The woman screamed, unable to let the fear of seeing a black woman paralyze her. She hollered with rage at Sierra. The yells continued as the woman jumped up to her feet. She charged Sierra with conviction. Except Sierra easily dodged the attack and grabbed the woman's hands. Sierra stood behind her, holding both her hands. The woman returned to her flaccid, fearful state.

"Fucking nigger!" she said, snot running from her nose, embarrassingly out of breath.

"Awe that's cute," Sierra said. "She thinks I care. You think I care? Huh? Answer me, bitch."

"See, that's the thing, Mr. Lawyer. I think you've been inside too long. Been playing dress up with those corporate people too much."

Antwan tried to speak up. He was tired of these kids demeaning his work and in turn, his character. Sierra waved the knife in his face.

"I'm not done. Sit the fuck down."

He retreated. Looked at George. Still had his head down between his legs. The white man twitched, and more blood squirted from his neck. The pungent copper smell was unbearable.

"It's not saying that they die," Sierra said still holding the woman. "It's that we do." Her voice became uncomfortably soft now.

"No matter how many records we sell, how many things we cure, how many trends we create."

She moved closer to Antwan.

"How many cases we save--."

"All they see, mostly, are a couple of things. Anger. Entertainment. Maybe three or four things if they grew up around us." Her own joke made her laugh. Cackle.

"A lot of us realized, a long time ago, that it was time for them to pay for their sins. For all the years of racist action. The years of liberal inaction. And they all knew it was coming."

"The government did," George said quietly.

"Exactly, exactly! Them niggas knew."

"That if black people as a whole, realized their true potential, and harnessed that with their anger, they'd be unstoppable," Antwan said, finishing the soliloquy.

"Ding ding, motherfucker," Sierra said. "It's their worst nightmare come true."

"No, fuck that," Antwan said. "They're still winning. They still have control. Do you see Detroit? Do you see how fucked up that city has become?"

"How can you not?" George said. "You know, Detroit used to be a Black city."

Silence.

Antwan still didn't have his answer about specifically why Sierra had been kidnapped. But he really didn't need George or Dre or whoever to spell it out to him. On one side, you have the Black Masks. Violent, organized, militant. Truly separated from the masses of the world. The feared niggas from down the block. Monopolized the ghetto and turned it into a paradise for thugs and outcasts. George's head was still between his legs.

Whether they called themselves The Blueprints or everyone else called them the Brunch Crew, Antwan only saw confusion in Sierra's eyes. He saw a young woman with the same amount of hatred in her heart as the Black Masks, but none of organization, no coordination. No purpose. A young woman driven by her obsession with a capitalistic state and the promises of black wealth. Mixing violence with money. A young woman and a young man nowhere near as visionary as they thought.

But, and Antwan couldn't hold back his tears any longer, it wasn't their fault.

Sierra pulled the white woman's hair once again. The woman grunted, decided to make her last words mean something.

"You'll never win," she wheezed. Sierra pushed her head closer to fire. "Wait---I mean, fuck---."

Antwan looked over at George. The young man had finally looked up and from the light of the fire, Antwan could see the redness of his eyes. He could see the tears still formed at the bottom of his eyelids. Sierra pushed the woman closer to the fire.

"There isn't enough money in the---oh God!" the white woman flipped from defiance to paralyzed fear every few seconds. A racist epithet followed by a plea to Jesus. Sierra didn't have anything else to say. In her mind, she was doing the white woman a service.

Antwan smelled the flesh burn almost instantly. The white woman probably wanted to say something, anything. One last thought to the niggas who her daddy had warned her were going to take her out. His late-night ramblings and hours spent on social media didn't seem so bad now. Or maybe she thought of her grandfather, who spent his time leading a militia in northern Michigan. She might have thought how she had let him down, let the legacy down. But maybe she could find some solace in the fact that she would be a martyr. A symbol for all white people to rally around. Rally and kill the niggers. Yeah, that pleased her.

She stopped screaming and let the fire consume her. As if to be in tune with the metaphysical, Sierra drove her knife into the white woman's head.

"Freaky bitch was enjoying it," Sierra said.

George stood up now, his weapon aimed at Sierra. Antwan couldn't move. He still wept. But he couldn't move, and he didn't want to.

"What you gun' do little nigga? We out here trying to buy back the block and you crusty niggas want to burn it!"

His hands were trembling. And to Antwan's surprise, George looked back at him. That hatred evaporated from his eyes, his spirit. The pain released like water from weak dam. 'What should I do?' was the expression on his face. Antwan was confused why it had come up during all of this. George must have seen situations like this on the daily. Antwan didn't dwell on it too long though. Dre owed him the favor of trying to get one of his recruits out of the Black Masks before initiation. After what he saw in ad square, after his talk with Jed, the urgency bit Antwan in the ass like a rabid animal. He quickly took the gun from George.

"Ahhh shit," Sierra said, waving the knife around. "Black Matt Murdock about to go crazy on me," she said.

George retreated, sat back down on the ground. His head once again in between his legs. Sierra was prancing around, mocking Antwan.

"You think you special. This nigga really think he special. HAHA!"

She was unstable. Unpredictable. Antwan tightened his grip on the gun. He caught a whiff of the white woman's burning body. The calm of the forest put him at ease. Behind Sierra, he could see the blackness of the trees, and he thought he saw a couple pairs of yellow eyes. Watching, betting, witnessing a struggle that had been going on for hundreds of years.

"You're crazy," Antwan said. "Leave. Go into the woods, find your way home. Or don't. Just leave us alone."

Sierra's face twitched. The smile disappeared from her face.

"You think you better than me? Huh? I know niggas that could buy you," she spit.

"I'm sure you do. But we can't keep this cycle going. You'll probably die to a nigga from the Black Masks, or you might make a career out of killing them. That's on you. But tonight, I'm not contributing to anymore of my people's pain. Please. Just leave."

For just a moment, he saw Sierra's eyes well with tears. But he might have just been imagining it. She quickly darted through the forest. Within seconds she was gone. Antwan dropped the gun.

"Javon is going to hunt me down," George whispered. "He's--- he's--,"

"Take it easy," Antwan said. "I'm not going to let that happen."

"What?"

"I meant what I said. I'm done with the cycle."

George sniffled, wiped his nose and stood up. Antwan put his hand on the young man's shoulder.

"Dre, Javon, whoever. I'm not letting them kill you. I'll protect you."

George couldn't contain himself. The fire had died down. The white woman's skin had absorbed most of the heat. Occasionally, her skin would pop, or her body would smolder. George collapsed into Antwan's chest. Antwan caught him, surprised at how light George was. And his crying, it wasn't soft. It wasn't contained or restrained. George wailed, probably scaring any animals in the vicinity. The unbearable pain rushing through his body, the pain that had given him purpose, exiting from his heart like an erupting volcano. After a few seconds, he went quiet. Head still in Antwan's chest.

"Thank you."

THE END

BLACK HOLE

COMICS + ENTERTAINMENT

Made in the USA
Monee, IL
06 June 2021